A MIDWINTER'S ☙ W9-BBX-589

A MIDWINTER FANTASY

Leanna Renee Hieber

L. J. McDonald

Helen Scott Taylor

Dorchester
Publishing

DORCHESTER PUBLISHING

November 2010

Published by

Dorchester Publishing Co., Inc.
200 Madison Avenue
New York, NY 10016

ISBN 13: 978-1-4285-1162-0
E-ISBN: 978-1-4285-0947-4

Visit us online at www.dorchesterpub.com.

A Midwinter Fantasy

CONTENTS

A Christmas Carroll

Leanna Renee Hieber

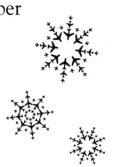

Team Michael, this is for you.
~Leanna Renee Hieber

Prologue

December 1888, at the edge of London's reality

Three spirits murmured to each other, standing in the luminous Liminal that separated the waiting Whisper-world from the dazzling, drawing light of the Great Beyond. The Whisper-world was quite the grey purgatory, while the Great Beyond, well . . . who possesses the words to describe Paradise?

The Liminal is a place where magic is discussed and made, from whence spirits receive duties and inspiration, where dreams are both created and abandoned. Where those who are worthy might become angels. It is a place where time is porous and malleable; it keeps its own clock. Here pasts are recaptured and futures glimpsed; here spirits from every walk of death—those still invested in parties on Earth—discuss their current designs on the living, for better or for worse.

The present trio at the Liminal edge was shrouded in shadow, and they contemplated parties in London, England, under the reign of Queen Victoria. Their clothing, too, represented various decades within Her Highness's extensive reign, long may she live. The spirits stood before a living portrait rendered by exquisite hands: the vast proscenium of an elaborate stage dwarfed their spirit trio. The set scene laid wide before them was a stately school on a moonlit night, dim, eerie, engaging . . . and awaiting its players.

The eldest of the three spirits stepped forward as if to touch this threshold upon which the past would play, a tall woman, appearing nearly forty and garbed in a plain dress. Her long, waving tresses—in life, they would have been a dark blonde—hung gamesomely down around her shoulders. Though she wore the grey-scale of death, the palette of the Whisper-world, her eyes were kind and her face very much alive.

She addressed the two spirits before her—a fair young woman and a raggedy little boy—in a boisterous Irish accent, as if she were presenting a vaudeville act, a mischievous light in her grey-hazel eyes. "Lady and gentleman, our forces of divine intervention present to you one of several scenes rather recently acted, starring our charges Headmistress Rebecca Thompson and Vicar Michael Carroll, here members of that honourable patrol known as The Guard, and the last of our miserable personal dramas to unfold."

She took the hands of her fellow spirits, and the Liminal clock set high above the stage frame—a device consisting simply of two vast, floating metal hands above shifting metal barrels of numbers arranged to display a calendar date—began to turn. The scene began to play, memory cast wide as if upon a photography plate, sounds emanating forth quite like magic. The spirits watched.

In the scene, distant music and laughter lured a tall, willowy woman with silver-streaked auburn hair from her book-filled office into the tenebrous hall of the stately, Romanesque fortress that was Athens Academy. She wore a dark woolen dress buttoned primly and proper as befitted her station as headmistress, yet sewn with just enough elegance to keep her from looking entirely the spinster. Up a grand staircase to a shadowy landing she crept, a wide, colonnaded foyer lit only by great swaths of moonlight and several low-trimmed gas lamps. Hanging back out of sight, she took in the antics of her longtime compatriots, this motley family fate had provided in her youth, the spectre-policing Guard.

A foppish blond man stood arm in arm with a gorgeous brunette, both swaying beside a broad-shouldered woman playing a waltz on a fiddle—a woman who looked eerily like the Irish spirit now watching from the Liminal. Nearby stood a distinguished figure in clergyman's garb, singing a soft and tender verse in accompaniment to the strings. From the shadows the headmistress stared at him as if she'd never known or paid attention to his voice, and for a fleeting moment she appeared enchanted. But it was the centre of the scene that clearly struck her a blow, the black-clad man and his ghost-pale partner who danced slowly through a wide shaft of moonlight.

The waltzing pair was clearly enraptured. Languorous steps, their bodies partaking in the close confidence only marriage could fashion . . . The girl in the moonlight was nothing short of an angel, graceful and blinding white, radiating love as pure as her skin, eyes and hair were colourless. Her partner stared down at her as if she were salvation incarnate, his otherwise stoic manner entirely transformed.

The headmistress donned pain like a mask. She retreated from the tableau, letting tears come as they would. Keeping to the shadows, she slipped down the stairs and to the corner of the foyer below, looking out over the courtyard. Pressing her forehead to the window, she sighed and did not hear the soft tread behind her.

His voice made her whirl. "I know that certain things do not unfold according to our desires."

It was the clergyman. He stood partly in shadow, his bushy, grey-peppered hair smoothed down from its usual chaos, and his blue eyes danced with an unusually bright light. "I know we cannot always choose who we love. And I know how it hurts to see the one we love look adoringly at someone else. I know; I have been watching you watch Alexi for years."

The headmistress registered his words, gaped, flushed and then returned to staring out the window, as if by turning away she might hide her transparent heart from his unmatched scrutiny.

"I cannot replace him," the clergyman began again, and waited patiently for her to turn. He continued with a bravery that seemed to surprise them both. "And I do not fault you your emotions, though I must admit a certain jealousy as to their bent. I do not expect to change anything with these words. I know I am bold and perhaps a fool, but I can remain silent no longer. Should you desire closer company . . ." His fortitude wavered and he could not continue the invitation.

He dropped his gaze and said, "I shall now return to a glass of wine. Or two. But as we're too old to play games and deny our hearts, I felt it my duty to speak. At long last. At long, long last." He then offered her his signature, winning smile that could warm the most inhuman heart, bowed slightly and retreated, leaving the headmistress clearly thunderstruck, standing alone once more in the glare of moonlight through the window.

The scene paused in its inexorable march of a now-past event, and the voyeur spirits in the Liminal turned to one another.

"What is to be done of it?" the younger female asked in her London accent, staring at the subject before her with both pity and recognition.

"And what stands between them?" said the little boy, in urchin's clothes, his voice a Scots brogue.

"They stand between themselves. And they stand grieving," the Irishwoman's spirit replied. "They need a good shaking, the both of them. Twenty years of nonsense, which shall end with us. If we do all we can, if we do what I wish, we'll end up with *this*." She murmured a brief Catholic prayer for intercession, all she could think to offer, and opened her hands in supplication. The Liminal responded, recognizing the tongues of all faiths. The great scene shifted.

The Liminal clock turned, the numbers trembling, the long hands quivering, as this outcome was not certain. But this possible future scene revealed a warm hearth and home, a blazing fire backlighting two silhouetted forms bending close as only lovers would. The trio of spirits gave sighs of appreciation, felt a gruesome weight of melancholy lifted.

The Liminal felt the change in their hearts, and the corners of its proscenium reacted; sparkling, vibrant, humming. The relieving of melancholy wielded great power. So, conversely, did the creation of it.

"But it's dangerous, the tasks they must be taken through," the little boy protested, knowing her intent. He shifted his feet on the glassy stone of the Liminal. "We could lose them to time and shadow. We could lose *ourselves*, be trapped forever if we're not careful. I do love hangin' from the Athens chandelier, but a nice rest might make a lovely Christmas present . . ." The loving scene before the fire faded to darkness with a slow hiss.

The second female nodded. "Even if it weren't nigh impossible . . . it's dangerous to weave souls through memories and time. Dark moments can rewrite themselves even darker. To take them through time, to risk changes? To change only the necessary moments, of their particular history, for the correct outcome? And, doing so with members of *The Guard*? Why, doesn't that make it even more perilous? Especially considering *him*."

The Irishwoman pursed her lips, undeterred. "True, we

only vanquished Darkness in form, not in spirit. We broke the cycle of the vendetta, but human misery will build him again. If we bring the headmistress into his world and she cannot overcome the poison inside her, if she's captured by the shadows, we'll have lost. I'll have died for nothing, The Guard toiled for nothing and the darkness that presses in around us even now will win her. But I'm willing to risk another sacrifice, to threaten my own eternal rest at the side of my beloved. For I believe in many things, but I believe most heartily in Rebecca and Michael."

"You'll dare bring them here?" asked the young woman, in awe. "And for you, what about your love, what will Aodhan—?"

"I assure you we've been up against far worse," said the Irishwoman. "I warred against the worst of the Whisper-world, remember! I tell you. I'll make a sacrifice." She called to the Liminal, announcing herself like a prophet. "Liminal edge, you tell those who beg your aid that you'll not change the course of lives without barter. But be clear I make my deal with you, not the devil, and I expect generous justice. Thus I place my soul on the line. I agree to remain trapped here in this uncomfortable between, unable to appear to my beloved friends and unable to gain the Great Beyond at my love's side until our two charges make the first honest step toward learning the lessons we must teach."

The Liminal stage had gone dark, a wall of black before them, the occasional tendril of Whisper-world mist curling across its surface.

"How . . . does one make a . . . deal?" the little boy murmured, breathless.

"Aodhan told me. My love traveled between worlds for ages and learned many things." The Irishwoman did not hesitate. She pressed her palms against the Liminal wall and hissed in pain, as if there were needles in that barrier. A deep black fluid oozed from her palms, phantom blood, sipping a bit of her life force before her wounds closed, her compact sealed. The Liminal sparked across its dark threshold like a fork of lightning, the air was charged and the portal was open. Clearly it was ready to begin.

She turned to her fellows with hope upon her grey face. "Sometimes a good haunting is just what a soul needs, even the most heroic. And we shall surely give them that. Come, we've not long before Christmas. It is the time of miracles."

"And the Liminal well knows it," said the boy, peering warily at the portal of infinite possibility. The edges of the frame again sparked, as if in assent.

The Irishwoman nodded. "Go, let us begin. Call upon them, the both of you. I daresay *one* of them will be thrilled to see you."

They all three closed their eyes in concentration.

The Liminal clock hands and numbers shifted to the hour and date concurrent with the mortal present, just days beyond the memory they had viewed. A new scene was born, and the living portrait now displayed a modest apartment filled with the same lively Guard characters, all save the headmistress and she who was lost.

The little boy spirit was the first to descend through the now-porous Liminal membrane, to pass through that proscenium portal and into the room. Immediately inside, there was great tumult regarding him.

The spirit of the Irishwoman chuckled at this, her greyscale eyes filling with fond tears. The other spirit placed a hand upon her shoulder, but the Irishwoman shrugged it off. "Go on, Miss Peterson." She gestured her forward, grinning. "I trust that I will eventually be able to follow you." Her voice was hopeful but her mood anxious.

As Ms. Peterson descended, the Irishwoman remained in the Liminal, watching the familiar, tumultuous melee of spectral and human interaction. "I'll forever miss that. *You,*" she murmured to the friends who could not see her.

After a moment, she moved into the thicker shadows. There she drew back a drape on another picture made manifest by the powers of the Liminal edge, a further masterwork in the museum of the cosmos, and murmured, "On a separate stage, the curtain now rises on Headmistress Thompson. Alone."

Indeed, just beyond sat Ms. Thompson, isolated in her academy apartments, her knees folded awkwardly upon bedclothes that showed no signs of having been slept in. Usually a model of efficiency, hard work and propriety, the headmistress was uncharacteristically undone.

The Irishwoman clucked her tongue. "Rebecca. Why aren't you with our friends? We scored a victory against Darkness. All of us. Why can't you make use of it?"

The headmistress's eyes were red with tears, her blouse askew. A white cat lay curled at her feet, and her thin hand stroked it almost mechanically, as if she dared not stop.

"I've no regrets, Rebecca. Not a single one," the voyeur spirit murmured. "It's time you felt the same." She turned back to the great stage opposite, inside of which her friends had resettled. Her two ghostly companions had disappeared and so she addressed the former Guard, those she considered family. "It's time *all* of you felt the same."

In the living painting that showcased her cohorts, the sturdy man who had confessed his heart in the earlier scene still sported distinguished age lines, unruly salt-and-pepper hair and clergyman's clothes. His blue eyes were wide and sparkling with an incomparable quality of compassion. But somewhere deep behind those oceanic orbs, somewhere deep behind the wide and contagious smile and the armour of good humour, lay the same private and keening pain that had just been on display.

"Twenty years of nonsense, Michael Carroll. Upon my dead body, I swear to you, you'll have a very merry Christmas if it's the last thing I do."

Chapter One

Vicar Michael Carroll turned the ladle in his pot of mulled wine and let the scented steam rise to his nostrils, unlocking emotion, memory and all those forces that such smells do around the Christmas holiday. He glanced out the window of the kitchen in his small Bloomsbury flat, which looked unflatteringly down upon an alley, and was pleased to witness a solitary flake of snow brush the thick, uneven glass before vanishing. It would be the first of many firsts this season, if the fates allowed.

Drawing himself a heaping tankard of Josephine's favourite cabernet, procured from the stores of her café and heated with bobbing chunks of cinnamon, fruit and cloves, he moved into his small dining room. The corners of the chamber were plastered at uneven angles, having settled awkwardly at the beginning of the century when the building was new. The window here only gave half a view of the avenue beyond, but he could see lamplighters plying their trade and nearing his street. It was not yet dark, and a purple sky reigned over parapets and smokestacks that grew ever higher and higher, the churning wheels of industry cranking them upward to challenge twilight's celestial throne.

He sat at a rough-hewn wooden table worn smooth by use, by company and the press of his own hands. Sliding his palms forward onto it, he eased into his chair, bracing himself and his heart, connecting with something solid and simple. The odd powers that had coursed through his body had once made his fingers twitch. Those powers were no more. Nonetheless, holding his palms firmly down, rooting himself to the table and to humanity, was one of his usual exercises. It brought him peace.

Michael, unlike his five compatriots in The Guard who had until very recently been charged with the Grand Work, had never cursed it. Theirs was a strenuous and at times lonely responsibility—though it didn't have to be—but it was ultimately rewarding. The Guard had been the law of the land, spectrally speaking. Though they'd left benign spirits well enough alone, each of their coterie had been granted a specific, beautiful power to arraign evil spirits and keep them from harassing the unwitting mortal populace. The Guard had controlled traffic of the unfettered and malignant dead all throughout London for twenty some years. They'd done the world a great supernatural deal of what Michael would consider Christian charity.

But he had to admit that his role in the Grand Work had held some irony. Literally the Heart of the group, he could open locked doors, touch a breastbone and flood someone's veins with joy, change the emotional contents of a room, shifting energy and intent like metals processed by alchemy. And yet he'd never gained happiness of his own, or the heart of the woman he'd loved for those twenty some years.

In the beginning they'd been simple teenaged youths, arraigned by a goddesslike force and called to duty. They'd been universally awkward and unlikely companions from disparate backgrounds and classes; they'd suspected little of their lives ahead. Michael hadn't known *anything* when he began seeing ghosts, when he began learning how his respective gift augmented their group. He hadn't known how long it would take for their prophesied seventh member to join their ranks—or that one of their beloved number would fall in recent battle. What he did know was that, from the very first moment he laid eyes on her, he loved the young and spindly brunette who would be their second in command. He'd loved Rebecca Thompson since Westminster Bridge in the summer of 1867.

She, in turn, likely from that very same moment, had loved the young man who would become their leader. Alexi. The battle with Darkness and the Whisper-world, in retrospect, seemed the easy part.

Michael pressed his hands harder against the table, slid them farther from his body, stretching his taut muscles and wrestling with his nerves like Jacob did the angel. He'd not seen Rebecca since they laid Jane in the tomb three days prior; she had gone to her apartments and locked herself in. She blamed herself, he could tell, wished God had taken her instead. Michael thought the sentiment might kill him. Nothing felt familiar. He'd lost his powers, Jane, and now he was losing Rebecca. His heart, so full of joy and love, was suffering a tumbling withdrawal from its preternaturally augmented height. It was a terrifying, dizzying fall.

"Pull yourself together, man," he murmured. "It's nearly Christmas."

His front door burst open, making him jump and splash warm wine onto his hand. Pursing his lips, knowing just who it was without even a glance, he finally looked up to behold the stern and striking figure upon his threshold. All in black stood his dear friend and unintentional rival, Alexi Rychman, former leader of the London Guard.

"Dear God, Professor. I truly thought, now that the weight of the known world is no longer entirely on your shoulders, you might at least allow yourself the more socially preferred custom of knocking upon a friend's door before entering."

"Old habits," Alexi intoned, his voice rich, low and commanding. It would always be thus, even though he had no group to lead any longer.

Behind Alexi, a moonbeam of a young woman stood with an apologetic look on her face. Michael grinned and forgot his irritation. "Ah, well, Mrs. Rychman . . . with you at his side, all debts are erased."

Alexi turned proudly to his entering bride. She was certainly the youth among them, Alexi not quite twice her age, but then again, where ancient prophecies were concerned, when gods were fiddling with mortal lives and taking their bodies as their own, age hardly mattered. Her fine taffeta skirts, in her favourite shade of rich blue, brushed the coarse wood of the door and rustled as she closed it.

She received Michael's warm expression with a radiant smile that transformed her death white face into a ray of magical starlight. There was nothing about her that was ordinary. The whole of Mrs. Persephone Rychman remained white as a spectre, even the hair piled atop her head in an elegant coif. But the light here was diffuse enough that she did not have to wear the dark blue tinted glasses that shielded her eerie, breathtaking, ice blue eyes from any harshness.

"My husband never allows me to get to a door first, Vicar Carroll, otherwise I might abate his most startling tradition," she said sweetly.

"Since we've lost so many traditions, I suppose we'd best keep the ones remaining," Michael chuckled in reply.

While he had wanted an evening alone—to plan, to ruminate, to dream—he could not deny that Persephone made all disappointments bearable. She had saved them all from spectral Armageddon, and her mere presence reminded him of hope. Even her husband, a cold and fearsome man, eased into something more handsome around his strangely beautiful wife.

"Come then, you must sit down, now that you've come calling and disturbed my quiet. I see your nostrils flaring at the smell of it, Professor, so I know you'll want a cup of your favourite brew."

Alexi nodded and drew out a chair for his wife. She looked up at him with fond eyes, her hand unconsciously grazing her abdomen where her corset stays were bound more loosely these days. Having almost lost what she'd hardly knew she had, under horrific circumstances Michael didn't wish to relive, he noticed her hand now rested there often, cradling the invisible life their beloved Jane had died to save.

Ducking into his small kitchen, he returned with a glass of wine for Alexi and a cup of steaming tea for Percy: as a parochial vicar for the Church of England, he always had a kettle of water at the ready, for he never knew when a parishioner might need guidance. It was more often that The Guard came calling. Would they still, now that they had lost their gifts?

The pair accepted their drinks, and Alexi wasted no time in admitting the reason for his visit.

"Michael, dear chap, now that we're no longer arbiters of escapees from the spectral realm, I feel it necessary that Percy and I take the genuine, lengthy honeymoon we were so rudely denied by the onslaught of spectral warfare. However, I think it ill advised to leave Athens Chapel unattended, should there be . . . spiritual backlash or any other such nonsense. I'll need your assistance to keep an eye open in case something flares up. Not that we could band together again without our powers, without our Healer . . ." Alexi's usually firm voice faltered, and everyone looked at the table. He cleared his throat. "I assume this is not a problem?"

Michael opened and closed his mouth. He didn't want more responsibility; he wanted time, now, to be a suitor.

Alexi read the conflict upon his face. "You've something better to do?"

"The good vicar does have a job, Alexi," Percy murmured.

Alexi looked unimpressed. "Be that as it may, I may need him to step in and assist Rebecca with goings-on at the school, too. I'm not officially an administrator, but I might as well have been. The headmistress deferred to my judgement in many things."

True, Rebecca often listened to him, but Alexi didn't have to be so smug about it. His unwavering air of confidence rode Michael far rougher than usual.

About to open his mouth and chide his friend, he stopped and considered the impulse. What was this? What was this overwhelming irritation he felt for his dear comrade? He had always suffered notions of fleeting jealousy or resignation, like any mortal, but never with such a sudden sense of petty anger. His great heart had indeed withered with the loss of his gift. He wondered if his inner foundation of faith, too, his touchstone of assurance, would prove similarly shaken.

Percy's voice roused him from his worried reverie. "How are you faring, Michael, in our new retirement?" She spoke softly, brushing her hand over his. Looking into her eyes, he fancied he could see her thoughts. Curious, empathizing, she was so intuitive despite her innocence, such an old soul in such a young, inexperienced body.

He shrugged. "Good, good. I spend more time at the church—never a bad place to be when one faces such a dramatic shift in life. There's more chance to think, to pray . . . I've plans, you know. You two are not the only ones trying to make up for lost time." Percy took a breath, but Michael continued before she could interject. "And how is *he* faring?" He indicated Alexi.

"I'm not sure he quite knows what to do with himself," Percy replied, allowing herself a little grin.

Alexi turned. "Please don't *you* go calling me insufferable, as The Guard has always done."

At that moment the door was thrown wide and a nasal voice was quick to comment, "Did I hear the word 'insufferable'?" Lord Elijah Withersby entered, a lean, flaxen-haired man in foppish satin sleeves, and he opened his arms to the assembled company. "Why, you must be talking about His Royal Eeriness, Minister of the Constant Sneer!" He bounded forward and clapped the grimacing Alexi on the arm.

Percy bit back a giggle, ever entertained by Lord Withersby's outlandish titles for her imperious, black-clad husband. Michael was glad she was so good-humoured about the teasing, The Guard's eldest tradition of all.

"Alexi, my dear man," Elijah exclaimed, "I know you simply cannot be away for long without missing me terribly, so I thought I'd oblige you. Rebecca said you were here on business. Hullo, Vicar! Wine, please!"

"Rebecca spoke with you?" Michael asked, on edge. "Did you see her?"

Elijah shrugged. "She barked at me from the other side of her door."

Alexi nodded. "Have we all called upon her then, and she has admitted no one?"

"So it would seem." Michael wasn't sure if his clenched fists were noticed, but he couldn't be bothered if they were. He sighed, rose and went for more wine. The instinct of hospitality ran deep.

A beautiful and impeccably dressed woman appeared through the front door. Rolling her eyes, she closed it behind her with the same consideration as Percy and moved to Lord Withersby's side. "Neither of you knock," she complained, offering fond, French-accented derision to both Elijah and Alexi. She looked at Percy with empathy, a twinkle in her eye. "We trail behind well-dressed animals, my dear."

Josephine Belledoux, the Artist of London's onetime Guard, and Lord Withersby, its Memory, had been lovers for longer than they'd cared to reveal. Not wanting to conflict with the delicate, pathetic love triangles already scoring the group, they'd thought it best to keep their happy pairing away from their cohorts. The truth of their relationship had been only recently admitted.

Michael returned with more mulled wine and pulled spare, rickety chairs from what could hardly be called a sitting room into the dining area.

"Yes, *I* am here on business, Withersby." Alexi eyed the turquoise fabric of Elijah's sleeve splayed upon the table. Reaching out to finger the starched, gilt lace upon the cuff, he withdrew in distaste. "What are *you* doing?"

"I don't know what to do!" Elijah cried, collapsing dramatically upon the table. "How on earth can I traipse about London as I wish, commandeer Auntie's house as I please, if I cannot bend anyone's mind to my bidding? If I cannot make them forget, if I cannot become invisible in their presence . . . Oh, the horror of living the *real* life of a gentleman!"

"Oh, Withersby, you're hardly a gentleman. You'll make do just fine," Alexi replied.

"He's maddening," Josephine muttered. "I'm painting more beautiful canvases than I've ever painted in my life, finally, subjects besides angels and death, and he won't leave me alone for a minute. *Mon Dieu.* I told him he should take up a sport, use all this excess energy of his—"

"You know, Withersby, I've shuddered to think what would have happened to you without our Grand Work to set your life's early course," Alexi remarked. "That said, you might enjoy what leisure your class offers you, now that you're free to fully take part."

Elijah stared as if his friend were daft. "You'll never understand the finer points of high society. Why, if I've taught you nothing, I'd thought you'd realized it's a requirement of my class never to be content!"

Everyone turned, eyeing Josephine with pity. "I know, I know, I'm a fool," she said, her French accent making her words drip with drama. "I tell him he needs a hobby, a new club, something. But no, he goes careening about the estate or pacing madly about our flat—"

"You've a flat?" Michael asked.

"We've always had a flat," Elijah replied. "But with the upcoming nuptials—"

Josephine interrupted. "That's truly the reason why we're here, Vicar, we need to set a date for the wedding."

Alexi turned to her. "You know, you don't have to do this."

Josephine chuckled. "Our fates were sealed long ago," she said with mock weariness, touching her fiancé's face with such obvious adoration that no sarcasm in the world could have countered it. "I accept as best I can and suffer onward. Right, Madame Rychman?"

Percy shrugged. "Alexi's not nearly the handful that Lord Withersby is. I find myself resigned to no fate but happiness." She smirked at Elijah, a sparkle in her eerie eyes. Alexi grinned triumphantly and snuggled his wife close.

It was still uncanny, Michael thought, to see Alexi smile.

Twenty years he'd known the man and all Alexi had done was scowl. The transformation truly was remarkable. But some things would never change, particularly such endless verbal fencing.

"Alexi," Elijah whined, "how *ever* will I have the upper hand now that you have this sweet young thing to take your part?"

Alexi shrugged. "Your fiancée will have to put on a better act of being your champion."

Josephine lifted her hands in mock chagrin. Elijah grabbed her fingers and kissed them.

Further discourse was ended as the room suddenly lit with a strange and shifting light, as if the air were a curtain blown in a breeze. A spirit burst through the wall—a young boy— and the temperature plummeted. Alexi jumped up and lifted his palms. The Guard all stood and reached for one another, ready for action. Percy rose from respect, having been brought late into their circle. She was not quick on the defensive, having been rarely ambushed by ghosts of the villainous variety, and she stared at this boy in recognition.

Alexi opened his mouth to say a benediction in a foreign tongue never meant for mortal ears, bequeathed only to The Guard. He anticipated the bursts of an angelic choir, braced himself for a charged and ancient wind that would whip up around them, magnifying their powers against the restless dead . . . But he could say nothing. He could hear nothing. There was no familiar blue fire crackling from his hand, no celestial music hanging glorious the air. He was a demigod no more. None of them retained such honours. They had earned this retirement, but clearly none of them had grown accustomed to it.

The spirit bobbed before them, a ghostly urchin, unperturbed. Michael recognized him, too: he haunted the ceiling of the foyer of Athens Academy, circling the chandelier, always watching the headmistress with interest.

Alexi's upraised arm slowly sank, defeated. Michael watched his former leader and felt for him; the general was back from the war with nothing to command, with over half his life spent in service. No, it was not an easy shift. For any of them.

Percy instinctively took her husband's hand. "It's all right, Alexi. Billy means no harm, he comes bearing tidings," she murmured. Her beloved sank into a chair, crestfallen, and Percy gave him one last empathetic glance before turning her attention to the spirit. "Yes? What have you come to tell me, Billy?"

The boy only had eyes for Percy, with an occasional glance at Michael. The one-sided conversation continued as the boy rapidly gesticulated. Percy nodded, clearly still translator to the dead, their medium, the only member of The Guard who had ever been able to hear spirits speak and the only one still apparently in possession of any of her powers. Translating had been part of her duty as The Guard's prophesied seventh member, if only one of her many gifts.

A second spirit bobbed through the wall, a once-lovely girl now cast in a ghostly greyscale, her clothing dated decades prior, her spectral curls weightless in a phantom breeze. Percy's eerie eyes widened. "Oh, Constance!" she cried, rushing joyfully forward. The ghost moved to embrace her with a cold gust of air. Percy closed her eyes and waited out the chill, as if this were a perfectly normal greeting—and for a girl who was born seeing spirits and calling them friends, it likely was.

"How I've missed you, Constance," she said. "Are you well and at peace?"

The female spirit spoke as animatedly as the boy, but she

seemed to be offering reassurances. She turned to the urchin and they both nodded—glancing again, Michael noted uncomfortably, at him.

"I think it's a lovely idea!" Percy exclaimed.

"What is?" the ex-Guard chorused.

Percy turned to them with a mysterious smile, her eyes lingering on Michael in a way that made him even more uneasy. "Oh, nothing, just a bit of a Christmas present these spirits have in mind." She looked demurely at the company. "Pardon me, Michael, but might the spirits and I discuss matters in the adjoining sitting room? I feel it is rude for me to carry on a conversation none of you is privy to and"— excitement played across her lips—"that I'm not at liberty to relay, it being private business."

Her husband scowled in clear displeasure at being left out. Percy dotingly stroked his black hair but offered no apology.

Michael gestured to the next room. Percy moved into it, the spectral boy close on her heels. Constance wafted to follow, offering Alexi a curtsey on the way out. Michael recalled having seen her at Athens Academy, too.

Alexi addressed her. "It is good to see you, Constance," he called as the spirit moved to pursue Percy. She stopped at the sound of her name. His scowl eased though his schoolmaster tone remained. "I owe you a bit of credit for making it quite clear, despite my inability to hear you, that I should teach my then-pupil to waltz. That thrilling lesson began our downfall; your friend is now my wife. As I didn't see you haunting our wedding, I assume the news might please you."

Constance's gaunt face brightened into a delighted smile that lit her whole transparent being, and she clapped her hands soundlessly in delight.

Percy poked her head out from the next room. "Constance, are—?"

The ghost said something, grinning, bobbing in the air.

Percy blushed. "Oh, yes, the professor and I are married. Isn't it wonderful?" She stared at her husband with renewed excitement, as if she could still hardly believe her good fortune, and Alexi's scowl was again vanquished by his earnest wife. A moment later, the spirits and Percy disappeared also, to discuss their mysterious business.

Percy. They'd found her so late in the course of their Grand Work, she'd been with them for such a short time before their powers were taken back, that Michael wondered what more they might have accomplished had she spent her entire life with them. Then again, she was only nineteen, and had he known her as a child it would have been awkward for Alexi to up and marry her. But true love overcame all obstacles, despite needing to await its time. Michael supposed if an immortal incarnation of Rebecca had taken up residence in one of his young parishioners and sought him out at an appropriate juncture, he'd think about her age a bit differently, too. As for its time . . . he had certainly awaited love long enough.

Elijah and Alexi fell to quarreling, filling up the silence with familiar chatter. Withersby demanded Alexi be present for his and Josephine's imminent wedding, but Alexi was set upon taking immediate time away. Each demanded theirs was the more important event, and neither budged. The debate then progressed to who, in truth, was the more difficult man in the realm of cohabitation. Josephine steered clear of a vote.

The two men whirled on Michael at the same time, both clearly expecting his acquiescence.

"You'll take care of the Athens particulars I delineate?" Alexi barked.

"You'll arrange the wedding?" Elijah insisted.

Michael took a breath and called upon the one gift that thankfully had not left him: his patience. He took a sip of mulled wine and examined his anxious compatriots. "Professor, you'd be hard-pressed to find anywhere I'd rather be than at Athens Academy, to help the headmistress," he said. "And Withersby, anything to get you into a church—may the Lord forgive me or bless my efforts." He smiled. "Perhaps it's best if Alexi and you aren't both under one sacred roof, though. I fear other guests might be harmed by chastising lightning bolts from Heaven should you quarrel so in His house."

Percy breezed back into the room. The spirits were gone. Alexi stared at her expectantly. She kissed her husband on the head, beaming. "I love Christmas!" she exclaimed, and took her empty teacup into the kitchen. If any of the former Guard were waiting for an explanation, they received none.

Michael picked up his tankard and followed her. As they both set their cups down upon a side table near the washbasin, the two turned to look at each other. "Truly, how are you?" they both asked at once. Percy smiled. Michael chuckled.

"You first," Michael prompted. "As I'm not sure I want to know what those spirits said, do tell me of your recent life. Be honest."

Percy's moonbeam eyes sparkled. "I'm very well . . . though I'm often reminding Alexi that he's just as impressive as he's always been, that he's just as important. The world needs mathematicians as much as it needs ghost hunters. More perhaps." She chuckled. "My, how he does like being in charge."

"Just think, my dear Percy, how long he's been in relative control of everything. He was tasked with directing our little group from the start. That control first slipped when we fumbled over Prophecy, when we met you, and it's been sorely tried ever since. He's had little opportunity to impress you, to show you our work when it was humming with maximum efficiency under his leadership. There was a time we were like machines in a divine factory," Michael promised her with a smile. "And he does so love to impress you."

Percy blushed. "But he already did, long before I ever knew about the Grand Work or The Guard. I'm waiting for him to trust me that I fell in love with him as a professor, not leader of a force against the supernatural."

"It will take time for him to adjust," Michael said. "In the meantime, I assume he'd like to orchestrate your every move? Though I must say, you handle him brilliantly."

Percy shared his half smirk. "Alexi's restrained himself from giving me direct orders, but takes great care to make sure I'm always comfortable, always provided for and always supported. I cannot say I mind. It's rather sweet to have a man like him doting. Especially in my condition," she said, brushing her abdomen. "Now, your turn. You'll not play the counselor and avoid being counseled."

Michael clenched his jaw, not wanting to speak of it. "I don't even know where to begin."

Percy knowingly shook her head. "But you two have already begun." She'd been the one to encourage him to confess his feelings to Rebecca in the first place, there in that darkened Athens foyer. Percy had been directly invested in this matter since she was first aware of it.

"Have we? Begun, I mean? It was a desperate time. We've not seen one another since we laid Jane to rest, all of us fiddling and making uncomfortable small talk, stifled by grief . . . It's been like none of us knows each other anymore."

"Alexi and Elijah were at each other again. I'd say life's returning to normal."

Michael bit his lip and gave in to temptation. "All right, I can't bear it. What did the spirits say about me?"

Percy smiled. "Are you a fan of Dickens?"

Michael blinked. "Of course. I'd have liked to have recruited him for The Guard, were we around forty-odd years ago. Who isn't a fan of Dickens?"

"Oh, Alexi, for one," Percy laughed. "He claims the man a consummate fraud in ghostly matters, but I think dear Charles is rather to the point. I suppose the poor man could have used a Guard to relieve him of his three plaguing spirits, but then we'd never have such a wonderful story."

Michael nodded, then paused, eyeing her. "But wait . . . What are you aiming at?" Dickens? Christmas? Ghosts? His uneasiness mounted.

Percy continued. "It would seem that spirits are interested in turning the tide. Reversing the roles. Rather than corralling spirits, as you used to do, they'll corral you. For a time."

Michael furrowed his brow. "Turn the tide? Whose tide?"

"Why, yours of course. They want to see you happy."

"Do they?"

"Oh, yes. My friend, Constance, she understands this situation all too well. I've missed her desperately." Percy offered a tiny, sad laugh. "The danger of having spirits for friends. You wish them peace but then, when they find it, you're terribly lonely without them."

Michael's heart swelled. It wasn't the first time he'd wondered if she was a guardian angel as well as a mortal young woman; kindness and goodness incarnate.

She took his hand and returned his fond expression, her white face all the more radiant. "There's a journey ahead. Await its coming."

Michael raised an eyebrow. "Expect three spirits? Before the bell tolls one?"

Percy shrugged. "Alas, while I maintain I deem Master

Dickens insightful, I doubt this will play out just like his *Carol*, Mr. Carroll, so I can't be sure of the time."

A thought occurred to him, and Michael felt his smile fade. "Percy . . . will it be dangerous? Will I be the only one—"

She shook her head. "Oh, no, it's really more for the headmistress than for you—"

"Is it dangerous?" he pressed, even more forcefully.

A shadow crossed Percy's face. "While your experience has taught you to not trust every spirit, I do trust *these*," she replied. Her voice was too careful for him to feel reassured. "And . . . I shall be on guard," she added.

"But your husband wants to whisk you away."

"Your long-overdue merry Christmas is more important," Percy stated, stretching up to kiss him softly on the cheek. "I will find a way to remain. For safety's sake."

Without another word she returned to the dining table. Michael followed, puzzling over this new development.

Elijah was insisting that Alexi would look much better in a verdant green than in his constant black, and Alexi was regarding him—and the notion—with disgust. "Yes, yes," Michael interrupted. "All your bickering must be attended in good time, and your various requests. But for now leave a vicar in peace, will you?"

His friends made their farewells, some of them eyeing him with surprise. Michael shut the door Elijah couldn't manage to shut for himself, returned to his table and sat. The tumult was out of his house. "Good riddance," he murmured. Then he stood back up. He went for his wine cup. It needed refilling.

He stared at his empty home. It was too bare. While never the lavish sort, he wanted something just a bit grander, as he could never imagine Rebecca Thompson in anything less than a well-appointed town house with windows and fireplaces in every room. It embarrassed him to dream of making a home with her here: how could he even presume? And it was terribly hard to entertain guests in so small a space. And he enjoyed nothing so much as guests.

His grumbling was a show; he'd delighted in company. Always a social creature; he was, after all, the Heart of the group. Or at least he had been. Yet for all the activity, the one person he wanted present was off somewhere else, likely tucked away at the top of Athens Academy in her small and cozy attic apartments, possibly pondering the same questions as he: Could they start anew? What would come next?

Pouring the last of his batch of mulled wine into his tankard, he sat with a common book of prayer, hoping a bit of Gospel could set his soul at ease. Tomorrow he would call upon her, right after his rounds. It was a man's duty to call upon a woman. They'd indulged for years in behaviours hardly common, excusing themselves each breach of etiquette, always allowing the Grand Work to take precedence over custom, but it was high time they began acting like the upstanding citizens of the Queen's great England that he wondered if they could ever become.

His hands shook slightly, so he set down the book of prayer and placed them on the table. The fleshy edges of his palms vibrated against the wood. He was a man in his late thirties, and he wasn't any surer of how to address a woman than he'd been at fifteen, when he'd first wanted to tell Rebecca Thompson how lovely and interesting she was. His tongue had been shackled then, and two decades had done nothing to unlock it. And, what opportunity would there be? It wasn't as though The Guard had seen one another every day, back when they'd had their powers, but Rebecca's recent absence worried him. There was no Pull to bring them all together, no spiritual call to arms that would assure him of seeing his beloved and thus being fed on her presence for yet another day.

Her presence. He'd subsisted on that meagre portion for just over twenty years, so how could he now ask for more? What was to be done about it, and what if he did something wrong? She was so tender, so raw and so utterly not in love with him. He was paralyzed with fear, and the feeling was unprecedented. For years he'd been the great Heart, so named by the goddess on that first day the Grand Work brought them together. Now he was a mortal man, a simple vicar. And a doubting one, at that.

He did not believe that heaven would cater precisely to his whims, so he prayed that whatever Percy and the spirits intended would indeed help. He could no longer open locked doors, and one heart had always remained shut to him, even when he could. Thus, though it went against years of instinct, Michael would accept a bit of ghostly intervention.

Chapter Two

Headmistress Rebecca Thompson sat curled upon her bed, hugging her long and slight frame and stroking Marlowe, Jane's familiar, a white cat as sullen as she. She peered into the beast's green eyes, hoping to see the luminous quality that once resided there, a sign of an otherworldly power. But that luminosity had vanished when the cat's mistress breathed her last, when the possessing spirits of The Guard vacated them all in a rush of wind leaving only a searing emptiness. The resultant vacuum felt wrong, and Rebecca regretted that she'd ever taken the Grand Work for granted.

She'd had a familiar as well: Frederic, a raven. He was nowhere to be seen, and Rebecca ached for him. She'd no idea how comforting it was simply to have that black bird outside on a windowsill, something that was hers, an ever-present companion. Poe had been ungrateful in his prose. Now that her bird had quit her chamber, Rebecca Thompson had never felt so alone.

Lit dimly in gaslight, a dark London night past her drawn window, she was caught between utter terror, incapacitating grief and a slight frisson of possibility. She had supped upon bland soup, tried to read, considered rearranging Athens Academy curriculum for the new year, reorganized her small pantry, changed the direction of her Persian rugs and nearly paced holes in them before at last curling up with Marlowe, her trembling hands gliding haphazardly over his fur, staring at her apartments, bewildered.

When the board of Athens Academy sent her a letter asking her to apprentice as headmistress at the tender age of sixteen, an act she assumed came from Prophecy rather than from her proficiency, she didn't dare say no. Their sacred space and the heart of the Grand Work centred around Athens and so it was fate that placed her in this building. But she'd wanted, as the rest of them had, her own space not so tied to the Grand Work. She wanted to retire separately, to a place neutral. But alas, she had been and perhaps would always be defined by the academy in her waking and sleeping hours.

Craning her head toward the window, she watched snowflakes begin to fall. As much as she may have wished to be elsewhere, she hadn't gained the courage to leave the apartment for days. Her thoughts were murky as she contemplated her broken state. She should have been the one to die, not Jane. For all her mistakes, Rebecca mused with sullen surety, it should have been she.

As early as she could remember, she had striven to be a woman both accomplished and reliable, gifted and strong. Once, she had been all those things. For years she had performed her duty to The Guard with aplomb, had been their Intuition. Then she'd nearly caused Prophecy to fail. She was a Judas. She was weak. She should never have been spared. Even saving the lives of her students and helping to prevent warring spirits from tearing up London brick by brick could not diminish her guilt.

She had no idea where her friends were on this cool winter night. Usually she could sense them, but since the forces previously driving their destinies were gone, the group was disconnected. She spared a moment of pity for the world at

large, people who'd never known what it was like to be teth-
ered in some direct way to loved ones, but then that passed.
Her bond was now sundered. Perhaps the rest of the world
was better off ignorant of such a thing.

Because she did not know where to find her friends, she
was hesitant to go out into the night and search for them.
Her melancholy did her the disservice of supposing them
assembled and having a grand time without her. Not that
the party could ever again be complete. Not without Jane,
their modest Healer, their keen judge of character and quiet
recluse, The Guard's steadfast hope and Rebecca's dearest
friend.

"What is wrong with you, Headmistress?" she chided
herself. "Pull yourself together; you've an institution to run.
You've never been unable to perform that venerable duty.
Oh, but for the grief and these nerves . . ."

There was just so much to *feel*—something she'd attempted
for years to avoid. She needed help sorting out the guilt-
ridden, lonely, excitable and confused mess that was her
present state of mind. But, to this end, she had no idea where
to turn. She would once have gone to Jane, to sensible, stalwart Jane, since she most certainly couldn't have turned to
Alexi, both her friend and her greatest agony. But Jane had
gone to the angels, to be eternally by the side of the man she
loved; she had no further time for the sorry human lots of
those back in London.

Rebecca allowed herself a moment of supposition: What
if Vicar Michael Carroll came and called upon her? What if
he roused her from melancholy as had been his job for
twenty years, confessing again the new shock of his love to
her? Yet, she'd ignored everyone who had knocked upon her
door, even Michael. She simply couldn't talk, exist or relate.
She did not feel, after everything she had done and what

was left of her soul, that she deserved such adoration. Not by such a kind and wonderful man. Surely there was something better for him than her tired, misguided self.

Tucking herself beneath her covers, shifting but not daring to let go of Marlowe, she shuddered. The air was full of murmuring whispers, like the voices of angels—or of ghosts. After years of dealing with spirits in silence, the whispering did nothing for her nerves. She had faced down demons and was weary from the toil, so if there were indeed supernatural forces breathing down her home, she prayed that these were angels.

Christmas. The holiday was all about angels. On every street corner were carolers; Christmas trees, all the rage since Prince Albert's use of them, sparkled in windows. Candles adorned sills, welcoming wassailing and friendly company; glitter and firelight beckoned angels to tend the lost shepherds and sheep of London and tell them of miracles.

She'd seen many unbelievable sights over the course of the Grand Work, but she wasn't sure if any of them had been angels. Sure, she'd seen winged things, and the godlike forces that drove the Grand Work had their angelic qualities, though they remained more of myth and legend. None of them called themselves angels and they didn't quite act like what she'd expect of one. So she couldn't say she believed in the creatures—being a practical woman despite how little she found strange—as she couldn't vouch that she'd encountered any.

Nonetheless, Rebecca had long held a secret hope every Christmas tide that an angel would come to her, just like in the stories, and point to a star of reassurance. It would be a private prophecy, just for her, and one that promised she might one day be able to unlock herself, to feel the sorts of warmth, joy and celebration that the rest of London so effortlessly benefitted from during this holiday.

Thus, this year, as she had for many previous, though she felt her betraying, tortured heart unworthy, she allowed herself a desperate prayer that a miracle of this season might save her from herself.

Chapter Three

"Alexi, darling . . . we cannot go on holiday just yet," Percy said as her husband took great care to settle her next to him before the fire in his study. As she'd told Michael, he had been achingly tender with her since they'd found out about the pregnancy.

Her husband frowned. "What do you mean? What on earth could possibly be more pressing than spending a quiet week lounging about with me, indulging me, loving me . . ." He traced a finger down her cheek, down her neck toward her bosom, following the line of her dress and sliding it aside.

Percy sighed in delight. "Nothing at all, husband, could be more pressing," she murmured, taking his fingers and bringing them to her lips. "And we shall go, I promise, but I'm needed here for a bit. Not for long, but I must help Michael have a merry Christmas." Alexi opened his mouth to protest, but she stopped him. "You and I will go away, as we've planned. We'll spend Christmas just the two of us, but there's work to be done."

"Christmas is not even a week hence!" Alexi said with a slight whine.

Percy smiled. "Have you learned nothing from Master Dickens? Spirits can work wonders in just one night."

Alexi raised an eyebrow. "Dickens? Claptrap. Is that what you and they were discussing?"

"It's their idea."

"Well, you and the spirits had best wrap up your salvation by Christmas Eve day, when I'll have you to myself for as long as I please," he stated, rose and moved to the door. His eyes narrowed, flashing darkly. "And if there's any thought of you going again into the Whisper-world, I swear to you I will open hell with my bare hands to come collect you."

"I don't doubt it," she laughed, used to his zealous protection and knowing just how to defuse it. "But that's hardly the plan, my love. I'll be a mere bystander. Someone who can hear spirits should be on hand. Trust me."

Her husband took a breath. Despite his domineering nature, he was adapting admirably to keeping his voice and his mood tolerably level. "I trust you, Percy, with all my life. In fact, I've learned to trust you more than myself . . ." Percy opened her mouth to thank him for the hard-fought praise she well deserved but he continued. "But I don't trust ghosts. I can't. You wouldn't either if you'd seen the same sights and performed the Grand Work for the years the rest of us did. It's one thing to help a spirit find peace. It's another to allow one to meddle with your life."

"Alexi, please." Her voice was calm and sure. She artfully managed to hold the rose of his love without grasping the thorns. "You must support me in this. You and I have such love between us. It's possible for all the world to have such passion, and if we are given the opportunity to help soul mates finally come together—"

"You cannot force them to love one another."

"But they do already!" she argued. "Michael *always* loved Rebecca, and she's only just now realized it. They simply have to trust it, and themselves. As we shall have to trust Constance, a spirit friend I would trust with any noble life. The pair will also need to procure a hearth of their own; the spirits insist on it. We'll employ our and Withersby's fortunes to that end, I suppose, and make it look like it came from Athens. Oh, Alexi, I want to see those two happy so badly it hurts!" A lump rose in her throat. "In addition, maybe this can alleviate my guilt. Maybe this can be my penance for . . ."

Realizing what she could not bring herself to say, Alexi moved to her side and bent a knee. "Darling, Jane's death was not your fault!"

Tears fell from her eyes. "I'm not sure I'll ever believe that. Nor will you ever overcome your own sense of responsibility. I know you." Her expression brightened suddenly, a hopeful look in her eye. "Oh! Perhaps Jane could help! Do you think she could? If Constance could return . . ."

Alexi only shrugged. They hadn't seen Jane's spirit since the night of the final confrontation with Darkness. "Though I'd love to see her, she went towards peace, to the arms of her ghostly love. How could we wish her to linger with us instead?"

"Of course," Percy murmured. "Perhaps seeing ghosts has spoiled us to the precious fragility of mortal life."

"Ah, I've had too many reminders of the precious fragility of life," Alexi murmured, kissing her cheek, then bending to kiss her abdomen; the living miracle within. "Having nearly lost all that I'd begun to live for."

Not wanting to lose himself to sentiment, the stern professor rose and cleared his throat. "Yes, indeed. Do make our friends' Christmases merry, Percy; do. You've such magic about you and I suppose it's only right that you should share it." He softly kissed her atop the head, turned on his heel and strolled toward the other room. "Come to bed, though," he called. "Where magic assuredly awaits."

It was an irresistible command.

Chapter Four

Michael went to the orphanage infirmary in the morning, as was his weekly custom and the duty he'd long ago requested.

As a child, he'd had no idea which vocation would call him. He'd been a strapping lad, strong and energetic, with a zeal for life that family and friends envied and admired. He had supposed he'd be a woodworker like his father, but then came The Guard. As their Heart, there was suddenly too much love, goodness and wonder within him to possibly contain; he'd had to give it to others—as many others as he possibly could—or it would overcome him with its intensity.

The church had been the obvious choice, and he'd pursued a level within the hierarchy that maintained autonomy and a bit of flexibility, so as not to conflict with outside work, his *Grand* Work. The vicar duties of guest preaching, visits to shut-ins, infirmary patients and children of orphanages had quite served his need. Now, however, the Grand Work was gone and Michael feared for his faith. They'd been inextricably tied.

Of course, duty was duty, and he could hardly explain to his superiors that he was suddenly unfit for his position; the guiding force he'd lost had been an ancient power that in the church's eyes might appear more than a bit pagan. He doubted the children would care even if he was pagan, and he hoped they wouldn't notice any difference. He still loved them.

Little Charlie's condition had worsened overnight, and the

nurse who ushered Michael into his tiny room looked grim. Wan light and a worn screen separated the boy from a comatose girl opposite who was wasting away. Michael was ever surprised the girl stayed dreaming, and he prayed those fluttering eyelids housed glorious visions: angels, beauty and joy, all the things little girls ought to be imagining in their blessed young lives.

Charlie's sickly face brightened. "Hello, Father!" The children all called him "Father" here, rather than Vicar, and Michael let them use the more Catholic term. He rather liked the familiarity of it, as hearing the word eased the ache of not having children of his own.

"Hello, Sir Charles. I was told you've been fiercely battling a most vile dragon, and I am here to commend you for your bravery!" He looked down at the fine buttons on the lower cuffs of his coat and surreptitiously plucked one free, placing it in the palm of the child. "Your medal of honour, sir. The Queen herself has heard of your service to the Crown, and she declares that even the great St. George holds you in highest esteem."

Charlie's grin took up his entire face, and his shaking yellow hands clutched the proffered button. He gave a salute. "Thank you, my lord Carroll. I accept this honour with a grateful heart and pledge my life to more such battles." He spoke cheerfully, as if the wheeze in his lungs were no trouble at all, nor the cough that rattled his frame. Michael always found it hard to keep tears at bay here in the sickroom of the orphanage, and it was never so hard as now. He steeled himself to remain strong.

Not that Charlie was frightened, as were many of the other wards; the boy was shockingly insightful, uncannily intelligent and calm. He cocked his head to the side, and Michael suddenly felt himself being examined much in same the way

Mrs. Rychman had examined him the day prior. It was disconcerting.

His discomfiture was interrupted. The air around him grew frigid, and one by one ghosts wafted through the modest brick walls and hovered behind Charlie's head. Michael's heart sank and tears welled up. Surely these spirits came to collect the boy. How God could take such a gifted soul escaped him, unless He was covetous and wanted such dearness closer . . .

Charlie eyed him with a dawning realization. "Oh! You can see them, too, then."

Michael hesitated. It wasn't something he admitted in public, his ability to see ghosts; it was a Guard's pledge to keep skills secret. Though their power over spirits was revoked, the ability to see them was not. He could see no harm in admitting so with this child. It would even be a point of commiseration. He nodded, a tear spilling onto his cheek.

"Don't cry, Father, it's not for me that they've come. It's for you. It seems *you're* the one in need of caretaking this day. That's what they said."

Michael's tears vanished and his heart quickened. "You can *hear* them, child?"

The boy shrugged. "Those of us who live in the shadow of death can often hear the whispers of those who have gone before us. Yes, we've been conversing, sometimes about them, sometimes about me. But today they've been talking about you. About your doubt." Charlie screwed up his face and continued. "How can *you* doubt, Father? You're the kindest man I know. You're what I imagine angels to be like. Archangels, even. Like your namesake. Doubting does not suit you, Father. I beg you, be done with it."

Michael fought off shame. "Would it were that easy, my child, to slay my dragons."

Charlie smiled sadly. "I wish I could give you the peace the spirits say you crave. But they'll help you. Do let them, Father. They mean no harm."

The boy shuddered violently, the ghosts' cool draft was having an effect, and Michael rushed to stoke the fire in the meagre hearth. Turning to address the spectres, he said, "Leave the child be. Come to me alone, if and when you will," he commanded sternly.

The spirits vanished, nodding.

Charlie was looking at him strangely. "That story you always tell," the boy breathed, narrowing his eyes in thoughtful concentration, "about the princess and her devoted knight. In every adventure they battle the devil himself, and then the knight returns the princess to her attic loft where she sits alone. You've told me the moral of these adventures is perseverance against forces that would take us under, and that I must be such a knight and must struggle onward to find my own princess to cherish, as all good men should. But . . . it's you who's the knight in these stories, isn't it? Who's the princess, Father? Why doesn't she accept you? And, must you always part ways? How can that be a happy ending?"

The two of them stared at each other for a moment.

"Those are questions for which I have no answers," Michael said thickly, breaking the long silence.

The nurse came with ointments and gruel, and so Michael was spared telling that familiar story. He kissed Charlie's feverish head before leaving, heavyhearted. His powers had once kept anxiety at bay. Powerless, he was becoming its slave.

But, there was a duty to be done. Likely the spirits would chastise him for cowardice. He must anticipate their demands and begin to try and prove himself before their harrowing journey began. Perhaps he could avoid it entirely. Even better, perhaps he could save Rebecca the trial to come. This, above all, strengthened his resolve.

He ascended the grand staircase of Athens Academy and up to the third-floor apartments where his princess lived, again taking up his knightly quest. "It will do no good to cloister ourselves away," he murmured, trying to rally his courage. After all, he was the suitor. He had to call. But his hand trembled as he lifted his fist to knock upon the door. Behind his back he tightly clutched two bouquets, and thorns dug into his palm.

"Yes . . . ?"

"Hullo, Headmistress! May I have a moment of your time?" Michael's voice jarred him as it was reflected back, loud and forcedly jovial, against the wooden door. "It's been . . . days."

Her booted footsteps grew nearer but hesitated. "Hullo, Vicar," he heard. After a long moment Rebecca opened the door. "I suppose."

Michael smiled—a reflex—and took in the sight of her. She seemed taller somehow, there against the door frame in her usual choice of prim grey dress that was blue-grey like her eyes. As it was winter she wore pressed wool, and a cameo brooch at her throat. She was always appointed with quiet elegance. Her face was, as ever, stoic, but those eyes betrayed tides of emotion. As for her hands, one was pressed tightly against the door frame, one was behind her back. He doubted they shook the way his did.

Not to be deterred, Michael reminded himself of the fact that generally when he smiled at her she could not help but smile back. He lifted one of the two bouquets out from his back, roses of an exquisite deep burgundy, and his cheeks reddened as he presented them. "For you."

"Oh, Michael, how lovely! Thank you," Rebecca said,

blushing as well. "Come in, let me put them in water." She gestured him into her small rooms filled with carved wooden doors and fine rugs, countless books and scattered pieces of art. "Sit, I won't be but a moment."

As she disappeared, Michael withdrew the second bouquet from his back, a cluster of yellow posies, made his way to his favourite chair in the corner of the sitting room, a Queen Anne partly facing the window, and sat. Staring at the Athens courtyard below, snow-covered, with its fountain angel lifting up wings, a book and flowers toward heaven, he silently asked the statue for her benediction.

There was rustling in the pantry. Michael shifted the flowers upon his knees, unsure what to say when Rebecca emerged. *Good God, this could not be more difficult if I were sixteen,* he thought wearily. *Why I didn't press my claim at sixteen I'll never know.*

Rebecca returned with the flowers in a vase and set them on a carved wooden table. Turning to Michael, she raised an eyebrow at the second bouquet.

"For Jane," he murmured. "It isn't as if we can ignore our grief. It rules our hearts at the moment."

Rebecca blinked back tears. "Indeed. It would be nice to lay them on her tomb." She paused, then said, "I would offer you tea, but I simply must get out of these rooms. I've entirely shut myself away here—"

"I know."

She looked at the ground. "Yes, I suppose you do. I am sorry if not admitting you before seemed rude. I was . . . I *am* unfit for company."

"I've never thought so."

If anyone had ever seen her truly vulnerable, unfit for company, it had been he. He'd always made himself available at times of her need. He wondered if she resented that—or feared it.

She glanced at him. There was an uncomfortable silence.

Michael rose and brandished the flowers, moving to the door. "Jane always would exclaim about yellow flowers whenever we passed them in the street, even en route to an exorcism or poltergeist. I bought her some for her birthday, once, and now I'm ashamed I didn't buy them for her all the time." He opened the door and gestured Rebecca into the hall.

"I'm ashamed of a great deal," she replied, following his lead. Her voice was thick. Starting down the stairs, they descended to floor level.

"You mustn't be. Not about Prophecy, not about Jane, none of it. Whatever you fear, none of us has ever been perfect."

"My gift failed, Michael. It failed because of my frailty. Would you tell Judas Iscariot not to be ashamed?"

They crossed the foyer, devoid of students gone on holiday, and rounded the corner toward Athens Chapel. Michael shrugged. "We've all of us parts to play. And you hardly sent a messiah to His death. Are you *still* grieving over choosing Miss Linden as Prophecy over Percy? Haven't we moved on?"

Rebecca looked sharply at him. "The part of the betrayer was never a part I wanted."

"I daresay Judas wasn't fond of it either, but it was necessary." He wagged a finger at her. "But don't go equating yourself to scripture, Headmistress; our dramas are not played on so grand a stage. And remember: that same gift went on to save Percy's life."

Rebecca sighed. "I suspect you'll be taking my ongoing confessions for some time. The past months weigh upon me so."

"It will be my pleasure," he replied.

She offered him a slight smile and looked away. He wanted so desperately to touch her, but the chasm between their bodies seemed impossible to cross.

The chapel of Athens Academy was white and modest, with a plain table draped in white linen for an altar and windows with golden stained-glass angels lining the walls beside unornamented pews. A painted dove of peace floated on the back wall.

"So strange, to come here and not have it open to our sacred space, eh?" Michael asked. "Strange, to have this simply be a chapel. So strange to be *normal*."

There were two alcoves in the back, like those that would house baptismal fonts but less elaborate; this was built a Quaker institution and thus there was no great pomp in the style. The founder of Athens had his tomb here and had left space for another. Rebecca had long ago abdicated her natural claim to it, not wishing to live floors above her imminent grave. None of The Guard had ever dreamed it would eventually be the resting place of their dear friend Jane, but it gave them some small comfort to know that she was close, that her mortal coil was interred here in this space that had been the doorway to so many incredible things, so near the raw power that had once driven their lives together.

Michael and Rebecca approached the tomb bedecked in fresh bouquets: other Guard had paid their respects. Rebecca stared at the flowers, her hand to her lips.

"They're all those yellow favourites of hers . . ."

"For as self-involved as our group has been, we listened to small yet important details," Michael said with quiet pride. He offered his bouquet for Rebecca to do the honours.

Her blush had returned. "And some remain oblivious . . ."

Michael was unsure what exactly she meant.

"Pray over her, Vicar. Please," Rebecca insisted, closing her eyes.

Michael searched his mind for appropriate Scripture and found it in Corinthians, an adulation suitable to the Grand Work that in recognizing separate gifts had created their family for life: "'Some people God has designated in the church to be, first, apostles; second, prophets; third, teachers; then, mighty deeds; then, gifts of healing, assistance, administration and varieties of tongues.' We miss you, Jane, you and your gift. All of our designated gifts left with you. We hope to somehow honour your name as we live on without you. We . . . we wish to see you again, but not if that would cost you your peace. Be our angel, Jane. You always were." Michael looked up. "Oh, Heavenly Father, I hope you recognize what gold you've collected unto your bosom."

He felt a cold draft and glanced around in anticipation. But . . . there was nothing. Perhaps he'd imagined it. Surely Jane was at peace; gone to the arms of a long-lost love. He could not begrudge her that. What more could they wish for her than love and peace? It was selfish, wanting to see her again. He forced back tears.

Rebecca's face was unreadable. She moved to a pew and sat. Michael joined her, keeping a decorous distance though he yearned to slide close and put his arm around her. Just for support, for commiseration, for contact. He yearned for simple contact. How could it be too much to ask?

The silence continued. Perhaps it was the sanctity of the church setting that was keeping them quiet, but Michael felt a riptide roiling deep within him, struggling and churning. *Please. Say something. I don't know how to begin, Rebecca. You know how I feel; I've already confessed. Your silence makes me believe it was all in vain. I admitted my love, but what are you going to do with it? Insist you still that you were the one God should have taken? Can you possibly know how that pains me?*

The quiet continued. Michael felt himself drowning in it. They were too old. They were too broken. It was too late for them. Any relationship they could cobble together would be a joke. He was second best and always would be. Knowing what they knew about the afterlife, even death wouldn't change that. He felt a heretofore uncharted depth of melancholy, and speaking his love aloud now seemed its own death sentence.

The room grew frigid, and a harrowing wind burst through, though there were no open windows or doors. A darkness came over Michael. He and Rebecca cried out in unison, and then there was a new silence; deathly empty.

"Oh, no, the spirits," Michael murmured. He thought he had time, that the ghosts would come at night, that he might prepare her. "I should have warned you! Rebecca, can you hear me?"

On his feet, he reached out his hands but found nothing; no pews, no Rebecca, only darkness. He'd failed. His cowardice had doomed them both to what surely would be a harrowing, ghostly course. Would she be ready for it? Or would it at last break her?

What in the Whisper-world were they in for?

Chapter Five

Percy was startled by Billy bursting through the wall, his torn clothes flapping about him where he floated in the air of the Rychman estate parlour. "It's begun, Miss Percy! They're at the academy. Are you comin' to be the guardian angel for the headmistress, then, like Miss Constance said?"

Percy rose to her feet. "Oh, yes, Billy, but I wasn't expecting it so soon."

The ghostly urchin shrugged. "It's one."

One in the *afternoon*. Perhaps it was a ghostly joke. This wasn't Dickens's story, this was their reality, so either way Percy could not expect it to play out in the grand tradition of famous literature.

"Do be careful, Percy. It's a danger, bringin' the Liminal threshold down on the living. Might trap us all if we're not careful. We'll need that light of yours to keep us from turnin' Whisper forever . . ."

Percy nodded. The spirits had explained the Liminal to her, and she knew she could not control it like she did other portals to the Whisper-world. But she was undeterred, despite her aversion to the Whisper-world and its contents.

The bell of the grand clock down the hall tolled, and she rushed into her husband's study. "Alexi, it has begun. I must go to Athens. What horse shall I take?"

He rose and closed the distance between them. "You think to go alone, that I'll not be by your side? Danger may come in an instant. The headmistress is my friend, too, you know. My best friend. I wish to help. I'll be on hand," he declared in a tone that clearly brooked no argument.

"Darling," Percy said in a soft murmur, her hands on his shoulders. "Don't you see you may do more harm than good? All I ask is that you leave me to my task."

Alexi's stern brow furrowed in confusion.

Percy explained what she felt was obvious. "If the headmistress were to see you during this vulnerable time . . . well, it wouldn't be without its complications, considering her feelings for you, it would likely set the task back. Come with me if you must, but please remain in your office. I'll run to you the moment the spirits are done. Though I've every faith in the couple of the hour, it's just best . . ." Her eyes glittered with sudden tears. "Oh, my dear, don't you see? I cannot imagine how difficult it would be to fall out of love with you. Thank God I don't have to," she murmured, cupping his chin and kissing him.

Alexi's cheeks coloured slightly, and Percy found it the greatest treasure in the world that she could make such a man blush. Fate be damned, true love was the only power she craved—and it was her own. She hoped the spirits would help grant it now to her friends.

"Come," she said excitedly. "While I keep watch, you must send Withersby and Josephine to the property, and you must plant the letter—"

"It will all be done according to plan, my dear," Alexi stated, and went out to ready the carriage.

Despite the delay in their trip, he seemed to have taken to the plan they'd discussed and to leading part of the charge. She didn't doubt for a minute that he wished his friends the very best and would do whatever he could to assure it. Percy had not mentioned the specific dangers the spirits discussed, lest Alexi worry maddeningly over her in ways that would not be helpful. But where the Whisper-world was concerned, one could never be entirely sure.

She bit her lip. So much of her life had been throwing herself toward things she did not entirely understand or trust, events where she was fearfully unsure of the outcome. She shuddered and offered a prayer that it would not come to what the spirits had warned her about, the grim possibility of an *extraction*. The Whisper-world fed on melancholy, provender of which the headmistress was keen; it might not wish to let her go. Percy might have to step in. Perhaps literally. And there was no conceivable place she wanted to revisit less.

She ran to her room and opened a jewelry box, plucking out a beautiful pearl rosary that had been a gift from the convent where she was raised. Before their recent battle, Michael had blessed these beads with the additional power of his gift. They were resonant with peace and love, and when Percy squeezed them in her hand, her heart was fortified, her own gift at the ready.

"Come now, Vicar, Headmistress . . . Let there be light."

Chapter Six

Michael was alone in the foyer of Athens Academy. He whirled. "Rebecca?"

"She'll be all right. You're on separate journeys. Parallel, but separate. Billy, the boy from the chandelier, has asked me to help."

Michael looked down to behold the small voice's owner. The ghost of a little girl reached up and tried to take his hand, but her own passed through. She stared for a moment, then up at him. "Hello, Father."

Michael blinked, processing this new development. "I can *hear* you."

"For now," she said.

"This is what was foretold to me?" he clarified.

She nodded.

Michael recognized the girl. He'd just seen her at Charlie's bedside, at the orphanage, whispering and murmuring about him. Little Mary, he recalled. She'd been in the orphanage all her life, quite ill for most of it. He'd always regretted that he wasn't there when she died. He'd been out saving another little girl from malevolent spectral possession. Would that doctors had such skills to cast out influenza.

Little Mary, in her drab orphanage dress, smiled. "It's all right, Father, you always blame yourself. It isn't *your* fault when we die. I knew you were with me, in *spirit*." She grinned at her little joke.

Michael reached out to touch her cheek but met only cold mist. The girl was right: he did always feel responsible, wishing there was some part of the Grand Work that extended to healing sick children. He'd assuaged his need by offering Jane the key to the orphanage, and every now and then she'd worked a few healing wonders inconspicuous enough to avoid arousing suspicion. It also kept the children believing in angels, which he felt was an invaluable service to the church. He believed in angels, though he couldn't recall ever meeting one. He didn't figure Percy counted, being flesh and blood and all.

"Come," the little girl said. "We must have you take a look at things."

There was a crushing darkness as all light was expunged from the chapel. There was a fierce wind and strange noises, whispering, so much *whispering*. But then everything went silent, slowly brightened, and Rebecca again found herself in the dim afternoon haze of the chapel.

But Michael was gone.

"Michael?" she gasped, whirling to find herself alone with a ghost. A young woman floated before her, in slightly dated fashion and ringlet curls about her lovely, hollowed face.

"Hello, Headmistress," the haunt said with an eager expression.

Rebecca blinked. They weren't supposed to hear spirits! Only Percy had been able to do that. Was she going mad?

The ghost anticipated her. "You've spent your life in service to this world and the next. Your entire group has earned a good rest, though I daresay none of you are prepared to enjoy it. Now it's *our* turn. Your powers have retired. Now we have power over you."

Rebecca's blood ran cold. "Where's Michael?"

"Safe."

"But where have you taken him?" Rebecca insisted. "If you—"

The ghost held up a hand. "Only the good of our kind have power over you at present, so do not fear. But you've separate journeys this night, ere you again stand side by side. And, be careful of the bent of your heart, for shadows are close at hand."

Rebecca shuddered, unsure what the woman meant.

The spirit smiled. "Your safety shall be monitored."

It was a small comfort. Rebecca pursed her lips. "I know you, don't I?"

"Indeed. Constance Peterson, haunt of the science library, at your service, Headmistress." The ghost bobbed a curtsey.

"And . . . why is it that you're going to help me?"

"Because I was called upon to help you. Because I understand."

"Who called upon you?"

"A friend. And . . ." Constance pointed upward with a sheepish smile.

Rebecca was silent. Perhaps her secret Christmas prayer was being answered? Perhaps this was divine intervention after all. Though, she'd never thought it would come like *this*. This was much too dramatic, the stuff of Gothic fiction, suitable for Alexi and Percy. Not her.

"We're all worthy of an opportunity like this, Headmistress." The ghost's eyes sparkled knowingly. "Even if few of us are so fortunate. You've never lived a normal life, Headmistress. You should not expect one."

Rebecca stared at her, ever trying to see sense in the fantastical. "You. How did you . . . 'see the light'? Did you see errors in your mortal ways and thusly have evolved? For a spirit, I trust you are well and fully at peaceable understanding to be able to lead me now?"

The ghost nodded. "I am indeed at peace, enlightened, free to do what I will, after help from Miss Persephone Parker. She found what I'd been looking for, just as she's now found her own heart's desire and taken his name. We're all looking for something, you know."

Rebecca nodded, her jaw clenching involuntarily. She felt an icy cold weight press down upon her.

The ghost scowled. "I can feel that, Headmistress; melancholy's dread march. You must stop. You must not hear the girl's name and cringe."

Rebecca looked away so that Constance would not see her shame. "It is a curse," she admitted. "My heart is cursed, and I want to remove it."

"That, Headmistress," said the ghost, "is our task. To cure the accursed. Come. We've much to do and I dare not tax you. While you've a most stalwart mind for a mortal, too much talk with spirits threatens sanity."

The young woman held up a hand, closed her eyes and murmured, invoking power. "Liminal; the journey, I pray."

In response, the air rippled like thin fabric and their surroundings melted away. In an instant they were back in time, in the science library of the academy, when it was fresh and new and all the chandeliers still sparkled like diamonds, before dust settled permanently into their crystalline grooves.

"Before you point out that it is indulgent of me to show you my past," Constance spoke up, "let me remind you that we recognize problems in others before we recognize them in ourselves. I humbly offer myself as an example."

The ghost pointed to a table, to herself. She had been quite beautiful while alive, full of health and vigour if the countenance she wore appeared hard, unrelenting, annoyed. She sat poring over a stack of books adjusted quite pointedly to block her from the view of a young man who sat unobtrusively studying different work at an angle opposite. The young man's face was gentle and kind. He slid a book between them.

The ghost gestured Rebecca closer. The memory did not come without pain for her, Rebecca saw, and she felt humbled Constance should torture herself for the sake of helping her.

The living Constance was staring at the biological reference book that had been shifted toward her; not at the scientific content, but at the scribblings in the margin.

Constant is my care for you, sweet girl, my Constancy.
  All I ask is that you, for one blissful moment, put aside your obsession long enough to look into my eyes.
  —P.

The young Constance scowled and slid the book back across the table, moving it around the fortress of tomes she'd stacked to buffer herself against his simple request. She was careful that their fingertips did not connect as he received the book. Rebecca noted this with a bit of pride; even under her own rule, students were not allowed to touch members of the opposite sex.

And yet, if the girl had taken this boy's hand, she couldn't have said she would mind. She'd likely not punish them; this seemed innocent enough. In fact, she found herself wishing Constance would brush his hand, for it would clearly mean so much to him.

Undeterred by her rejection, the young man turned pages and found a new illustration, one that spoke to him, and he began to write. Rebecca opened her mouth to admonish him for defacing school property when she read what he'd scripted so carefully next to a diagram of the human heart:

Can science explain everything, my Constancy, when my heart beats only for you?

Constance returned the book, writing on the opposite margin a shaky reply:

Dear P., though you share my library table, I cannot commit any part of my heart, for I fear I do not have one to divide. The course of my blood flows toward science alone. —C.

She looked up at the boy and peered over their books, her voice a whisper: "Science is a man's profession, Mr. Clarke. I am a woman, and I must make a choice, whether to live as my sex, or to deny it and take the man's profession I crave. The demands of our age unfairly divide us. I'm sorry I cannot choose you."

Mr. Clarke appeared crestfallen.

Constance turned to Rebecca, tears in her phantom eyes, her greyscale face taut with sorrow. Rebecca recalled all the young women to whom she'd boasted of choosing to run an institution rather than a household, justifying her life choice. But it had been a damned lonely choice, especially when secretly pining for a chance to run the Rychman estate.

"I realized my mistake too late," the ghost said. "My greatest folly was to deny a lovely soul who asked nothing more than to remain by my side. Of all the places I could have been a scientist *and* a woman, it was here at Athens; these blessed bricks never asked me to choose. I never gave him, *us*, a chance, despite having no true objection. I pushed him away for three years before the fever took me." The spirit's eyes narrowed, and her voice was cool. "You've pushed someone else away for twenty. Why?"

"I don't know," Rebecca replied.

"Is there any more beautiful a calling in life than love?"

"I have *loved*," Rebecca hissed. "Desperately."

The ghost nodded. "So did I. I loved science—something that couldn't love me back. There's safety in that solitude. Do you understand?"

Rebecca could only nod.

"Safety, but no solace. I haunted this Earth until Miss Percy found that book, revealing the one critical experience I denied. There come many callings on Earth, and heaven allows us them all. You'd do well to realize the same, and to do it before you're dead."

"But that's just it!" Rebecca began, her eyes wide. "I . . . I don't think I merit being alive right now. I think the heavens made a mistake."

Constance's eyes glittered threateningly. The deceased had an uncanny ability to make one shiver, it was certain. "Ah. Indeed," the ghost replied. "And this is not the only time you've wished yourself dead." These were condemning words and they chartered their next course. Rebecca didn't know what the Liminal was, this force Constance wielded, but it responded.

Rebecca had no time to protest. The environment whirled, spun and shifted, and suddenly she stood in a darkened foyer of Athens Academy. There was the distant sound of an argument.

Rebecca turned, wringing her hands. "Oh, not this. Please, not this. It is my penance, I am sure, for my failures, but please . . ."

Constance gazed upon her with pity. "We've not much time, and I'm not the only visitation. There's something you didn't see, then, that you must see now. And through your pain you may yet make it right." The ghost sighed. "And I beg you, do so while you yet *live*. Come."

Rebecca gulped, trying to prepare herself. She knew exactly what she was about to see, and her body felt colder than if a horde of spirits was accosting her.

Constance led her toward her office, where the door was shut. The ghost gestured her forward. Rebecca fumbled at the door but passed through as if she too were a spirit. These were chimerical things, past memories; thinner than paper; visions, illusions . . . yet potent and all too real.

Rebecca's throat constricted. A younger Professor Alexi Rychman paced in her office, his dark robes billowing about him as he moved, his face set in characteristic consternation. She herself sat stoic, though she remembered her pain.

She looked at herself, in this moment fifteen years or so younger, and noticed the lines of worry already beginning to form, the thin mouth so prim and composed, those blue-grey eyes that stared at the imperious man before her, secretly drinking in his striking, stifling presence.

"Damn it, Rebecca," Alexi hissed. "I am no closer to telling you when Prophecy might come than I was years ago when the Goddess heralded our destiny and pronounced us The Guard. How *should* I know how long it will take?"

"It isn't about when Prophecy might come, Alexi, but how you're thinking of it. Tonight at the exorcism, when we stumbled at the force of that devilish blow, when you buckled in strain, I heard you mutter, 'My bride shall make it well.'"

Alexi stopped pacing and turned. "And?"

"Alexi—Prophecy won't be your bride. She'll come as a companion to all of us, not some predestined lover of yours."

Young Alexi's features went slack. "What do you mean?"

"The prophesied seventh member was never specified as *yours.*"

"Yes, she was," he replied.

"Tell me the precise words the Goddess said that make you think so."

"Why, *everything* she said." But Alexi thought back, clearly trying to latch onto a specific phrase.

"Nothing more than insinuations." Rebecca closed her eyes, using her gift of texts, the library of her mind, and plucking free an exact transcript of the Goddess's words: "'I hope you will know her when she comes, Alexi, my love. And I hope she will know you, too. Await her, but beware. She will not come with answers but be lost, confused. I have put protections in place, but she will be threatened and seeking refuge. There shall be tricks, betrayals and many second guesses. Caution, beloved. Mortal hearts make mistakes. Choose your seventh carefully, for if you choose the false prophet, the end of your world shall follow.'" Rebecca stared hard at Alexi. "What in that promises you a lover?"

"Everything," he replied. "When she comes, I will love her. You may be the Intuition of the group, but your belief does not therefore supersede mine. On this point I am sure, and that's final. Good night, Headmistress." The young Alexi exited in a rustle of black fabric, and the room expanded; breathing was easier.

It was the first time this particular argument was voiced, the elder and wiser Rebecca recalled, and most certainly not the last. They argued these precise points for the next fifteen years until Prophecy finally did show up, a snow-white girl unlike anything The Guard expected, and Rebecca would grow blinded by jealousy and make dangerous mistakes in an effort to disprove an undesirable fate.

Yet, it was not this failure that Constance wanted her to see; it was the next torturous few moments. Rebecca watched herself sit stiffly in her chair, watched her eyes cloud, watched her shoulders tense against the thick wool of her jacket. Such pain, Rebecca felt and saw, shocked by its magnitude. Such pain, all to love a man who was saving himself for some future stranger, when she was yet so close and could grasp those black robes and pull him near . . . Even looking back, knowing all she knew, she could not think herself wrong for urging caution in the matter of Prophecy, or for loving him. She had never been able to help it. But then, as now, such love was futile. Empty. Hopeless.

A sound came from the windowsill. Frederic, her raven, a single blue breast feather indicating his service to The Guard, had alighted upon the ledge outside. He rapped again upon the casement.

"He'll never love me," her younger self said. "I do not want this fate. I do not want to patrol the dead if I *feel* dead, and this shall surely kill my heart. I don't want this destiny, for I am ill suited to it." Her face held no expression, though Rebecca recalled all too well how her body had shuddered against her corset bones, how her heart lurched in agony. She'd never been fond of emotions, and they'd certainly never been more useless or cruel.

Her young self rose, went to the window and dragged a finger across the glass, absently mollifying the bird. Then she walked out of the office, her elder self and Constance in silent pursuit.

The younger Rebecca descended and burst from the school into the cool London night. A host of spirits followed, curious, worried by her air of misery, and they turned to one another in consultation. Frederic was immediately upon her, squawking and swooping to get her attention, but she paid him no heed. The bird went so far as to pull on a lock of her hair, but this only caused her to whirl, batting at him and hissing in the language of The Guard, "Leave me be!" The bird offered one more gruff call before flying off.

Frederic, her stalwart companion. One couldn't know how such a creature might be missed until he was gone. Rebecca suffered a pang watching the raven fly off. She wished to run forward and chide her younger self: how foolish it was to go out into the night unaccompanied, how it was begging for trouble. She remembered how this had crossed her mind, and how she hadn't cared. In that moment she'd cared for nothing but finding a drastic solution to the unnecessary complication that was her heart.

Out into the dark London night she glided, in and out of the pooled light of gas lamps as if she were already a wraith, past clattering carriages, avoiding puddles of filth and ignoring the occasional inappropriate comment hurled from the safety of shadows, likely by gentlemen with wives awaiting them at home. Rebecca remembered how sickened she'd been by humanity as a whole, how she'd wondered why they even deserved any protection.

"To hell with them," she heard her younger self hiss. "To hell with all of it. There is nothing here worth saving, not even myself."

The hazy night held the buildings in a wet fog that rose from the riverbank, and young Rebecca moved through it to the crest of Westminster Bridge. She stared down at the deep black Thames, at the cargo ships and ferries so far below and at countless manner of traffic, all ringing bells and making noise. She stepped onto the ledge, grasping the parapet beside her. She pulled up her skirts as if preparing to climb, intending to pitch herself into the air, to hurl herself to freedom, to end it all.

Constance touched Rebecca's sleeve. "You may think, Headmistress, that this is just a recollection, and will unfold just as you remember. But the Liminal is far greater than mere memory. It can change. So I beg you, beware your heart, right at this moment, lest it alter the outcome before you."

Rebecca turned back to watch herself, her heart pounding in fear, terrified to speak lest the wrong words send her tumbling . . .

Her younger self trailed death in her wake, literally. The spirits that had followed her from the academy rushed close, trying to save her from her sorrow. They bobbed before her, making a barrier though they knew full well she could slip past and through their transparent bodies to her death if she tried. Still, they attempted to make her see, tried to make her pause and think. Rebecca remembered this scene as if it had happened yesterday. But, this time, she could hear what the spirits were saying.

"Headmistress, don't!" the spirits cried. "Don't you understand the balance hinges on *all* of you? It affects the whole city, everyone we love. Don't you see you can't just break rank, walk away and kill yourself? You mustn't! And, Athens—what about Athens? And The Guard? Michael. What of poor Michael?"

As the spirits exclaimed, phantom images began to float through the air like reflections upon water. A shimmering picture of a dusty Athens came into view, its fine Romanesque windows shuttered and boarded. The scene included Rebecca's friends, all in black, flowers hanging limply from their hands. They descended those formidable academy steps to never again enter its now-locked doors. Spirits were everywhere. Too many of them. The Work was faltering.

Michael stood at the rear of the procession, his once jolly and engaging face entirely devoid of colour, of life, of anything recognizable. His luminous heart was doused. It was the most terrifying sight Rebecca had ever beheld, watching this unfold on the mist before her eyes, her hand to her mouth, tears in her eyes.

Constance spoke gently, but gravely. "In this delicate space between time and memory, any one of these phantom reflections could become reality. If you accept it, down you go into the cold, deadly kiss of the Thames. What say you?"

"No," was all Rebecca could manage, in a desperate murmur.

In a panic she rejected those images. She did not want to see or to bring about this future. Yet her younger self still stood precarious.

Constance gestured behind her. "See here what you missed."

From a dark alley, a figure broke from shadow. He wore a dark, modest coat, his hair was disheveled, and his cheeks glowed bright with a blush even in the dim lamplight. His beautiful blue eyes were wide with panic, and he was prepared to run forward and save her. But he was far enough away that, even if he ran full tilt, he might not cross the distance before she fell.

"Michael," Rebecca gasped into her hand. "Oh, Michael, I did not want *you* to see this."

"He was the Heart," Constance murmured. "He felt it before he saw it. Before Frederic summoned him, he was already on his way."

"He was there," Rebecca choked.

"He always has been."

It was a solid truth that turned Rebecca's stomach.

"Now you must watch and accept," Constance added.

As Michael ran forward, she saw that he held something large and black in his hands, something surprisingly docile for being a wild creature. It was Frederic. Michael held the raven in his palms, its blue breast feather aglow. He released the bird with a soft prayer, and it flew to the younger version of Rebecca on the bridge.

Rebecca watched herself pause. She remembered how she'd reflected in that instant, seeing the swarm of spirits wishing to block her. They did not want her to join them, she'd realized. Not yet. And when she'd felt Frederic alight on her shoulder, she'd reached a trembling hand up to his talons and her heart had grown less heavy upon contact.

The blue glow of the bird's breast feather faded. Rebecca saw now that Michael had used Frederic as his gift's conduit, to impart what his hands were too far away to bequeath. Her younger self's foot shifted, slid back off the ledge.

"What am I doing . . . ?" she heard herself mutter. Tears were pouring down her younger cheeks. Frederic rubbed his head against her, and she stroked his feathers. "I'm so sorry, Frederic. I love you. Thank you."

Michael had saved her. His talent for leavening the heart had bridged the gap until her gifts could regain control. Instinct now reassured her younger self, but Michael's gift had pulled her back from the edge. The bleak alternate future dissipated like fog in a breeze.

Rebecca glanced over at him and absorbed the intense relief on his face. It was beautiful and poignant, his tears tiny glimmers in the gaslight. He stepped back into partial shadow but did not leave.

A spirit approached her younger, shaking self, and though silent, she'd understood as the ghost, a young woman in century-old clothes, perhaps who had thrown herself off that same bridge, carefully mouthed the words, "Thank you."

The elder Rebecca heard the words this time, and she was moved to reply, "No. Thank you. Thank all of you."

Constance, who had stood as still and as impassive as a statue, smiled.

"That simple exchange, that thank-you," Rebecca murmured, "fed my lonely soul for years. I knew that while I wouldn't receive the love I craved from Alexi, that crowd of spectres alone was evidence that I did have a purpose."

Her focus shifted to Michael, still standing in the shadows. "Why didn't he say anything?"

"You know him," Constance replied. "You know why."

"Because he knew the shame and horror I felt," Rebecca said, watching those sentiments so evident on her younger incarnation's face. "He was not worried I would try again, and he felt my embarrassment would overshadow any benefit. This was a private moment so unlike me, something I'd never share . . . That was why he said nothing."

She turned to Michael's shadow and said words she'd never known to utter. "Thank you for being there, Michael Carroll. It's not the last time you and Frederic would prove my valorous knights, but thank you for being my champion *here*, when no other living person was." She faltered as she recollected the grim images presented as an alternate future. "And I don't want to ever see that heart of yours broken. That was a sight more terrible than the face of Darkness itself."

Little Mary floated at Michael's side. He was forced to watch the scene on Westminster Bridge and wondered if Rebecca was watching it, too, from elsewhere. And, what would she see? Were each of them trapped in their own memories, the events once again unfolding? Was this what the ghosts had in mind? If so, to what purpose?

The scene grieved him now like it had then. Worse, even, for his love for Rebecca had only grown. He again wanted to run forward, to take her in his arms and ask her what on earth was she thinking, she the strong and stalwart second in command, she to whom they all looked for strength, guidance and sensibility. He yearned to kiss her madly and wipe all thoughts of Alexi Rychman from her consciousness, just as he'd wanted to do then and hadn't.

He turned to the ghost and said, "I am a coward."

"Are you? Or did you surmise that it would have been worse if you shamed her by your appearance? Didn't you really know that strong silence, your secret guardianship, was a better choice at that moment?"

"I maintain that I am a coward." Michael set his jaw, unwilling to be praised.

The little girl smirked. "It is true that it is safer to love someone unattainable than to love someone in reality. This moment could have changed everything. You were as scared for yourself as you were for her, weren't you?"

He stared at the ghost. "You're wise for a child."

"Death expands the mind," she said airily, then grinned. She touched his hand, and suddenly they were at a dance.

Rebecca threw her hands up at the bright light. Everyone was dressed in finery, and there was music.

It was the same autumn as the scene at the bridge, though some weeks afterward. The academy ball. The glorious ballroom of Athens was thrown open for one day, its gilded and glittering interior packed with guests bedecked in jewels and garbed in fine dresses and frock coats, accessorized with buttons, bows, lace, silk and perfume. In addition there were ubiquitous floral bouquets, confections and the finest in modern music played by a string quartet. The students relished this one day of freedom to stand close, to chat, to *touch*, and even the chaperones were not fully averse to camaraderie and flirtation. Rebecca herself remembered hoping to find an opportunity.

It was her year to chaperone, and she remembered thinking that while she was headmistress it was still a chance to look stunning. She'd put Alexi's name on the chaperone list as well, praying that perhaps he'd notice her this time. He hated such frivolities, and she knew he'd likely stand in the corner and scowl, looking every bit the brooding, Gothic hero of sensationalist novels, a trait that garnered him endless teasing from The Guard. But if Alexi dreaded the event, all the better if she looked stunning. He might be discomfited in the very best of ways.

She saw herself in a corner sipping the champagne reserved for the faculty, indeed looking lovely in a rich red gown that matched the colour of Alexi's favourite accessory, his crimson cravats. Complemented by all the staff, she chuckled at the raised eyebrows of every student who had never dreamed to see their headmistress's uncovered collarbones. Her younger self didn't yet know that Alexi would never come. That he would claim family business with his sister. That she would soon feel the bitter sting of rejection.

The room brightened just a bit. "Ho-ho, Headmistress! Why . . . My God!" came a voice through the open side doors. Michael strode in, wearing a fine navy suit coat over a charcoal vest and lighter cravat that enhanced the oceanic blue of his eyes. His usually haphazard hair was combed neatly, his sideburns trimmed to accentuate a firm jaw, his dark brown mustache shaved away to reveal a firm mouth. The only wrinkles on his kind face were laugh lines.

Had she seen then how handsome he looked, how engaging and endearing? Had she felt the breeze of fresh air that was his constant good cheer? Watching how his smile drew out that of her younger self, Rebecca remembered being glad to see him. She remembered thinking what a good husband he would make for some kind and uncomplicated woman, for some soul as devout as he, someone saintly and flawless, some angel. She still felt he deserved that, but her older self gasped at the way he looked at her. The desire and appreciation she saw in his eyes made her realize his intentions were anything but saintly.

He *wanted* her. She'd grown used to the idea that she was not the type of woman a man would crave, but this . . . Something shifted in her body and Rebecca moved forward into the scene, yearning to be closer to Michael, to warm herself at the fires in his eyes.

"I hope you don't mind my stealing into the party," he said to her younger incarnation, his hungry appreciation curtained by winking camaraderie. "You know I cannot resist social engagements."

"Oh, *please*," the young Rebecca said with exaggerated weariness, raising her hand to her head. "My students' shock at seeing their headmistress in her finery has palled. Do save me."

"I'd save you from anything," he replied, "even yourself." Then he must have realized how that sounded, for he offered a gracious explanation: "And by that I mean how dangerously fetching you are in this dress, Headmistress. You ought to be warned!"

Her younger self blushed, ignorant, but the older Rebecca saw exactly what he meant. Suddenly she knew how very truly he spoke, and how he had striven to save her, to rally her, to care for her, each and every time they were together. When they hunted as The Guard, when they sat at their favourite café, when they commiserated as friends—he was always there for her. More memories flooded forth, countless scenes flashing before her eyes: grim confrontations of malevolent spirits, glad conversations at La Belle et La Bête. Dining at the Withersby estate. Strolling about Regents Park. Running off to intercept violent poltergeists. There had been so many moments where this man had made her smile and laugh and forget that there was such a thing as pain and spectral horror in the world.

So many times he'd saved her, with tiny, life-affirming gestures. No one else had such power over her, she realized. And no one else had ever looked at her like this. She recognized his look; she'd aimed it for years at someone unattainable. But had she even shown this same fire? For there was a *fire* in Michael's, and that was a thrilling concept: the *fire* of love, not just the cold emptiness of the unrequited. What a silly game they'd played! How silly she was not to have taken each of these small moments and made sense of them.

Something must have been writ upon her face, for Constance looked pleased and the flickering ball vanished. Rebecca swayed upon her feet.

"A good beginning to your journey," the ghost said. "Everything you need to know you already do. Here, somewhere"—her transparent finger poked at her temple—"and on its way here." She pointed toward Rebecca's heart. "Trust the journey. You'll be a lovelier woman if you choose happiness."

The ghost flickered, and, reeling, Rebecca found herself at the entrance to the Athens foyer.

"Farewell, Headmistress, do find your peace, for it shall

aid in securing mine forever. We rest happier in heaven if we've helped those on Earth." Constance's gaze darkened. "But if you falter . . . you might bring us all down with you. And now the next guide shall take you onward."

Chapter Seven

Students twirled past Michael where he stood oblivious within memory. Little Mary seemed just as captivated. The headmistress was stunning in her crimson gown; it brought out a bloom in her cheeks, accentuated her every feature and highlighted the pallor of her smooth skin.

"Is this just to torture me?" he choked out, overtaken by fresh desire.

"No, no," Mary said. "It's to remind you. To embolden you. You called yourself a coward, and that cannot be. But, come. Billy's got you next."

She took his hand and warned, "You'll feel seasick. The Liminal presses hard against this academy to drag the two of you through the veil of time like this. But thankfully these mysterious stones can take whatever's thrown at them, can't they? I heard your recent battle here was rather brilliant. Now close your eyes."

Michael did not hesitate; he closed his eyes and felt the world change again.

Rebecca glanced around, wanting to bid Constance a final farewell. Instead, a familiar spirit floated at face level: the young boy from the chandelier, a spirit she'd made a fond habit of greeting.

He grinned. "My turn, mum." He had a Scots accent.

"Well, hello there, young man," Rebecca said, finally able

to talk to the boy and glad of it, but the world was suddenly a dizzying blur in front of her, and her question was lost in her throat. Years whirled by. She, Alexi, The Guard and students came and went, appearing and disappearing, moving in hurried motion through this hall and foyer of Athens, and all the while the young man from the chandelier watched and smiled. Each day, a wink was offered up to him by an aging Rebecca. And, suddenly she understood: he was showing her everything he'd seen in two decades.

She found her voice. "I don't know your story, young man."

He shrugged. "Street urchin. Ran away from an orphanage up north. Bad lot, that. But not much better, London. Fell ill. Nurse who worked at Athens took me in, died up there." He gestured toward the wing with the infirmary. "But this was home, as much as I ever had one, while I was here. Didn't feel like leavin'. Liked it when you winked at me. Only mum I've had, really," the lad admitted.

Rebecca turned away. She had wanted to be a mother once, as she supposed most women did.

"But enough o' that," the boy said gently. "This is about you. Keep watchin'."

Rebecca cleared her throat and watched the whirlwind of images. Alexi stalked across the foyer and back again like some great, swooping raven. Rebecca saw herself pace to and fro, realized how unnecessarily stern she looked. "Most certainly, unnecessarily stern," she muttered.

But then Michael would enter. He would make no pause, see no other sights, just make his way surely and directly across the foyer to her office. Each and every time, there on business or as a friend, her door was his only destination. His hesitation outside struck her. He would stride confidently forward, then stop and stuff his hand in a pocket. Did he tremble slightly? He'd close his eyes, loose a prayer, perhaps, and finally, after that less-than-confident pause, knock. It happened over and over.

Rebecca shook her head. "Good God, Michael, you're not *nervous*, are you?"

"Always," Billy replied. "Every time, he was. Reminded of it now, too, as he's living this, right now. Or, reliving it."

"Why is Michael enduring this trial?"

"To learn."

"What on earth does *he* need to learn? He's always been the perfect one, the one that never needed any help." Rebecca's breath gave out. "I'm the broken one."

The ghostly boy's hand touched hers. It was a freezing connection, but Rebecca subdued her shiver. The contact was fond, however uncomfortable, and she appreciated the gesture.

"He needs to trust his heart. Especially now. He fears he's worthless since his power is gone."

"Why, that's ridiculous! His heart was always beyond capacity. Just because our Guard spirits went and—"

"Have you ever told him so?"

Rebecca looked at her feet. "No."

"Do so. But first he must believe it himself. You need not be separately broken to together make a whole, but separately whole to remain unbreakable. Only that makes a healthy home."

Was it so easy to just say yes and make a home together, as the ghost intimated? Perhaps it was. She eyed the boy. "You're wise for a child."

"Staring down eternity will make one so," he replied, but he bobbed his head and she could tell he was greatly pleased.

Despite herself, Rebecca chuckled. "I imagine so."

"So," the young ghost continued, "while you may think

you've a thousand things keepin' you from happiness, a thousand flaws and mistakes, here's a man who thinks himself a coward. He wonders if he has enough to give you. He's nervous every time he's alone with you. All for love." The ghost's eyes grew a bit cold, and his face ominous. "You both live in fear, and I tell you the whole of the spirit world fears you cannot overcome it. You've given much of your life to these blessed bricks. Do you want to give your eternity to hauntin' them? There are two paths here. Now from the darkness, choose."

And then Billy gave her a small but decisive push and everything went black.

"Percy, come closer!"

Constance appeared at her side, and Percy started. She had maintained her perch overlooking the foyer, rosary in hand, sitting on a bench on the second floor of Athens, remaining inconspicuous but on guard. Constance and Billy had been told to call upon her if something needed attention. Nothing had raised an alarm until now.

"The Liminal presses in, right into the heart of us, she's in the Whisper-world now," the ghost warned. "The shadows will be close and they'll not want to let the headmistress go. She's a perfect candidate for a state like mine, forever haunting these bricks."

Percy moved to the edge of the landing. She'd been mesmerized by visions below, all done in a misty, giant picture frame, the hazy clouds of shifting images filling the foyer and then vanishing as the memories moved elsewhere. She'd never seen anything like it; hundreds of images superimposed upon one another, shifting in and over and across in curling tendrils of smoke and mist, like ink bleeding into water to form ever-changing shapes, all of them individually poignant. These were private matters played out in mist, and so Percy did not strain to make out the particulars; all she heard were murmurs, and all she saw were greyscale silhouettes.

But, then, Percy wasn't exactly sure what she was looking for. The precise nature of angels, demons, ghosts, guardians and the worlds between wasn't something any of them would ever master. But Percy chose to believe in angels. While she'd never seen them, during the course of the Grand Work she was *sure* she'd heard them. She hoped they heard her now and could sing at her side.

Constance grimaced. "The Liminal can change many ways. Let's make sure it twists the way we hope. I've seen two possible futures, one I like a great deal better than the other! Come to the threshold edge. Fate cuts along a razor-thin line."

Chapter Eight

All was darkness. The chill went to the bone, and Rebecca shuddered. She might appear as stoic and fearless as their leader Alexi, but she knew her frailty all too well.

"Mortal hearts make many mistakes," she murmured, ruminating on her various failures. The longer she stood in the dark, the more the chill of death itself began to seep in. She wondered if she'd been abandoned in some corner of the dark netherworld.

"And what is this, then?" she asked, feeling nothing on her skin but cold, seeing nothing in her gaze but blackness. There was no echo of her voice; it sounded flat, enclosed, like a coffin.

She stretched out her hands in a panic, wondering if she was indeed entombed. But she was free to move. She was standing upright.

There was nothing at her back. Nothing before her. But considering the extent of the darkness she dared not take a step. "This must be the 'yet to come' part, Master Dickens? Did you have any idea what you were toying with, sir? I maintain your tale was overwrought," Rebecca murmured. "Tell me, is this where I see my headstone and repent my every sin, where I pray for a second chance? I *do* regret. Repent. But what if there's no second chance? Is darkness to be my final judgement? Is there to be no spirit guide through this last, harrowing phase?"

There was a long silence. Rebecca had held a glimmer of hope, had begun to feel the lightness of a heart opening to its true call; she had begun to truly see the man who loved her as she is and always was. But all was precarious. In vain. Too late. There was no one to guide her.

"Oh, no! Don't ye dare let go of that glimmer, Rebecca Thompson, or I can't do my duty and we'll all be bound to these damned stones! And who would want to see ye happier than I?" came a familiar, chiding Irish brogue, an accent always heightened by anxiety. Suddenly there was a grey light, a silver halo around a solid woman who wore the greyscale of the dead.

"Jane!" Rebecca cried and threw her arms around her. "Oh, how we miss you! Wait. Am I dead?" In this existence, in this time and place, Jane was solid.

"No, you're not. Yet. But the spirits are all in agreement—"

"That it should have been me!" Rebecca cried.

"No!" Jane hissed. "That's not the answer."

There was a rumble of thunder. Lightning illuminated the shadows, and Rebecca screamed as pillars of human skulls were revealed marching off into the endless distance. Shadows lurked behind those pillars, and Rebecca squeezed her eyes shut, not wanting any further illumination.

Jane shook her head and whispered, "None of that nonsense, now. Watch your words in these parts."

"Where are we, exactly?"

"This is the Whisper-world, Rebecca."

"Here? *Me?* I'm not supposed to be here, am I?"

"No, it's dangerous while you're alive. You're on the edge of a dark realm. Ahead of us sits the Liminal threshold. A powerful place not to be trifled with. It's what allows us this final examination."

She led Rebecca forward. As they moved, the darkness

lightened; the air became a luminous silver, and her muffled footfalls over the wet stone sounded across something more like glass. The air was less dank in her nostrils, the breath of sadness less oppressive.

"Are you happy, Jane?" Rebecca asked. "Where is your ghostly love, your Aodhan? I've prayed so dearly for your peace."

Jane spoke carefully. "I chose my path. Aodhan awaits me in the Great Beyond, but I can't go to him 'til I see you choose *your* path. No matter what happens, I regret nothing. But if you fail . . ."

"What . . . what will happen?"

"I'll be trapped here forever. It's the price that the Liminal asks. But I love and believe in you that much."

"Oh, Jane—"

"Hush your mouth, we've work to do."

A great proscenium of a stage was gleaming before her. Both females looked onto a scene that Rebecca recognized from her very recent past. The scene was still, frozen, waiting to leap to life. Rebecca's heart raced. It was a darkened Athens, right before the spirit war.

Hearing music from the upstairs foyer, she anxiously turned to Jane. "In Dickens, the past was the purview of the first spirit alone. How are *you* showing me this?"

Jane pursed grey lips. "I thought you didn't like Dickens."

Rebecca paused. "Well . . . I suppose he's my only reference here."

Jane smirked. "You're an infinitely more complicated creature than Ebenezer Scrooge, Headmistress, and so the same methods of salvation cannot apply."

Rebecca sniffed, straightening her shoulders. "I didn't think he got it exactly right. Too dramatic."

Jane laughed. "Oh, but he got it exactly right. Yet while

we're not following his script, we *must* teach you and repeat until you really see."

"I see—"

"Do you?" Jane insisted, placing an icy hand upon her chest. "No. You're not free. Not yet."

"No," Rebecca agreed, looking down. "I don't know that I'll ever be free."

Suddenly, she emitted a torrent of confession. "All I've hoped for in life is to valiantly serve those who depend upon me, to be an efficient, respected headmistress, a member of The Guard, an upstanding citizen. Of course I wanted to be loved in return by Alexi! I wanted a home and a family with him. But our Grand Work had its own agenda, his heart its own call. So now, as I stare down my life, I find my past ruled by cowardice and second-guessing. What could I have done differently? I'm nothing of what I wish to be."

So satisfyingly low, the words felt good the moment they dripped from her lips. But their effect was anything but. As they escaped, Rebecca's guilt only magnified. Sorrow crested in her blood, and the darkness around her intensified, pressing in, urging her to simply wallow in a deep well of never-ending self-pity. She could drink from this bubbling font of misery, as she had every night for twenty years, from now unto eternity. The better air she had begun to breathe again went rancorous, the shadows around them lengthened.

"Rebecca," her friend warned. "This is a deadly place to go melancholy. Do not ingest such a drug—"

"But I've so much pain—"

"Well, *mitigate* it before it's too late!" Jane exclaimed. The Liminal stage of possibility went black. Shadow pressed in upon Rebecca's heart, and she recognized the sensation. While The Guard had briefly halted Darkness, its ruler, the Whisper-world was its own entity and lived on, attuned to misery and fear, an ethereal, subtle and dangerous predator. That predator was hungry for a restless soul. Her misery was just the sort of food the Whisper-world craved.

Suddenly, in the distance, far outside the now-black picture frame through which she gazed, in the thick shadows becoming recognizable as Athens, there came a bright white gleam, like a star, widening. It was a beautiful light, a familiar light, and there was a petite figure within and drawing inexorably closer.

"What's that?" Rebecca breathed.

Jane offered a partial smile. "A guardian angel, watching out for us beyond the Liminal edge. But we mustn't test her. This realm wants her for its own more than any of us, and if she has to come in for you"—Jane shuddered—"who knows what it might do to her again. Look what surrounds you in the Whisper-world. Do you want to join them?" She gestured to the shadows, to figures Rebecca saw there that moved listlessly, shapeless, aimless.

Jane continued. "These souls are here because of second-guessing themselves, because of mortal frailty or selfishness. You're hardly the first to come. What keeps them here is their inability to let go—which is their *greatest* crime. To err is mortal. To not forgive is the stuff of the Whisper-world. Who knows why events needed to unfold as they did, to press, madden or even kill"—she gave Rebecca a meaningful glance—"some of us as they did? Who are we to question? We must forgive."

Rebecca could not meet her gaze. She gave a sob and the air thickened further.

Her friend sighed. "You're a powerful woman, Rebecca, but stop thinking you've power over everything. You can't make someone love you who doesn't, and you can't change what fate has already wrought. You cannot live well if you're unable to discard regrets! In the end, this isn't about me, or Alexi, or Percy. It's about you—and the man who's always loved you. The man who was meant for you, though you never let yourself believe it. You hid from the reality of his love in the dream of Alexi's. Try, for once, to be unselfish. Be *grateful*."

Rebecca bit her lip, helpless. "Show me the scene," she gasped, turning to the Liminal stage. "Help me see what I must . . ."

The Liminal agreed, and the bright guardian star remained visible, a soft glow in the corner of the stage frame as the past began to play its chosen scene:

The Guard were all assembled on the dark third-floor foyer of Athens Academy, where Jane played the fiddle for the waltzing Percy and Alexi. Elijah and Josephine were arm in arm, and Michael was . . . staring at Rebecca. She had been too focused on the waltzing couple to notice before, always too preoccupied.

She wasn't much to look at here, having already given over to an identity built around efficient administration. And yet, there Michael was, staring at her with the same desire he'd worn on his face when she'd done herself up for the ball years prior. Here she was drawn and shadowed, her face a grimace, so sure she could never be loved—some part of her was still certain of that—and yet . . .

"He must see something I cannot," Rebecca murmured, baffled to see that he not only desired her but cared for her, ached for and knew her—truly *knew* her, knew all the complications of her life like no one else possibly could—and here he was, likely as scared as she to reach out and take what he wanted by the hand.

"After all you've seen and been through, he still looks at you that way. He always will. You must trust it," Jane said.

"I . . . don't understand how. I don't know that I—"

"What? You don't deserve love? That's the talk of a person who jumps off bridges, who does terrible things or lets terrible things be done to her. You are not she. You must not fear that look, and you must not fear what it means. You must open your eyes to what shines in him and embrace it." Jane pressed her hand to Rebecca's heart again. "But there's a catch here, a hiccup. Thinking you understand and *feeling* that you understand are two different beasts. Stare what you fear in the face."

"I've stared down death," Rebecca said.

"But what about *love?* Because that, Headmistress, is your greatest fear. Look at it," Jane insisted, guiding Rebecca toward the frame.

Rebecca stared. She watched Michael Carroll and let herself entertain the idea of what it would be like to receive, accept and possibly return his look of adoration and everything it contained. It was true, she was afraid. Pining, unrequited love was indeed of one dimension. This look, this heart, this love of Michael's was all-encompassing. Yet it was not desperate, cloying or imbalanced; it was simply solid. It could be her foundation.

She'd never conceived of anything quite like this. Her heart began to expand from its tiny, huddled, clutched position and allowed for something new to take its place. She felt like a phoenix being reborn—

But, she was not a woman who liked earth-shattering change. She was fond of routine, not the unknown. The unknown was terrifying. Her heart huddled close again, clutching at its familiar loneliness, a reflexive contraction. An interior door somewhere slammed closed.

The shadows were ready for her this time, lurching close. A distant beat of horse hooves, a cacophony of whispers, hisses and deadly threats filled the air. The rushing river of restless souls again gurgled in the distance, its currents churning upward, beckoning her to drown herself at last, in waters worse than the Thames . . .

"Rebecca," Jane chided.

An inward chill spread inside her, the sort of dread she'd felt when facing demons and the stuff of eternally damning horror. The cold had hooks into her, a fluid invasion and perversion such as blood into a pure spring. It was as if a possessing spirit had slipped cold, wet fingers in around her heart and was digging a hole. That unwelcome guest found her melancholy and made a nest within, birthing a wasting madness and inescapable loathing. Rebecca cried out in physical, mental and spiritual pain.

But then there was that bright angel's light again, coming closer, as if from across a long room—as if from across Athens's foyer. Brighter, brighter . . . The shadows sliding inside Rebecca seemed to jump back scalded, no longer as bold if still nipping at the hem of her skirts. She felt her body warm; the forces that wished to keep her prisoner were for the nonce held at bay. That light was no match for this shadow and Rebecca longed to warm herself in it.

Jane glanced from the light to Rebecca, gauging her progress. "I've told you before, you and Alexi would never have been a good fit. All you'd have done was scowl at each other. You loved him because he was safe, because he felt familiar. Because you didn't trust anyone else, didn't trust that anyone could love you, hardly even yourself. But at some point you have to let go and be loved, for there are people who love you."

She pointed. "Look at Michael Carroll. Imagine turning the tide from the first moment you know him, *from the very first moment.* This should be a good trick," she added in a mutter. "Please, God, let it work. Maestro, from the top . . ."

Jane snapped her fingers, and the world whirled into something entirely different. But familiar. Suddenly Rebecca was a youth on Westminster Bridge. It was a grey day in autumn, and six unlikely children had been called to police spirits throughout London. It was the first day of the Grand Work. It was the first day she fell in love with Alexi Rychman. The very first day.

Rebecca watched her spindly, awkward, confused self waiting and shifting upon her heels, not knowing what trials and tribulations lay before her. Alexi hadn't arrived yet. Instead, she and Michael were alone. Why hadn't she remembered that they were the first to arrive? He was staring at her with such kindness and admiration, *from the very first.* And his smile . . .

This, she realized, was destiny. She'd cursed a fate that hadn't provided for her, but fate had provided and she had turned away. She was destined for Michael from the first, but she'd been intimidated even then.

"Can you see?" Jane murmured.

"Yes," Rebecca breathed. Honestly. She did. "I see that it's right."

She stared at Michael, at her young self and her current self, and she truly saw him, completely, for the first time. With clarion focus she knew that he would never be second-best. He was, simply, *best.* For her, he always had been.

Her huddled heart exploded with joy. Her body shifted, expanded; her every muscle, so tightly clenched in quivering fists, finally let go. The transformation was whole and glorious, a revelation that could never be undone, a knowledge so sure that it put all other pain in distant shadow. Her love of Alexi had no power here. She was broken free from the unwitting spell he'd never intended to cast. The gentle heart before her, fiercely passionate for nothing but her, had overcome all. It was the greatest power yet seen in all manner of strange in her life of spectral mayhem.

She turned to Jane in wonder, and the friends shared a beautiful, moved silence. Rebecca saw the new light in her eyes reflected in Jane's.

"Now," her friend pressed. "The last question. Do you forgive yourself for the past?"

Rebecca faltered, the word "forgive" an impossible obstacle. She felt the chill of shadow pierce her again, finding that hollow, tender place and ripping the fresh stitches. She groaned, a terrible swinging pendulum in the pit of her heart, bloodied and razor sharp. Oh, to feel such joy, only to regress again and feel it ripped away . . . The scene on Westminster faded, and she was again in grey shadow.

Jane was talking again, giving words of reassurance to again turn the tide. Rebecca couldn't hear her. The shadows encircled them both, and they seemed too powerful. These shadows didn't think she deserved a second chance; they wanted her a wasting form, unable to pass on, doomed for eternal regrets. Why had she made so many mistakes? Why had she wasted all the time she'd been given with Michael? What was left for her when so much time had passed and the Grand Work was done? She began to weep.

Her shoulders felt a gentle pressure. Jane held her. But Rebecca still could not hear her. She saw the hideous form of the defeated Whisper-world lord, Darkness, a form of bones and rot, a force comprised of everything one wished humanity could just leave behind. Rebecca saw him in her mind's eye, in that serpents' nest within her; reassembling.

Digit by digit, vertebrae by vertebrae. Eyes of hellfire and a tongue of damnation.

But she recalled that she had life yet to live. She had the power to retaliate, just like when her feet were on the bridge's edge. She did not want Darkness, so recently torn apart, to so easily be put back together. Not by the mere regrets of her weak, mortal heart. She did not want Darkness to win her as a bride. She would not *let* Darkness win her.

"I reject thee . . ." she murmured to shadow.

She wanted the bright hearth of Michael's heart. She would be lured, fooled and seduced by misery no longer. Jane was right: the heavens had made no mistakes. Darkness only wanted her to think so.

"And now I see," Rebecca murmured. "Forgiveness."

And suddenly everything was light.

Chapter Nine

Percy maintained her position in the Athens foyer and watched how the shadow shapes responded to her light through the portal before her, how she curbed them. This was her power, her gift, and it had saved them all once before. While it hurt, dearly, to let it burn, it was worth the discomfort to know that she could turn tides, that so long as she focused, she could strike back and declaw misery's talons.

"Oh, Percy, look how it worsens," Constance murmured, bobbing in the air beside her. "The headmistress chose correctly, at least I think, but it's not over."

The whole vast room had grown dark over the course of the journey. There were terrible murmurs and whispers through the portal hung like a curtain in the middle of the foyer, seeping out into their mortal reality, and the blood chilled in Percy's veins. She rushed forward to its very edge, staring in, straining to see the dim figures beyond. A dark mist rose within, and Percy could hear its familiar hissing, trying to invite her in, insidious and also eerily seductive. This edge of shadow was a dangerous place for coming and going. And it wanted her, like it had before.

As if through a veil, Percy recognized the headmistress, unsteady on her feet, surrounded by flickering shadows. The headmistress was in the midst of a battle.

"This is the Liminal?" Percy asked.

"Yes," Constance murmured. "It's here that the greatest

change of a soul can take effect. The danger is necessary because the transformation can be the richest. The Liminal can be a beautiful place, but it edges the Whisper-world, and with any darkness present . . . Well, it amplifies *all* things."

The mists of the Whisper-world swirled up around the edge of Rebecca's skirts, clearly trying to hold her like shackles. But, Rebecca fought. And, who was the spirit beside her?

Percy's heart swelled in sudden recognition. "Jane!" she breathed. Close enough to touch her friends if she reached through the portal, Percy kept to the side, a bright candle at the base of a vast altar. She dared not step up and inside, not because she feared for herself, but for the child she carried.

Jane looked out from the portal and smiled. "Hello, Percy. Could you spare us just a bit more of your light? Rebecca's done what she must, but we're still precarious. You're just the one to tip the scales."

Rebecca didn't seem able to hear past her internal fight.

Percy squeezed in her hand the rosary Michael had blessed, staring deep into the offending, greedy shadows that wanted to make sadness a forever state throughout Creation. The burning in her breast intensified, searing. The unfortunate effect of a divine power using her mortal body was that there were limits, but as Percy had herself once lived a life domineered by melancholy, she was more than ready to give what she could for this battle. She'd be damned if such melancholy was going to hold Rebecca and feed the beast they'd already bested.

"Headmistress, go on. Release your tears," Jane was saying. "Don't hold them in or give them power. Shed your tears upon the stones and leave them. When all is done, step into the light."

The headmistress looked up. She seemed to hear. Her

cheeks were wet, but her face was more open than Percy had ever seen it.

"Let that caged heart of yours free," Jane urged. "I love you, Rebecca. I always have and I always will. You're right about forgiveness. It's time to begin again."

The friends embraced, and Rebecca's healing tears flowed faster. Seeming to realize what came next, the two said good-bye—and Merry Christmas.

Jane stepped from the portal. She appeared at Percy's side, floating, changing from her solid form in the Whisper-world to her transparent, spectral buoyancy upon Earth. Inside the portal, Rebecca looked around, squinted out at them, apparently seeing only light and feeling that she was alone. More tears had to drain before she could start life anew.

Placing a cool draft of a hand on Percy's shoulder, Jane murmured, "Let her have a good cry; she needs it. Let sorrow drain into the river. When she's done, carefully help her off the ledge. Now that the headmistress's change of heart has freed me, I must be off to shake final sense into a vicar."

When Jane grinned, Percy returned the expression. "Sense? Indeed." But her heart was heavy; they'd have to say good-bye again.

"I'll be back to spook you and your beloved," Jane promised, anticipating her. "I know Alexi will be insulted if I don't give him his fair haunting. He'll never forgive me."

"Thank you. It's so good to see you," Percy murmured. "But, I am—we all are—so sorry to have lost you. Grateful for your sacrifice, but sorry."

Percy's inner light, that otherworldly beacon of hope, flickered. Jane rolled her eyes. "Not you, too! All of you with your regrets," the Irishwoman scoffed. "My fate was what was meant to be. Now, tend your light." Jane turned to Constance, floating patiently at Percy's side. "Good work, my lass. Stay here with Percy 'til the last, and then I daresay we've all earned our blessed peace and then some!"

Constance nodded, and placed her ghostly hand on Percy's shoulder. Percy's light burned brighter for friendship. Being a beacon was exhausting and painful, and she wondered if her skin would bear the mark of a burn.

Graceful, dark movement from the floor above caught Percy's eye. Alexi stared down at the scene from the floor above; down at the roiling portal, the headmistress's vague form within, at the ghosts of Jane and Constance, and then at his luminous wife. Tears stood in his dark eyes. He made no move to stop Percy, or to move her away from the perilous edge where she stood guard, only stared at her with awestruck pride. Jane smiled and waved up at him.

"Merry Christmas!" Jane whispered and vanished.

Alexi blew Percy a kiss and turned away, leaving her to her miracles as she had requested. Percy's light was sustained anew.

Rebecca looked up. The light yet blinded her, but she was done; her tears had run their course. Everything was different.

She stood. "What do I do?" she murmured, seeing only the light, unsure.

"Come," said a sweet voice. "Give me your hand."

Rebecca reached out toward the light. A soft, small hand met hers and pulled. There came a whirling sensation. She found herself stepping down onto firm ground in the foyer of Athens Academy. A small pop sounded behind her, and the portal, shadows, mists and encroaching danger were no more.

It was indeed the sturdy marble floor of her academy; she was in the school she had run with strength and aplomb, the place that had given so many opportunities otherwise absent to its students and staff. God, she loved this building.

Her eyes found those of the guardian angel whose light had helped her fight the greedy Whisper-world: they were the eerie, ice blue irises of Persephone Rychman. The young woman's inner light, as white as her skin, faded as Rebecca moved to safety. She was breathing heavily, as if from great pain and exertion; but save for a bit of sweat on her brow she seemed otherwise composed. Her faintly rouged lips curved into a small smile just as radiant as her spirit.

"Welcome back, Headmistress!"

Rebecca swallowed hard, at a loss for words. "Indeed. Th-thank you, Percy."

There was a short pause.

"Merry Christmas!" Alexi's young wife cried, and she threw her arms around Rebecca.

Rebecca took a moment to take stock. There was no jealousy. There was no pining. There was only possibility. The spirits had granted her new life. She felt entirely, wholly, utterly *new*. She returned the girl's embrace, no longer tentative.

Percy pulled back and grinned again.

Curtseying before either of them could say another word, the young woman trotted off up the staircase . . . and the vast room seemed suddenly all the more empty for the lack of her. There was no remaining bitterness as Rebecca's unwitting rival disappeared. This girl had never wished to be her rival; she had only embraced fate. Something the headmistress intended to do from now on.

"They did it all in one night," she murmured, wandering to her office, a grin on her face. "Spirits. Good spirits. Of course they did it all in one night. Of course they can."

Dickens was to the point after all, damn him. She realized she didn't mind being proven wrong.

It seemed her surprises weren't done. There was an envelope on her desk bearing the official seal of Athens. From the board of directors. Rebecca's heart was in her throat, for she feared something had finally snapped. Perhaps closing the school to battle Darkness had brought about repercussions? Perhaps the board had heard that she'd been acting odd of late, which she most certainly had. But her tension vanished as she read, and a grin again spread across her face.

> *In recognition of your exemplary work as headmistress, the board of Athens Academy has voted to secure you more spacious housing near but not on the grounds of the academy. We will convert your existing apartments into space for visiting faculty, there being a number who wish to learn from and champion Athens's impressive and progressive model as their own. Enclosed, please find the keys for 6 Athens Row.*
>
> *Merry Christmas.*

It looked like Alexi's handwriting but she couldn't be bothered to verify it.

A home. A real home, just down the block. Of course she'd not want to be far, but . . . a home! Not some attic perch or cloistered closet filled with memories of loneliness. She'd now have a hearth. She had someplace to begin her new life, someplace to invite the some*one* she wanted to be part of it. Now that she was whole, now that she knew the heavens wanted something of her—demanded it, in fact—a glorious future awaited.

She nearly ran out the door.

Chapter Ten

Considering all the spiritual upheaval the school had seen, it was lucky Athens was tucked into an area of Bloomsbury and placed at such an odd angle: the red sandstone fortress was surrounded on all sides by alleys and the backs of other buildings. Billy and Mary floated at face level, their arms crossed, and they were just outside the front doors of the academy, in the cold. The breeze felt good on Michael's flushed face; bracing.

He was still reeling from admitting his constant nerves when coming to call upon Rebecca. Surely that made him seem less of a man. But Michael had done as the ghosts wished, moved in his own footsteps through years and years, all seen from the spinning temporal axis of Billy's chandelier vantage. The boy and Mary had taken turns urging him on, and now he was certain he could knock upon the headmistress's door without trembling. He wanted her and loved her more than any fear could obstruct.

"So ye see," Billy said, taking a paternal tone, "it isn't that you fear for your Guard gifts gone. You fear for the very human gift of love being accepted. You fear havin' what you desire. You've feared it all along."

Michael nodded, dizzy.

"So now what are you waitin' for? You, of all people! We'd have thought you'd seen plenty to give you perspective. Do ye need to be frightened by something far more terrifying? Do you want to go back and fight Darkness again? He could live again, could take your bones as his own . . ." Billy threatened. He made a motion and there was a tearing sound. Where the front door of Athens stood, a dark maw of a portal opened to the Whisper-world. A rushing river of bones gurgled by.

Michael gulped. "No, thank you. I'm grateful to battle the heart, instead."

"And are ye going to win this battle this time, Vicar?" cried a voice in an Irish brogue. Stepping from the portal, a woman floated down to hover over the Athens stoop.

"Jane!" Michael cried. He rushed forward.

Jane wafted close, giving his cheek a phantom kiss of cold condensation.

"I . . . I can *hear* you, too!" He was amazed and pleased.

She grinned. "You're still under my spell."

"*Your* spell? Are you all right? Is Rebecca all right? Where is she?"

"Oh, yes, I'm grand. She's grand. She's still inside, working a few things out. Percy's watching her, the dear heart. Time's a bit funny here and there, especially crossing in and out like we've been doing, toying with the past. It doesn't all add up, exactly . . . but then again, that's the Whisper-world for you, full of baffling wonders and terrors. When has it ever added up?"

Michael's face darkened. "What do you mean, she's 'inside'?"

"Inside the Whisper-world. The Liminal, to be exact. It's dangerous, but that's where a soul best gets changed. Would you like to go? Do you *need* to go? Or might we move on to the next phase of this ridiculous and beautiful production?"

Michael shook his head, and his fists clenched. "The Whisper-world? We're not meant to go in there. That was the whole point of the war of the spirits—that we couldn't go in, that Alexi couldn't run in after Percy, that we'll go mad if we go in. What do you mean you've taken her in? I'll go in after her and get her out!" He prepared to run inside the gaping portal.

Jane made a motion and the portal snapped closed behind her. "Why, Vicar Carroll, such spirit," she said.

Michael eyed her with desperation. "You know I'd do anything for Rebecca. Always would have."

"Except say that you love her," Jane accused.

"I did! Much too late, but I did! Can't that count for something? Where is she? Promise me she's not in danger."

"Michael, my dear, if anyone was suited for the mental rigours of the Whisper-world, it's our headmistress. You, dear heart, would be destroyed by the sadness of that place. You'd be unable to break free; it would cripple and scar you forever. Let this moment be. Let *her* be. Focus on yourself."

"When can I see her?"

"Momentarily. I promise."

The tension in Michael's shoulders eased, and his fists uncurled. Jane would never leave Rebecca without recourse. He stared at the greyscale spirit, noting how only colour and transparency differentiated her from when she lived.

"Oh, goodness, what is it now?" she said, smiling as his eyes welled with tears. She'd always loved his sentimentalism but teased him for it.

"It's so very good to see you," he explained. "I think the idea of the Grand Work made us take for granted how much we care for one another. Are you well? Are you at peace? It's so frightfully good to see you, but I didn't mean to rouse you as we prayed at your—"

Jane drew her cold fingers across his eyes, and the draft

dried Michael's eyes. "I happily chose to linger on, to help make this right. And there's only one thing I've left to do. Tell me, Vicar, are you ready to start again? It's my favourite trick, this."

She didn't wait for a response when she snapped her fingers. In a blink, Michael was suddenly fourteen years old again, standing on a street corner and staring. He'd been summoned from his home as if by a great bell, knocked to the ground by a great wind, and his heart exploded with new sensations. His eyes were full of ghosts. It was the first day of the Grand Work, and he was living it.

Living it, indeed. He was no longer watching himself, as he'd done in Athens; he was *in* this memory. He stared down at his hands and flexed them, felt the vigour of youth pounding in his veins. His consciousness was fully aware, though these events happened years long past. With a little giggle he ran full tilt until he reached the crest of Westminster Bridge. If time and memory were both flexible, perhaps there were ways of making things right.

She was waiting, young and spindly-legged, the most beautiful thing he had ever seen. Strands of her brown hair were caressed by the wind, and she glanced around nervously, clutching her skirts and shifting from foot to foot. She'd been the first to arrive, the first of them anxiously awaiting destiny.

"Hello. I'm Rebecca," she said. She opened her mouth to say something else but stopped, staring intently at him. Something on his face had stilled her.

Michael took a step forward. He reached for her hand, and she gave it willingly.

"Hello, Rebecca, I'm Michael," he heard his young voice say. But his old heart shaped new words, released the thunderbolt of knowledge he felt but had once feared to utter. "And I will always love you."

The young Rebecca gasped. She blushed furiously and smiled a welcoming smile.

History changed.

Chapter Eleven

Released from time, from memory, from the magic of the past, or perhaps caught in some sweet mixture of the three, Vicar Michael Carroll stood at the back door of a building he did not recognize. He felt a new man. He wasn't sure what he was suddenly doing on the steps of this lovely town house, or how he'd gotten there.

He looked around for Jane. She was nowhere to be seen, but his heart pounded with the same vigour he had just felt. He wasn't sure if what he'd seen had truly happened, or if it had been a dream, but either way he yearned to find Rebecca, to walk up to her right now, again, a lifetime later. He would approach her with that same surety and change history again.

A sound on the street made him turn: a slowly approaching carriage. The curtain on the window was flung aside, the glass opened, and a snow-white face beamed an expression of joy up at him where he stood on the steps. She waved.

Mrs. Rychman's eerie eyes were shaded from the winter glare by dark-tinted glasses, and she turned to someone behind her and uttered a sort of admonition. "I have to tell him something," she insisted, and soon the door was flung open and a firm male voice barked for the driver to stop.

Before her husband could help her out of the carriage, Percy had lifted up her skirts, disembarked from the carriage and trotted up the stairs to Michael's side. Professor Rychman exited behind her, standing tall and imperious, his black hair, frock coat and carriage a stark contrast to the white of his wife and the snow on the street.

"Hullo, dear girl," Michael said, squeezing her hand, "I'm not sure what has happened, but Jane told me you were at hand, so I'm sure I owe you some sort of—"

"The town house is unlocked," Percy blurted over him. "Your key on the table. The headmistress's key is in her office, with a letter from the academy board explaining the change in quarters. You *must* have a home, Vicar," she added earnestly. "A fresh new start, with no memories but those you two now make. The spirits told me so; they insisted upon it. You must have a home free from the haunting of memories gone by, and you shall make new memories to inhabit *these* bricks. Spirits understand the need of such things: hearths and homes, it's why they haunt them. There is very little more important."

"Indeed," Michael said, having never thought about such a detail. "Most sensible."

"Merry Christmas!" Percy cried, throwing her arms around him. She released him, lifted her skirts and scurried back toward her husband, who awaited her with a small smile tugging at his mouth.

"But . . . where did this home come from? To whom do I owe . . . ?" He stopped short.

Percy waved her hand as if it didn't matter.

"This building is the property of Athens Academy. How it was paid for is none of your concern," Alexi said, his tone all business, though Michael knew there was warmth beneath. "As Percy said, the board voted to give the headmistress better lodging. Go on, Vicar, we've all got Christmas merrymaking to do. We're hosting a New Year's celebration at the Rychman estate, don't you know. Do come with your fiancée."

"My fiancée . . . ?" Michael registered the words, processed them and stepped back a pace. Then he grinned and nearly jumped in the air.

"Go on, she'll be here any minute!" Percy squealed, and dragged Alexi back to the carriage. He gladly helped her up, and they started off.

Michael entered the front hall of the town house. There were spicy scents and warm, alluring lights. Ignoring the stairs that ascended, surely, to bedrooms and studies, he entered the main room to find it well furnished and decorated, with a blazing hearth.

"My God," he murmured, staring at the painting above the mantel. Josephine was right: she was painting more beautifully than ever. Her distinct style was no longer limited to guardian angels, as required by the Grand Work, and now her subjects were free and entirely her own. Tumbling masses of sumptuous flowers, bursting with both colour and life, threatened to spill directly onto the mantel below.

He heard a hiss from the rearmost room—a kitchen, likely—from which warm and intoxicating odours flowed. Someone was mulling wine, a fine cabernet. "Go, go out the side. One of them is here!" hissed a voice with a French accent.

Michael rushed forward. He was in time. In the kitchen he found Josephine, who had prepared a feast that overflowed from tables and countertops. Lord Withersby was lighting candles, careful to keep his absurdly excessive mauve sleeves from catching fire.

"Hullo, friends." Michael grinned.

Josephine and Elijah turned, sheepish. "Sorry, old chap," Elijah murmured. "We wanted to have this all done and ready before you got here, but the spirits sure were quick about it, weren't they?"

Michael didn't know what to say.

Seeming to understand, Josephine took his hands. "Have you lived a whole life over? For us it's only been a day. You must promise to tell us all about it!"

"Josie, it's private," Elijah scoffed. "If the spirits went rooting around in our pasts, do you think we'd want to share?"

Josephine raised an eyebrow, shocked at her fiancé's unusual moment of discretion. "C'est vrai. I suppose for once you are right."

"Listen," Michael said, grabbing Elijah, "whom do I have to thank—?"

Elijah waved at him to be silent. "I've a message from the orphanage. Little Charlie's health has turned a corner. He said an angel came and commended him for his help. You should have him over for a nice dinner, he said he'd like that—and 'God bless us' and all that nonsense." Withersby grinned. Michael pressed his hands to his face in a prayer of thanksgiving.

Josephine removed her apron, showing herself in a far fancier gown than anyone should have been found cooking, and threw one last handful of cinnamon sticks into the wine. "Finis." She turned to Elijah. "Allons-y, ma chere." She turned to Michael. "Joyeux Noelle!" Kissing him on both cheeks, she darted into the main hall and out the front door.

Elijah plucked a piece of paper from his vest pocket and pressed it into Michael's hands. "Get done with this quickly and stop us all from living in sin. I love you!" He kissed Michael's forehead and darted out the door.

Michael opened the paper. Stunned by his good fortune and his even better friends, he entered the sitting room and sat before the hearth, tears of joy in his eyes. While The Guard couldn't be more different as individuals, Michael doubted there'd ever been such care between other humans.

He held a certificate for two rings, courtesy of Lord Withersby's favourite jeweler.

He felt as though his heart might burst from the magnitude of his blessings. It was hard to imagine that just yesterday he'd been feeling that his world was collapsing, that he'd lost everything. His heart was as full as the first day he joined The Guard. He'd lost nothing. He had everything yet to gain.

Heedless of the falling snow, flakes melting immediately against her flushed cheeks, Rebecca was down the block before she knew it, at the address specified in the letter. She went to turn the key in the lock and found it already open. The interior was lit. It smelled like heaven.

She did not take the stairs to the upper landings because a crackling warmth drew her toward the parlour. Inside sat a dapper man upon a divan, his hair more kempt than Rebecca was ever used to seeing, and his oceanic blue eyes were wide and brimming with promise. In what surely must be firelight, it seemed as though a great aura hung about him, as if he were channeling an angel. Or perhaps they were illuminating him for her. Lighting the way.

Michael Carroll. This was the man she'd been meant to love all along, the dear friend whom she *had* loved all along. And now she understood the truth. He was her past, her present, her . . .

"My Christmas yet to come," she murmured from the doorway.

Michael's eyes snapped up to behold her, and his face, somehow joyous even without expression, shone like a sun when he bestowed upon her his magnificent smile. The light was, in fact, his own. Jumping to his feet, he rushed to the threshold and took her hands. From there he escorted her into the parlour, where surely a hundred candles were lit. The pungent smell of spice wafted from a back kitchen. The walls were bare save for the most gorgeous canvas she'd ever seen: Josephine's rich style, uninhibited, the voluptuous beauty of flowers that had Rebecca feeling as fresh and untouched as those blooms.

"Welcome home, Headmistress," Michael murmured, drawing close. He lifted a key. "I assume you've been given one, too. It would seem this is our home, Rebecca. If you'll—"

She silenced him with a kiss.

It was a soft but deepening kiss, one that began as a mere taste and appreciation of the press of lips but progressed toward a hunger unquenchable, a release of tension, a discarding of years gone by, a desperate need to savour the present and a promise of what was to come.

She pulled back. Michael gasped and touched his lip. "Am I dreaming?"

Rebecca chuckled and shook her head. "No. But . . . are you all right?" she asked, wondering if he felt as oddly drained yet vibrant as she. "Did the spirits put you through quite the tasks?"

"Oh, indeed. I'd much to learn. To trust, mostly. I've been so scared. I'd lost heart, though that seems impossible. I feared that in losing our Grand Work I'd lost what little I had to give you."

Rebecca placed her hand on his cheek. "You've the greatest heart of any man who ever lived, with or without the power of The Guard. I know this. I truly *know* this. I am new. I am reborn, like the phoenix, our incarnate patron. Now, please, please, show me how to love like you. Teach me, for the headmistress is ready to learn—and to love you in return, from now until the end of our days, if you will have it so."

The joy upon Michael's face outshone the fire in the hearth. "Amen!" he cried.

Taking her in his arms, he kissed her reverently. Achingly slowly, he kissed her in a progression of passion, demonstrating all the courses of his epic emotions, all he was capable of feeling. In caresses and presses and torturous promises of expanding passion he showed her who he was, and who they would yet become.

Their clasping embrace sent them to the divan, their limbs wrapping tightly, no caress or gasp or devouring kiss enough to express the pent-up passion of twenty unrequited years. Yet there were no regrets. Only possibility.

Soft carols played on church bells nearby, the bells of Michael's parish, songs promising a child was to be born who would bring love to the world. For two lovers reborn in a second chance, it seemed oddly fitting.

Epilogue

As their carriage traveled away from the town house of the soon-to-be Carrolls, Percy removed her glasses and gazed at her husband. The force of her dramatic, ice blue eyes was mesmerizing as ever. "Oh, Alexi. Thank you for postponing our proper honeymoon. Won't it be glorious to attend the two weddings of our most beloved friends? Isn't it wondrous how the world is full of ghosts and angels, muses and magic?"

He placed an arm around her. "Tell me, Percy. How, if spirits can do all this to humans . . . how did we not know it possible? How could The Guard, arbiters of ghosts in this great city, not be privy to these cataclysmic shifts spirits can wreak?"

"Dickens knew about them," Percy teased. "Hardly claptrap."

Alexi opened his mouth to retort but she continued. "*Because*, Alexi, what happened here was done with love. Your job was to halt malevolence from penetrating this world, not goodness, these sorts of miracles weren't in your purview. But love conquers all, especially in this season. My dear," she breathed, "there is so much good in this world, and in the next world, and even in the world between. Such incredible opportunities! Jane took hers to become an angel, and now the world of the Great Beyond will open to her. Perhaps that's the difference between spirits and angels; it's in the *becoming*."

Alexi's furrowed brow eased, dazzled. "You are one of the angels of *this* world," he murmured.

Percy blushed, nuzzled against him and denied it.

The carriage jostled on. Snow again began to fall on the cobblestones, kissing London crystalline pure, dusting its sooty eaves with the white of renewal. The city was reborn, too. There *were* angels on the streets, or those who might be angels. There were angels in the hearts of all those who worked wonders, in all who do, and in all who will.

Of course they can.

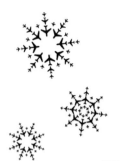

The Worth of a Sylph

L. J. McDonald

To everyone who has a place in a good family,
whether formed from blood ties or not, and
especially for those without. And to Oliver, who's
always been my family.
~L. J. McDonald

Chapter One

"I hate you! I never want to see you again!"

Mace paused on his way up the front walk as he heard the boy scream through the open front door. Lily would be very annoyed to learn it wasn't closed. It was the start of the long Winter Festival, and though it had been a mild season, there was half an inch of snow on the ground and the bushes were frosted with a clean coating of white. That didn't stop the humans from trudging out to visit their neighbors, though, mimicking some old legend about a strange old-time man who went door-to-door throughout the entire world, giving the people he met gifts of food and healing. Mace had never cared for it. It made the humans he was charged to protect move in patterns he wasn't used to and distracted the hive. More, this year he resented the idea that anyone would be coming to this door. Mace didn't feel the cold, but he knew that humans did, and Lily wasn't as young as she used to be. Fire sylphs supplied heat to all the homes in Sylph Valley through underground vents, but the Blackwell house was far from the main furnace rooms and a sudden draft could be dangerous to an old woman.

He went up the porch stairs, careful not to stomp, though there were no babies to wake in the house and hadn't been for years now. While the argument continued inside, he took off his boots, shaking them to rid them of snow before he set them neatly beside the others and closed the door behind him. There was no lock. No one was stupid enough to try and break into any house in the Valley, especially not one in which a battle sylph lived.

Lily's voice echoed down the hall toward him, almost as loud as Jayden's had been. "Are you prepared to be on your own already?" she yelled, her famous temper at its peak. "I really don't think so!"

"I'm going to Crem's!" Jayden screamed, and appeared in the doorway to the kitchen. He stopped at the sight of Mace. There wasn't any fear in him, not after having lived with the battle sylph all his life, but the boy stood for a moment, staring at him with an expression Mace couldn't be bothered to interpret.

"I'm going away," he said suddenly, boldly.

"And?" Mace replied. Lily should never have taken Jayden in. At fourteen, he was by far the youngest child she still fostered, and she didn't have the energy to keep up with him. Jayden always seemed to want something, and now was apparently no different. He stared at Mace with a great hunger in his eyes, waiting.

Whatever it was that he wanted, he didn't get it. Mace continued to stare back at him. Finally, Jayden flushed red and ran past, grabbing his coat and boots and rushing out the door, his mind nothing but anger and that stupid morass of emotions all young humans seemed to go through before they finished growing up. Mace hadn't bothered to keep track of the number of boys he'd felt undergo this struggle while in Lily's care. The girls he'd try to help through the changes, but the boys could take care of themselves. Jayden's had always been an especially thick soup of feelings, but maybe that was because the boy forever seemed to be around. Anytime Mace was home, Jayden followed him.

Putting the youth out of his mind, Mace continued into the kitchen, set at the back of the house with a window overlooking the snowy garden. The stove was currently stocked high with wood and pumped out a great deal of heat to supplement what the fire sylphs provided, even though it was nowhere near a mealtime. Nor did Lily bake. It was the Winter Festival and everyone else in the Valley seemed to be mixed up with the silliness of baking and visiting, but the Widow hadn't bothered with that in years. Mace shot a suspicious look at her, studying the emotions she'd been able to hide from him while he was on the other side of the Valley.

She was angry at Jayden, frustrated and tired. More, she was cold, her shawl tight around her shoulders despite the heat from the stove. Lily Blackwell, still known as the Widow to almost everyone in the Valley except Mace, was eighty-two years old. Her white hair was thinning where it was gathered into a bun, her back hunched and her hands gnarled. She leaned on the cane he'd carved for her, glaring at the door through eyes that were rheumy and, he knew, not as clear as they used to be, despite the Valley's healer's efforts. As far as he knew, no one could cure age, and humans were short-lived creatures indeed, compared to the near-immortal sylphs.

Noting his regard, she lifted her gaze to evenly meet his. Thanks to their master/sylph bond, she could feel his worry even as he tried to suppress it. Lily didn't like to have anyone worrying about her. For nineteen years, since the day the collective was established, she'd been caring for most of the Valley's orphans—many of whom had lost their parents because of Mace himself, back when he'd still been a slave. He'd been frozen in the shape of a suit of armor then, forced to obey the orders of a male master he'd loathed. Jayden was decades too young to be one of the orphans Mace had created, though, and he'd arrived after Lily meant to retire. Mace's heart ached that she was stuck with the boy now, in what should have been her quiet twilight years. He ached even more that caring for Jayden might be shortening the time she had left.

She felt him thinking that.

"Don't," she said, turning and shuffling over to get a kettle of water and put it on the stove. Jayden was the most useless of her children, but he wasn't the only one still living in the house. Mace hoped that one of the sweet adult girls still living there had been the one to fill the kettle and scour the kitchen to its current cleanliness; Lily shouldn't have been doing that herself anymore. At least no one had needed to go to the well at the bottom of the garden in years. Now there was a barrel in the side of the kitchen with a pipe leading to it. Once a day a water sylph topped it off, and Mace had made quietly sure that Lily's house was the first on her rounds.

"I'm going to smack that boy one of these days," Lily said, shuffling to the cupboard to get some tea. Mace beat her there and she grudgingly allowed him to retrieve it for her and measure a few spoonfuls into her old clay pot.

"He could probably use a good smack," Mace agreed.

Lily smiled, a touch of amusement in her emotions at the thought, though if anyone was going to do the smacking, it would be her, not him. For all that he looked like a large, heavily built man of indeterminate age, that was only illusion. Mace was actually a shape-shifter from a different plane, only able to keep his place in this human world due to the tie he had to Lily Blackwell. She kept him here, but in turn he had no choice other than to obey her slightest command. He didn't mind. Obedience was part of what he was. He was a battle sylph, a defender of the hive and a prospective lover for the hive's queen. Unable to accomplish that second goal in his original hive, he'd come through a mystical gate into this world instead. He'd done so in pursuit of a woman, only to have her murdered and him bound to a man he despised. Jasar Doliard had been dead for a very long time now, though, and Mace had taken Lily to be his new master. It had been a practical decision at the time, but the arrangement had worked well for both of them for close to twenty years.

She didn't have him do any of the disciplining of her children, though. While Lily was quick with a wooden spoon on the back of the knuckles, Mace's instincts were more intense. She very likely didn't want him turning Jayden into a pile of fine ash on the floor, no matter how annoyed she was with him.

Lily smiled, her thin lips twisting. She always knew his thoughts. "He's a good boy when he isn't being needy," she reminded Mace. "I'll let him stay at Crem's until the end of the week. Horsing around some before the festival ends should calm him down."

"Are you sure?" Mace asked. Not that he wanted the boy hanging around. In an ideal world there wouldn't be any human men, and Mace looked forward to the day when Jayden left home—likely after the girls departed as well—which would leave just him and Lily.

She studied him again, and Mace wasn't entirely sure what she was thinking. She was being contemplative in the way that always made him . . . he wouldn't say nervous, but alert. Lily had a practical but devious mind, and much as he cared for her, he couldn't always anticipate what she would do.

"How was your day?" she asked.

"Good." He went to pour her tea. "Very quiet."

"Which means no one died." When he quirked an eyebrow at her, she laughed. "Don't look at me. I know how you battle sylphs are. Nothing but instinct."

As if that weren't a good thing. As if it didn't keep them

all safe. He poured her tea, added a dollop of honey, and brought it to the table.

"Thank you," she told him, and took a sip. She savored it for a moment, holding the steaming cup between her gnarled hands.

"I've been thinking," she said at last. "I see everyone getting ready for the Winter Festival and this year it seems almost sad." She set the cup down, leaning her cheek against one hand while her elbow braced on the table. It wasn't a position that Mace had ever seen her take before. "I don't know as many people as I used to. So many of them aren't with us anymore, and I know I'm not going to live forever."

He opened his mouth.

"Don't even think about arguing with me about this." Mace's mouth clapped shut. Lily lifted her cup to taste her tea again and set it down with a sigh. "I think I've done you sweet creatures a bit of a disservice."

Mace raised his eyebrows, not having any idea what she was referring to.

"With demanding right at the start that you be bound to women past their childbearing years," she explained.

Ah, that was it. There were younger women with battle sylphs in the Valley now, but when Mace was first linked to Lily, when there were only a handful of battle sylphs, Lily herself had been about the average age for a master, and she'd been in her sixties. She'd been concerned at the time that the younger women would come to regret the decision, since no battle sylph could give them children and would definitely object to sharing their masters with a human husband. Not all women wanted husbands or children, but Lily hadn't had the time then to seriously consider the ramifications. From the look on her face, she'd done so since.

"I didn't realize back then how long you creatures live,"

Lily admitted, "and I've seen how you react when your masters die."

Actually, we turn into wrecks, Mace thought, with no desire to experience it himself. Sylphs' souls were bound to their masters, and if love was involved, they were in danger of shattering when they lost them. Many recovered and went on, of course. But others, those who'd been lucky or unlucky enough to forge a truly deep soul tie to their masters, they never got over it. Mace cared for Lily, loving her and regretting nothing about being with her, but they both knew that soul tie wasn't there. They'd been good for each other, but he'd survive her death in the end.

Lily studied his face, nodding in satisfaction as she saw that. Still, she wasn't done.

"I don't want you handed off to whoever just happens to be around after I go," she continued. She lowered her other hand and gripped her teacup with both. "I don't care how typical a reaction that seems to be; I don't like it. You're not some sort of prize cow to be given to its next owner."

"What are you suggesting?" Mace asked.

"That you be open to having a second master now," she told him.

He blinked.

She glared at him. "You should have a choice, and so should she. Put some thought into it, instead of being stuck with someone who may be completely wrong for you."

She had a point, he realized. Mace had seen more than one sylph with a master who was totally unsuitable, but once someone became a master, there was no changing it. Yet, while Lily's words were true, he could only stare at her, unsure what to say.

Lily smiled. "I'm hardly planning on dropping dead tomorrow," she reminded him. "But I don't want to worry about this, either, and I want to meet the woman. I want to make sure for myself that she's good enough for you. And . . . I'm hardly able to provide for all your needs anymore."

That was also true. Mace still made love to her, but it was rare and done with the gentleness of stroking a dove, fragile and soft. That's what Lily had become for him, and his fear of breaking her with his lust was something he'd obviously not hidden as well as he'd thought.

Her smile turned into a smirk for a moment and then faded back into that grim practicality he'd always loved. "Look around the Valley and see if there's a woman you think you could spend another lifetime with. Perhaps someone you could truly love as deeply as some of you silly things do. At least, be open to the idea." She looked at him directly. "I give you permission."

"All right, I'll be open to it," he promised, knowing she meant for him to make love to this unknown woman: he would need to in order to be sure there was hope for a bond. Regardless of his words though, he had no intention of actively doing any such thing. He leaned forward to kiss her, his mouth gentle against hers. Lily bent into it, one gnarled hand reaching up to stroke his cheek, clean of hair in this form, the way she liked. He'd be open to her idea, and he would find a new master once she was gone, for otherwise all that remained for him was banishment and loneliness. Right now, though, he couldn't imagine anyone replacing her, and if he was honest with himself, he didn't think there was anyone out there that he could form a true soul tie with. Not the way Heyou had with the queen or Ril had with Lizzy and even Leon. He wasn't that lucky.

He'd long since surrendered any hope that someday he might be.

Chapter Two

The boy was gone.

Mace found out about it when he was in a council meeting, where he sat on the board to represent the sylphs. Leon Petrule was talking, still the Valley's chancellor at fifty-nine, though Mace had heard rumors that his wife gave him three more years to retire or she'd cut his ears off. Mace had been thinking to himself that he doubted the human would ever allow that to happen when he felt Lily's usual calm placidity flip over into horror and rage, and he was bolting for the door before he even realized he was moving.

"Mace?" The queen gasped from the head of the table. There was no order in her tone, so he kept going, shifting his form and racing for the nearest sylph vent to the surface. People ducked out of his way, running from the black cloud that was his natural form. They always did. In the Valley, all battlers preferred their human bodies, and the stronger ties they gave to the human women they loved. To see a battle sylph in his real shape was to know that somewhere nearby was a threat.

What's going on? asked Ril, the other battler on the council, speaking directly into his mind. Ril's tension was obvious, and it spread through the rest of the hive. In another minute, the battlers would all be rising.

My master needs me, Mace told him. He felt Ril's tension ease. This was personal, not something that would involve the hive as a whole. Mace had seen other battlers run off for no reason more pressing than that their masters were feeling lusty, but his Lily had never called him for that. Their love-making was controlled and planned. Other than the time one of her orphans decided to fall out of the tree in the front yard and break both his legs, she'd never put out a call that drew him from his work.

She wasn't at their home. Instead, Mace tracked her a short distance away, to another neighborhood with houses similar to their own, most of them decorated with the pine branches and garlands that heralded the Winter Festival. The parties that marked the event were only days away now and people were already starting to go from door to door, visiting their neighbors and wishing them well. Lily hadn't gone on such a visit in years and hadn't made Mace go in even longer, and though the house Lily stood in wasn't one he'd ever accompanied her to or even visited on his own before, he knew the family who lived there, just as he knew every human in the Valley.

Mace landed before the front door, shifting back to human shape, and charged inside, not bothering to knock. The door led straight into the living room, and the couple standing before Lily jumped at the sight of him. Even if they hadn't recognized Mace, they would have known what he was from his blue uniform with its gold trim, worn by all battlers so that there were no mistakes made by human men. Angering a battle sylph might just turn out to be fatal.

"What's going on?" Mace demanded.

The woman before Lily held a boy, her arms around his neck and her hands clasped so that the knuckles were white. Her husband stood nearby, swallowing nervously at the sight of the battler. The boy was rebellious and scared.

Lily spun toward him, years seeming to drop away in her

concern and anger. She looked glorious to Mace. "I came to get Jayden. He was never here!"

She was upset about that? "Where did he go?" Mace asked. It had been five peaceful days since the boy left. Still, he mused, even a human could travel a long way in that amount of time. Perhaps Lily had a reason to be upset.

Crem's parents felt concerned to him. "He didn't come here," the mother told Mace. "We didn't know he was supposed to be staying with us."

Lily muttered something under her breath that was completely unrepeatable.

"We d-didn't know," the father stammered. Most sensible men were afraid around battle sylphs, Mace especially.

The young boy's defiance grew, and Mace looked down at him. "Where did he go?" he repeated.

"I dunno," Crem said.

"You're lying," Mace told him flatly. The boy jumped. His parents looked at each other. "Where is he?"

"I don't know," Crem said again, and Mace's hand shot out faster than any of them could react. It locked around the boy's throat, and he hoisted him up until his shoes were four feet off the floor. Both parents screamed, but Mace ignored them—though he did feel a little bad about the mother's fear.

"Where *is* he?" he asked a third time.

The boy was ashen-faced, his father trying to work his terror into enough anger to attack. That would only get him killed, so Mace stared at him. The man blanched and backed up. The mother clenched her fists, though, readying herself for a charge that Mace wouldn't be so quick to retaliate against.

"MACE!" Lily barked. "Put him down!"

That was definitely an order. Mace set the boy down. "Where did he go?"

The boy started to cry. "To Eferem!" he sobbed, turning to find comfort with both his parents. "He went to Eferem!"

"Why?" Mace asked, totally baffled. The kingdom of Eferem wasn't quite the threat it used to be, but he couldn't imagine anyone wanting to go there.

"Tell us why, child," Lily demanded as Crem kept crying. His parents felt like they very much wanted to tell Lily to take her concerns and get out of their house, but neither of them wanted to face Mace's reaction.

Crem eyed the battler over his shoulder, his face covered in snot and tears: little boys were especially disgusting. "He said he wanted to show you. He wanted to be a swordsman," he spat, "but no one here gets to. So he took a mail convoy to Eferem."

To be a swordsman? For Eferem? Mace had heard of plenty of stupid human motivations before, but this was definitely up there. He looked at Lily to see her regarding him, and he had a sudden, very uncomfortable understanding of exactly what her next order was going to be.

Chapter Three

Ruffles adored him.

Mace padded along the dusty road, all four feet moving smoothly. A great deal of work had been done in the Shale Plains since the Valley was established, but the battling sylphs who'd wrecked the original grasslands so many centuries ago had done a thorough job. It took a long time and a lot of work to get the land to come back to life and stay that way without constant attention. Mace had heard that one day the plains would become one of the wealthiest farm belts in the known world, but that probably wouldn't happen in the lifetimes of any of the humans living in the Valley right now. So it stayed a mostly barren, shale-filled dead zone, filled with slowly spreading wild grasses. The sylphs used them to anchor what little soil there was while they labored to create more. In that soil lay the Valley's future, which made the effort worthwhile.

It also made traveling a pain, though Mace was doing so in the most efficient way possible, other than flight. He trotted along the side of the sylph-made road in the shape of a large, darkly mottled mastiff. It wasn't a shape he was used to, but it was no different than any other form he could take, and certainly it was easier than having to bring horses, which he'd need to take care of.

At least Ruffles was capable of taking care of herself, since the dog was trained to hunt. She was a shepherd/mastiff mix from the Valley's anchor pool—animals specifically raised and trained to be bonded to sylphs who didn't want or couldn't handle human masters. Though they usually preferred it, sylphs didn't need to be linked to a human in order to stay in this world. Nor did they need one to feed from, as they'd previously believed. Any large-enough animal could provide a sylph with energy and a hold on the world, and when the master was an animal, there was no chance of the sylph receiving abusive orders. For some emotionally wounded sylphs, that was a good thing, though Mace knew of one earth sylph with a dog who was very good at getting across the concept of "Take me for a walk," and they all did "Feed me now" quite effectively. Anchor animals were usually fat.

Most sylphs didn't want to have to rely on the anchor dogs, though. Their love was unconditional and simple, but for many, it was too simple. They could give energy and companionship, but no sylph/dog bond could ever come close to the soul tie they all craved from a human master.

In this case, Ruffles was a better choice to take along than an eighty-two-year-old woman who needed a cane. Mace didn't know how long he would be gone, and he did need to restore his energy levels on a regular basis. That was Ruffles's job. She was a year old, ninety pounds, and furry, her tongue hanging out and slobbery as she ran at his side. She was meticulously well trained, used to sylphs and their ability to change shape, and even in dog shape, Mace was impressed at how well she obeyed his nonverbal orders. She paced him easily, having been kept fit by her trainers. Mace had never bothered to pay attention to any of the anchor dogs in the Valley before, but with sylph instinct, now that Ruffles was his master, he wanted to protect her. Her emotions were uncomplicated, and she was ready to follow him anywhere, so long as he wanted her.

Given he was the one used to following, it was really rather nice.

The two trotted down the road, wending their way through the spread-out ranks of a mail convoy, the only sort of transport that traveled at this time of year. Mace suspected these men were only doing so now in order to get to their homes in time for the Winter Festival. In the Valley and Shale Plains they were safe from attack, but outside sylph-patrolled lands the roads weren't always guarded. The men rode with swords at their belts and crossbows on their backs.

From the look of it, Crem was right: Jayden had left the Valley by working for an earlier convoy. This one probably wouldn't have needed the extra manpower. There were only a half dozen riders and a short string of pack mules loaded high with mail. This was likely the last convoy to leave until spring, and the men peered down at the passing dogs in puzzlement. Mace ignored them, but Ruffles slowed, wagging her tail up at one of them when he clucked. His emotions showed the man thought he was looking at an unattached animal.

Mace swung his big head around. "Leave my dog alone," he growled.

The man jumped, the others gaping with their jaws open. Ruffles gave them all a very doggy grin, and she broke into a loose run, easily keeping up with Mace as he himself ran, intent upon leaving the irritating convoy behind.

At this time of year, traveling at a rate of thirty miles on a good day, the trip from Sylph Valley to Eferem's capital took a week for a standard merchant caravan. For a couple of dogs the journey would be much shorter, not that Mace was expecting to have to go all that way. Not if he could possibly avoid it. Eferem at the best of times was a city he never wanted to see again. Eferem in the grip of the Winter Festival could only be a hundred times worse. Humans were far too invasive into personal space for his liking at this time of year.

At a battle sylph's flying speed, the trip to Eferem's border could be done in hours, but Mace didn't have that option. For one, Ruffles wasn't likely to understand being carried inside of him, unable to see, but feeling every twist and turn of the flight . . . The thought of what she might *do* while inside him was beyond disgusting. More importantly, the treaty between Eferem and the Valley forbade sylph battlers from passing over the border, save in defense of Eferem itself. Mace had considered that a human rule, not that he would have gone by the border without a very good reason, but the absoluteness of the requirement had been forced on him.

The rules had been given to him while they were at the Anchor Center, the attendant off picking Ruffles as a dog specifically trained to keep up with an active battler. The lazy beasts sprawled out in the front area of the center hadn't appealed to Mace at all. They'd been mostly mutts, all of them looking at him as though they'd just love to have him jumping to bring them dog food for the rest of their lives. Mace understood the importance of the animals, but he didn't want to cater to one.

"I suppose we'll have to build a dog house for it after you get back," Lily remarked, sitting in a chair beside the fireplace. She'd insisted upon coming and he'd carried her the entire way, cradling her inside the warmth of his natural form. She was a bit pale, but there was a flush of the anger he still felt inside her, along with the worry. Her concern about Jayden was driving her nearly to distraction.

"Yes," he murmured, determined to tie the boy to the house when he brought him back.

Lily frowned down at a mutt sitting beside her and staring up at her, its tail thumping against the floor. "I don't want this animal inside my house," she decided. "Muddy things. I'd be cleaning up after it all the time."

Mace hesitated. He had no tie to the animal, but soon enough he would, and deep inside, the thought of leaving it outside wasn't a lot different from the thought of having to leave Lily outside.

Lily looked at him, picking up on the sudden emotion inside him, but before she could say anything more, the door opened and the queen walked in. Solie had always been a lovely girl, but she'd grown over the years into a beautiful, confident woman, and the battle sylph who followed behind her had paced the appearance of his own age to match hers. They looked as though they belonged together, and Mace could see the soul tie between the two. Their bond was much deeper than any Mace had any hope to experience, and he bowed to both of them in respect.

"My queen," he said.

Solie smiled at him, while Heyou grinned. "Hi, Mace," he teased. "Hear you lost somebody. You know, I don't have to keep a twenty-four-hour guard on *my* kids."

Mace straightened up, studiously ignoring him. Of course he didn't. Of Solie's children, both fathered with the help of two different human men, one was a quiet, contemplative boy, more interested in studying than going anywhere, and the other one *was* guarded twenty-four hours a day by a battler that never left her side. Seeing he was being ignored, Heyou just grinned wider.

"I'm sorry that Jayden is missing," Solie told Mace. She'd always made it a point to remember everyone's name that she could, and for that, the humans of Sylph Valley loved her nearly as much as the sylphs did. Mace nodded back, pleased at her concern, but even more annoyed at the boy for doing anything to upset her. Solie just shook her head. Thanks to her status, as long as she was close enough, she could feel his emotions as easily as a sylph, and she could feel his ambivalence. A moment later, he knew she could feel his ambivalence turn into something else entirely.

"I want you to be very careful in Eferem, Mace. You know how tenuous our peace treaties are. I want Eferem to be more than just our neighbors—I want them to be our friends."

Both sylphs stared at her, Heyou's mouth turning down into a frown. "You're about to take all the fun out of this for him, aren't you?"

Solie ignored him, eyeing Mace, and he felt the lack of compromise in what she was saying. "I'm not telling you to hide what you are or why you're there, but I don't want you to be obvious about it."

"Meaning?" he asked slowly.

"Meaning no going to your natural shape unless you absolutely have to. Don't flaunt being there to Eferem's troops."

"You really are taking all the fun out of it!" Heyou wailed.

"And no killing," Lily added. Mace turned to look at her, sitting at the fire with the light of the flame flickering on her wrinkled face. "You're only going to retrieve a single boy. You won't have any need to kill anyone."

Mace looked at his master, wanting to argue, wanting to protest, wanting to point out that, treaty or not, Eferem wasn't their friend and he didn't know what he was going to face. He wanted to say that he was one of the most powerful sylphs in the entire Valley and it was beneath his dignity to skulk on the ground and chase a child who meant nothing to him anyway. He wanted all of that and he looked into her eyes, those eyes that had ruled him for so many years, and then he looked down.

"Yes, Lily," he agreed.

"Well, crap," Heyou muttered. "Now I'm not going to ask if I can go along."

At least Ruffles didn't mind the style of their journey. She ran at his side happily, tongue hanging out and tail wagging, even as the snow fell around them and turned her into a white caricature of herself. Since the shale was sharp enough to cut her pads, they kept to the road through the plains. She seemed tireless.

"Seemed" was all it was, though, and Mace made his pace match hers. She was happy just to be out with him, and curled against him when they stopped to rest well shy of the forests of Eferem. Her emotions were peaceful and happy, calming without being demanding, and Mace nuzzled her, wondering why Lily hadn't suggested this solution for him for when she passed away. Many sylphs who'd had the strongest bonds now took anchor animals when their masters passed, not wanting to face the pain of potentially losing another human again so soon. Dogs didn't live as long, but there was no risk of a true soul tie with them.

He supposed that in the long run, Lily knew it wouldn't work. Ruffles could give him energy, and she loved him with all the doggy fervor in her soul, but she couldn't give him the deeper connection for which he'd come through the gate from his world. He needed companionship, equality, conversation. He needed a sentient lover to feel complete, not a pet, and though he'd long since given up on finding it, part of him needed the deeper-still soul tie like the one Heyou had with their queen. Still, for all that he'd only taken her on for the sake of this journey, Ruffles was his for life, for the bond between them could only be broken by going back through the gate—which he would never do—or by death.

Mace licked the dog's ear until she fell asleep, warm against him despite the snow that covered them both. She had a home with him, and he wouldn't risk her safety any more than he'd risk Lily's. They'd find the boy and they'd go home, and that would be the end of it.

He lay beside the sleeping dog, not needing to sleep himself, and waited for her to wake. Ahead of them, the forests of Eferem were just a haze barely visible through the snow, and he cursed the stupidity of a boy who would choose this time of year to run away. At the same time he was grateful, since it had brought him Ruffles.

Once it reached the border of Eferem, the stone highway that cut across the Shale Plains turned into a rough, twisting dirt road heavily marked by potholes and ruts from the progress of wagons and horses. Mace doubted it would be used at all if it weren't the quickest way to both Sylph Valley and the mountainous kingdom of Para Dubh to the east. The fact that it was in such bad shape was a sign of what Solie had been saying. The kingdom of Eferem wasn't at war with them, but they'd rather ignore the Valley than be friends. Solie was working to change that, but it was slow going.

The road needed so many repairs that after a few moments of thought, Mace abandoned it and led Ruffles up a deer path into the woods. Here, for them, the way would be quicker. There wasn't much point in staying on the road in hope of tracking Jayden, anyway. The boy had gone through a week before, long enough for the best tracking hound to lose him, and while Mace looked like a dog, he wasn't one. His sense of smell was heightened, as was his hearing, but he didn't know what scents would be helpful to pick up. He didn't even know what Jayden smelled like, so he just ignored his nose. He'd only find the boy by questioning humans. If the boy had left the convoy, an angry youth traveling alone at this time of year would attract notice. Or so Mace hoped. At any rate, even if he hadn't, the convoy itself should be remembered. Humans liked mail.

It had been almost twenty years since Mace last came this way, and he'd never expected to return. His last visit had been when he was a bound sylph, traveling with his master in pursuit of a woman Mace never wanted to harm. That wouldn't have mattered, though, if they'd found her. Mace would have killed her on command, no matter his personal feelings. After all, he'd done it before. Luckily, things hadn't happened that way, and instead everything had changed. The only orders floating in Mace's mind right now were Solie's admonition not to take his original form except in an emergency and Lily's commands to bring Jayden back without killing any people. He would succeed, even if it was just the boy's body he returned, even if it was just the boy's bones and it took a thousand years. Lily thought she understood sylph behavior, but she didn't. Not really. Even without the soul tie, after nearly twenty years of being hers, her slightest wish was his command.

He and Ruffles made good time through the woods, pausing only to help her hunt down a rabbit to eat. It was easy. Ruffles sniffed the beast out, and the instant it bolted, Mace used the tiniest amount of his fighting energy to kill it. While Ruffles feasted, he shifted to the form of an eagle and flapped his way up into the dim, gray sky to take a look at their surroundings.

There wasn't much. The clouds were dropping a steady stream of snow that made it hard to see anything other than the dimmest, closest outlines of trees. Mace didn't bother with sight, though. Though his ability to do so was limited outside his natural shape, he looked at the patterns of life instead, dismissing any vegetation and animals for the more complex patterns of human beings.

There were a great many only a few miles farther on. Circling there, Mace remembered. When he'd come this way before, there had been a town in the woods, a place called Falloweld, which served the men who trapped animals in the surrounding forests. Mace hadn't thought of the place in a long time. At least, he hadn't thought of the town itself. There were other things about it that he did remember with great, unspoken fondness.

He dropped down, landing in his human form again beside Ruffles and retrieving his clothes. As an eagle, he'd been too small to carry them inside of him. She glanced at him and continued with her meal, used to seeing sylphs change shape. Anchor animals were acclimated to that from puppyhood, even if they were never called on to serve, and they faced everything unique about sylphs except for a battler's hate aura. It was considered cruel to expose them to that. They also weren't trained to ride inside a sylph's mantle, since no battler in the Valley would volunteer to help teach them.

The battler dressed while he waited for her. The clothes were real, and while the eagle was too small, his dog form was just big enough that he could carry them inside, since he only needed to look like a dog on the outside. There were battlers skilled enough to shift and have their clothes simply appear real, but Mace had never bothered to gain that kind of competence. Lily had made both his shirt and pants for him, and while they were plain cotton, they served him well. Better yet, they smelled of her from when she washed them. Other than his uniform, he couldn't imagine wearing anything else.

From the look of it, they'd arrive in Falloweld shortly after noon, sooner if they continued cutting through the woods. It would be better to go by the road from here, he decided at last. He'd have to interact with the humans in the town, and he didn't want them to think he was anything other than one of them. Even humans back home sometimes reacted oddly to battle sylphs, and in the Valley they weren't used solely as mindless weapons, as in the other kingdoms. No one in Eferem who was outside their capital had likely seen a battle sylph in years, and even before then they'd been rare, so he wasn't sure what they thought about his kind. Likely they only knew rumors of the truth, and he didn't know what any of those were or how much they were believed. Mace didn't even want to imagine how awkward it could get here if they realized what he was. It was entirely possible the Fallowelders would refuse to help.

Ruffles finished her meal and lifted her head, her tail wagging and her muzzle bloody.

"Come on," Mace told her, and he set off, his big shape vanishing in the misty light of the snowy woods, the dog padding patiently by his side.

Chapter Four

Falloweld had grown since Mace last visited. What had been a rough collection of buildings and a single inn had become a fair-sized town. It was also far less rough than it used to be, the homes well built and cared for, though the entire place was surrounded by a log wall that looked both very strong and new, and also as though it didn't belong. There was a single-gate entry on the side he approached.

While he was allowed to pass, Mace was watched by the guards as he did. He was observed pretty closely by the people in town as well, even as they moved around in that annoying visiting routine that marked the Winter Festival. Mace frowned as he trudged through the snowy streets. He had his orders to be discreet in his mission, and he looked like an ordinary human, but he wasn't used to actually pretending to be one and had forgotten some fundamental truths about how frail they were. It was December, snowing, and cold, and he'd arrived as a stranger in town with no wilderness gear or even a cloak. Even as they went on their way, invading their neighbors' homes and forcing their gifts on each other, they shied away from Mace. It wasn't that these folk were suspicious of him—not so much—but they seemed almost frightened to see him. Not for who he was, he realized after a time, but for what his arrival seemed to mean. It was almost as if they'd seen him before in their streets, or someone like him.

A few looked as though they wanted to talk, but Mace wasn't interested in their concern. His plan had been to start his search at the inn. He didn't see a reason to change that.

Despite Falloweld's growth, Mace still saw a few buildings he recognized, and it wasn't long before he reached the center of town. There, the same inn that his master had stayed in all those years ago was still standing, though expanded now with an extra wing and a new stable in the back. Its walls were clean and well mended, and despite the snow, light showed in the windows. Mace heard laughter from inside. The exterior was decorated for the Winter Festival, and he could see that someone had taken an entire small tree in and set it up. In the Valley, people went visiting each other's private homes, but from the numbers he could sense inside, it appeared Falloweld spread the tradition to businesses as well.

He went inside, Ruffles padding contentedly at his side. Back in the Valley, anchor dogs were allowed in any building their sylph might go into, but he learned the inhabitants of Falloweld didn't feel the same way the moment he stepped through the door.

"Hey! Whoa! Get that dog out of here!" the innkeeper shouted from behind the bar, gesturing with a large mug. "No animals allowed!"

Mace hesitated. If the man had been brandishing a knife, he would have been tempted to blow him to pieces, though of course Lily's orders wouldn't have allowed that. As it was, everyone was staring. With an annoyed frown, he backed out the door and settled Ruffles in a sheltered spot with a very firm "Stay." If she was frightened by anything, he'd know and come for her. She licked his hand and he went back inside.

Everyone was still staring at him, murmuring now. Mace was used to that but still irritated, and to add to the matter, everyone he saw was male, showing none of the fearful respect he was used to getting. He was tempted to just walk out, but this was still the best place to start. The mail convoy he sought would have gone through this town. If the convoy hadn't stopped at this inn, the innkeeper still should know where it went. It was even possible that Jayden was still here, though Mace couldn't sense him. He'd never paid much attention to Lily's male orphans, but he knew them well enough that he could identify their patterns. That was true of Jayden especially, since the boy was always around. Mace only had to get within a few hundred feet of the youngster to spot him.

He went across the room to the innkeeper, who'd just had one of the patrons at his bar whisper to him and was now regarding Mace with rather more concern than before. There was a bit of fear under the bluster, but it still had nothing to do with any realization of what Mace actually was. Mace couldn't read minds, only emotions, and right now that didn't help him much.

He stopped on the other side of the bar, looking down at the man.

"You lost your cloak," the innkeeper noted. "You get attacked by those bandits?"

"What?" Mace said, surprised. He hadn't heard anything about bandits, though of course he wouldn't have cared, so long as they stayed off sylph land. "I'm looking for a boy. His name's Jayden, about fourteen. He would have come through here a week ago with a mail convoy out of Sylph Valley."

To his surprise, the man's expression turned to dismay, and the talking started up in the inn again. Mace looked around in bemusement, listening to the conversations for information, but it was the innkeeper who said something that made sense. Sort of.

"Oh, hell. Look, we didn't know where he came from.

The postmen didn't stay long enough to say much. I mean, we knew about it, but we didn't know who to tell."

Mace eyed him. "What are you talking about?"

The innkeeper took a deep breath, obviously not happy with what he had to say next. "A mail convoy got attacked by bandits on the road a few days ago. They came through here afterward and didn't stay long; they'd lost everything, and no one wants to stay here anymore, thanks to those damn murderers." He paused. "They said that the bandits told them that if they didn't get a recruit, they'd kill everyone. They said a boy volunteered to go with them. No one's seen him since."

"Damn bastards," a patron growled. "Just wanted to toy with him, I bet. They don't need recruits. They got enough already."

"Won't be long before they attack us, I tell you. That wall won't be enough to keep them out."

"Someone's got to petition the king for help!"

"We've already sent to him. Won't see nothing until spring, if we see anything at all."

Mace looked around at the different speakers until an older man with sparse hair and a facial similarity to the innkeeper leaned over and patted his arm. He smelled of ale. "He was a brave, brave lad. He your son?"

"No." Mace pulled his arm free. This was going to take longer than he'd hoped. "Where are these bandits?" He didn't ask why the townsfolk hadn't risen up themselves against them. They weren't battle sylphs.

The innkeeper's brow lifted. "Are you planning to go after them? By yourself?"

"Of course."

They laughed. Mace would have been annoyed if he'd cared. They seemed to think he was crazy, though, and he hoped he wouldn't have to reveal his identity just to get them to take him seriously. This whole "discretion" approach really wasn't working as well as he'd hoped.

The innkeeper howled, wiping his eyes. "You're going to go after them. Bandits. In winter. Alone. Just who the hell do you think you are?"

Mace frowned. "My name is Mace, and I need to know—"

"Mace?" The man gaped, his emotions flipping instantly to surprise. A complex twist of emotions overlaid with disgust replaced this as his entire personality changed, faster than Mace would have thought possible. His eyes narrowed. "Have you been here before? About nineteen years ago, in the winter?"

"Yes," Mace said, having no idea why the man was asking. He'd been a giant, silent suit of armour then, and he'd never stepped into the inn. He'd been left out in the stable for the night, with only a single visitor.

"Bastard!" the man thundered, his face flushing red as he reached under the bar. Surprised, Mace just stared at him until the innkeeper brought out a cudgel and swung it hard against the side of his head.

It was a blow meant to kill, fueled by a sudden, passionate rage. With a normal man the attack would have been fatal, but Mace's head only rocked to one side and back. The innkeeper gaped, and Mace reached across the bar, grabbed him by the front of his shirt, and threw him across the room. The man howled and crashed into a table, knocking it over and scattering the people sitting around it. A moment later, everyone seemed to be piling atop Mace, joined in some form of semidrunken solidarity that was familiar to a battle sylph, if annoying beyond belief.

A chair smashed across Mace's back and an ale mug struck him. Truly annoyed that Lily banned him from killing anyone, the battler grabbed one fist that was speeding toward his face and flung its owner off to his right. He then backhanded another. He didn't try to kill either man, but his blows were more powerful than a human's. This didn't deter his attackers, however. The men in the inn were obviously family, and the more of them he knocked down, the more the rest seemed determined to get vengeance.

Mace wasn't prepared to be their victim, no matter how much of this was a fear reaction because of bandits. Stepping forward, he bent down as a man came at him, catching him around the waist and straightening. The man's roar of anger became an unmanly shriek as he found himself abruptly flipped upside down, held behind Mace's head. Mace let him go and stepped forward, letting the man crash heavily onto the wood floor.

By this point, the innkeeper had struggled to his feet, standing unsteadily and waving at the rest. "Bash that guy's head in!" he shouted. "That's the bastard who ruined our family's reputation! Just don't wreck my inn!"

Right. There was a table beside him, a heavy thing made of scratched wood. Mace grabbed the end of it with one hand and threw it at a group, careful to aim just high enough that they could duck, much as he wanted to take their heads off. That gave more than a few of them pause, some of them realizing at last that this wasn't a normal fight. Not that Mace cared. He just knew that he hadn't come here for this, and he didn't have the patience for it.

Throwing the table wasn't enough. The men kept coming. Seeing no other option, Mace released his hate. Every man in the bar, whether drunk or sober, angry or afraid, froze. The hate of a battle sylph was a palpable thing, an aura that covered and overwhelmed, causing terror in the hearts of humans and the urge to fight in other battlers. For the years when he was bound, Mace had used it to hide his emotions from his master, who was empathic with him. He hadn't used the aura in years, but even now it marked what he was and made those near him afraid. It was a warning. They wouldn't accept him as one of them? He wouldn't pretend anymore.

"Oh, gods," the innkeeper gasped, his face utterly white. "She wasn't lying."

Half the occupants of his bar were already running for the door, and the only regret Mace felt was the fear he sensed in Ruffles outside, who couldn't understand battler hate and was bolting in terror. He was just turning to go find her when the door to the kitchen banged open, hitting the wall so hard that even Mace turned to look.

A woman stood there, thin and tired, her hair done up in a messy bun and her clothes faded and worn by toil. Her face was lined with old worries, but even as Mace looked at her, the lines were dropping away, amazement returning her youth as she stared at him, her arms covered in soapy water to the elbows and her apron stained and worn.

"Mace?" she whispered.

"Yes," he replied uncertainly, staring at the strangest reaction to his hate he'd ever seen in his life. He let the aura drop.

"Mace!"

She screamed and ran forward to throw her arms around him, burying her face against his chest. This close, he could smell her soap and her scent—one he'd smelled many years ago, during a night spent banished to a stable with only a single visitor. Smiling, he put his arms around her.

"Sally," he said, and she started to cry.

Chapter Five

Sally was seventeen when she came to him that night nineteen years ago. Mace had been standing in an empty stall, though of course the entire stable was emptied of animals to try and accommodate him. Jasar had been especially petty since the journey began, not having wanted to travel in the first place and being angry with Mace for other reasons. He'd tormented his battler to distraction, making him angrier and angrier until, by the time they reached the village, Mace was steaming with hatred and not caring how far he broadcast it. He'd been wallowing, Mace knew, especially since Jasar was too small-minded to be bothered by his hate, but he hadn't been able to stop himself. He'd just wanted to hate, to make sure everyone shared his misery.

That changed when Sally came in. He was so busy imagining tortures for his master that he didn't even realize she was there until she spoke. Mr. Mace, she called him. The second he heard, he shut down the hate. His master he'd see die a thousand different deaths, but he'd never deliberately hurt a female of his own volition. She'd called his name again, so afraid of what he could do to her but so brave, and he'd stepped out of his stall to see her.

Her beauty had almost undone him. He'd seen many women in the castle where Jasar lived, and he'd had many of them as well, slaking his needs on them and preventing his own madness, but Sally was different. She wasn't dressed in a noble's finery or a servant's uniform. She wore a simple homespun dress, her hair curling around her face where it came loose from the bun, and her hands curled in her apron, twisting the fabric in a way that made his heart surge. She was innocent and sweet, and deep inside her he felt the needs that she was afraid of facing in herself, needs she certainly hadn't come into this stable expecting to experience.

She asked him to stop scaring everyone in the inn. He nodded in agreement: he only wanted to hurt Jasar, and to Jasar the hate meant nothing anyway. Instead Mace felt the deep longing she had, the loneliness and surety that no one could ever want her, and he drew it into himself, blending it with his own never-ending desire before sending it back to her. He heard her breath catch and wanted to take her into his arms. Instead she fled back to the inn. He let her go, despite longing as always for a woman's touch. This was what he was made for, even more than the hate and the violence. He was meant to be a lover.

He thought this woman wouldn't have him. He had offered—in the only way he could, given that he was forbidden to speak—and she'd fled. She came back, though. Deep in the night, after the rest of the town was asleep, he saw the brief flicker of a hooded lantern at the window to the stable, followed a moment later by a slim, shadowy figure darting inside. She hesitated, but she had courage and Mace could feel her desire, could feel the burning knot deep within her, and his own lust surged, projecting straight to her. She gasped at the feel of it, trembling, and he stepped forward to take the lantern from her before she dropped it into the straw.

She stared up at him as he set the lantern aside and turned the wick up a little so that she could see. He didn't need it; he could see in the dimmest light or use his senses to find his way. He was aware of far more of her without his eyes anyway. Most importantly, he knew exactly what she needed and what she'd come for.

She wasn't so sure, despite the bravery he felt deep inside. "I don't know why I'm here," she whispered.

He was tall and bulky in his armored shape, his interior seemingly empty though Jasar hadn't specified what was supposed to go *inside* the armour when he commanded Mace's form. Many women had learned in fact that he wasn't empty at all. This female barely came to the bottom of his breastplate though, so Mace knelt down before her, reaching up to cup the sides of her breasts with his hands. She gasped at that, and he brought his thumbs around to brush her nipples. She whimpered, and he pressed a little harder, just enough to feel her pleasure increase, stimulated by his aura of desire as much as his touch.

She wanted more, and he lifted his hands away to unlace her bodice. She let him, her breath quickening, and he opened the heavy fabric to free her breasts in the chemise. The front was cut low, normally kept decent, if tantalizing, by the bodice. Mace just pushed the cloth wide, and she cried out as he took her bared breasts in his hands, squeezing them rhythmically as his thumbs made circles around her nipples.

"Oh, this is why I'm here," she gasped, her head falling back. Her entire body was taut, pleasure quivering through her, but he contented himself with her breasts, rubbing the visor of his face against her. All his moments had been stolen before this, quick flashes of sex taken in hurried minutes in which he always feared someone would come and see, women with skirts tossed up to permit him, often biting their own hands to keep from screaming while he filled them. He'd never had leave to take his time before, and he meant to take advantage of it. This woman came to him willingly. He had the leisure to make her never regret it.

Mace stroked every inch of her body, baring her slowly as he set aside bodice and chemise, then went to work on the ribbon that held her hair, loosening it and running his hands through her locks before dropping his hands to loosen the ties around her waist and lower her skirts and undergarments. She leaned forward while he did, planting little kisses all over his visor and helm.

She was beautiful naked, her body soft and curvy. Mace pulled her toward him and she came willingly as he sat back on his heels, twining her arms around his neck as she continued her kisses.

Stroking his hands down her back and buttocks, he pulled her legs wide and settled her against him, the tip of his phallus pressing against her softly swollen nether lips. She shuddered against him, her mouth stilling on his cheek, but there was no resistance and he pushed her down, sliding himself sweetly into her.

Sally cried out, her back arching and her entire body tense. Mace nuzzled her neck, massaging her back as she grew used to the feel of him. She was tight, though, and he increased the amount of desire he was feeding to her, to counter her flash of pain.

It didn't take long. She shuddered again and started to move, lifting herself uncertainly on him and then down again, taking more of him into her. Mace wanted to talk to her, to whisper in her ear as he moved his hips, slipping a little more of himself into her with each thrust. All he could do was growl appreciatively, one hand caressing her back as the other massaged her inner thighs, helping her to relax and spread them wider, giving her more room to slide down him.

Finally, he was all the way inside her. Shivering, she leaned back, her eyes smoky with desire, and Mace wiped a tear from her cheek. "Should I be doing this?" she whispered, and he nuzzled her neck. "I feel, I feel . . ." Mace moved inside her, arching his hips up, and she bucked, biting down a sudden scream as the abruptness of her orgasm took over. Gasping, she started to lift herself up and down against him, and Mace lay back on the straw.

She moved against him as if she'd been born to it, her pleasure already growing in her again. Mace stared at her in wonder, stroking her breasts as he moved his own hips against hers, their rhythm already settling into a fast, wild pace that had her climaxing again as his own pleasure started to overwhelm him.

She peaked a third time before he let himself finish, just as she collapsed against him in exhaustion. Mace wrapped his arms around her, carefully shuffling himself up so he was half leaning against a wall and she could lie on him, her cheek against his chest and his length still within her.

"I didn't know anything could feel like that," she whispered, limp. Mace stroked her hair in answer. She shifted herself a bit and looked up at him. "You're still hard," she said, blushing.

Mace rumbled a laugh.

Biting her lip, she squeezed him experimentally, that courage still there and even stronger now. "Again?" she asked hopefully.

Mace obliged her at least three more times.

She left before dawn, exhausted but happy. She told him her name then, and that she'd welcome him anytime. She told him the latter with downcast eyes, but he could see the flush on her cheeks went all the way down inside her chemise to the breasts he'd held and nuzzled such a short time before. Mace would have loved to oblige, but Jasar took him away, and then the queen rose and he was made the battle sylph of Lily Blackwell. He'd never thought to return.

He'd certainly never thought she'd still be waiting.

"It's a gift," she whispered, her face still pressed against his chest. "The best Winter Festival gift ever."

"More of a nightmare," her brother muttered. He was the innkeeper, and Mace felt his disapproval clearly. The rest of the family was there, men and women both, though the other visitors to the inn had left, many with bruises.

Battle sylph or not, Mace felt the family's determination to get rid of him if they could, along with a very real degree of disgust and shame for the slim woman in his arms. For whatever reason her brother and the rest of them had attacked Mace, it wasn't because they thought it was the best thing for her. There was resentment there. For whatever reason, they hated him and they blamed her for it.

Sally knew this, and she kept her face against him, saying nothing. Mace stroked her hair and looked at the innkeeper, whose name was Falon.

"What have I ever done to you?" he asked.

Falon gaped at him. "Done? You have the bloody nerve to come here, now of all times, and ask that? After you ruined my sister?"

Mace raised his eyebrows. "I didn't ruin her."

"You seduced her!"

"So?"

The men all stared at him, horrified. It was different in the Valley, Mace reminded himself. Whom a woman chose to sleep with was her own business. They must have called Sally a whore here. That was close to a death sentence in the Valley for any man who said it. At least, it had been in the first few years before the queen found out her battle sylphs were attacking anyone who disparaged a female. After that, they could only attack men who hurt them. These days, no men dared.

"Leave him alone," Sally whispered, lifting her head and looking fearfully but defiantly at her brother, that bravery he remembered still shining far back in her eyes. "He didn't mean any harm. He's a good man."

"He's a monster!" her brother shouted, and Mace growled as he felt her tense. Falon winced but glared at him. "You have no place here."

"He does!" Sally wailed. "I've been praying for him to come back!"

"Why?" Falon shouted. "For the sake of your other monster?" More family members nodded in agreement, muttering.

Sally winced, her breath catching. She was about to start crying again, and Mace felt that if she did, he was going to hurl a few more tables around.

"What monster?" he snarled.

Sally looked up, her eyes filled with tears and her face as beautiful as it had been nineteen years before. "Please, Mace. You have to rescue our son."

Chapter Six

Her child was named Travish, a boy born nine months after her one night with Mace, one whom she'd doted on while the rest of the town rejected him as a bastard. That she'd declared him to be the son of a battle sylph—a story from which she hadn't wavered for even a moment—only made it worse for them. Sally had no husband, and her son grew up bitter and unwanted by anyone but his mother.

Staring around at them, Mace loathed her family, especially after the decades of blame and loneliness they had put Sally through, but he honestly couldn't blame them for not believing her. "How can he be *my* son?" he whispered to her, not wanting the others to hear.

She stared up at him, her eyes filled with tears. "He's yours, I swear he's yours. I've never gone to anyone else. Please believe me."

How could he, even when she was looking up at him with those pleading eyes? Sylphs couldn't get human women pregnant. Even Solie's children had needed to be fathered by human men, much as Heyou pretended otherwise. Despite what he knew, though, he nodded for her, glad she couldn't feel what he felt. Her answering smile was beautiful.

"Now what?" her brother snapped, his face still flushed. The happy festival decorations seemed to make a mockery of the tension in the room. "Having that thing as the father just makes Travish even more of a beast."

"He's not a beast!" Sally screamed, stepping forward to confront Falon. Mace didn't know if this was a common thing or if she was drawing strength from his presence, but he felt that same courage that had brought her to the stable so long ago as he crossed his arms and stood behind her, watching warily. He didn't know how he felt about all of this—he certainly didn't want a human son—but he'd support Sally. He'd support any woman, but Sally especially. Claimed son or not, he felt he owed her something and he felt that same spark for her that he had before. Where her family hadn't crushed it out of her, she was alive and vibrant, courageous and strong. That part of her sang to the battler inside of him, crying out with the voice of a queen.

"He's a bully and a thief and a backstabber! And now he's working with those brigands!" Falon shouted in response. "He's probably telling them all about how to ruin this town!"

"What else was he supposed to do? No one would hire him! He had to work!"

"And robbing and killing people is work?" Falon demanded.

At that, Mace understood the tension he'd felt in the town when he arrived. Even as they pretended with the Winter Festival that nothing was wrong, these people were terrified. "Are these the same bandits who took Jayden?" he asked.

Falon hesitated, eyeing him. Sally did as well, her face pale. "Who's Jayden?"

Mace stroked her hair. "A runaway boy I was sent to find." He lifted his chin toward Falon. "He says that the bandits took him."

Falon glanced away, but his emotions were answer enough. They also told Mace that the man didn't want to be recruited into going to rescue anyone—which was fine, since there was no chance that Mace would ask. He could destroy the bandits on his own, once he got close enough to track them.

Eferem was a large kingdom, though, and he needed a place to start.

"Which way are these bandits?" he asked.

"No one's sure," Falon said, clearly still worried he'd have to provide some direct guidance. He was also ashamed of his fear and lying because of it.

Sally took Mace's hand. "I'll show you," she promised.

They found Ruffles and headed out, Sally dressed warmly in furs and Mace taking the shape of a heavy gray horse. He changed form right in the square before the inn. The people here had rejected Sally's word about lying with a battle sylph? Now they'd all know she was telling the truth. He left with the town's eyes on him, Sally proudly riding bareback.

He cantered eastward, moving along a cart track for a while and then onto a deer path. Sally didn't know exactly where the brigands were—no one did—but they were suspected to be in the woods to the east, away from the main roads and certainly away from the Shale Plains and Sylph Valley. A group like this would never have been able to establish itself in any area that battlers guarded. Nor, apparently, were they stupid enough to attack any Valley merchants, or any groups heading into the Valley. It was only the convoys heading away from the Valley and the people of Eferem itself who were suffering.

It was late in the afternoon and snowing, but Mace chose to go anyway. He didn't want Sally to stay in this town. He wasn't worried about exposing her to bandits; he'd keep her safe. The bandits weren't half as bad as her family. He didn't want her anywhere near the people who'd dragged her down for so long, and the farther they went from Falloweld, the more her happiness increased. She was away from her family. She was going toward her son. She was with her beloved.

Mace had no issues with the fact that she loved him. That was a simple concept: you met, you connected, you loved. It was easy. It was the fact that she believed he'd fathered a son on her that had him confused, so he pushed the thought away. He had three missions now: rescue Jayden for Lily, rescue Travish for Sally, and keep Sally safe.

There was really only one way to guarantee Sally's safety. In the Valley, no one would care about her finding pleasure outside of wedlock. He just hoped that Lily had really meant it when she told him to search out a new master. If he brought a woman home and she reacted badly . . . Mace didn't want to think about that. He just wanted to get Sally to safety and maybe even see if he still fit in her life. He wasn't sure yet that she would make a good master to him, and he'd seen enough battlers end up with bad ones in the last decades that he would be very careful of whom he gave control of himself to, but there was that spark in her. That goodness and strength that made him want to protect her, to love her, and to feel her quivering underneath him as she cried out her pleasure into his ear.

"Travish is a good boy," Sally was saying, unaware of Mace's thoughts as she sat on his back with her knees gripping his barrel and her fingers twined in his mane. "He's just so frustrated with everything. He was teased terribly when he was a child, and my father hated him. So did Falon. They thought I'd wasted myself and ruined the family." She sighed. "Travish just wants to be respected. He's never had that before. He wants to be something more."

Mace snorted. That was the kind of thinking that had got Jayden into this mess. Everyone was what they were. There was no need to want anything else.

Then why did you come through the gate? a treasonous voice whispered into his mind. Why not stay in your original hive, where you could have remained a guard and simple warrior for the entirety of your life? Mace decided not to think about that, either.

"Tell me about Jayden," Sally said, her fingers tangled in his rough mane.

Mace had made a few modifications to his horse form, just as he had with his dog form earlier, and he could speak. "He's one of Lily's orphans," he said.

"Who's Lily?"

He tossed his head, making his way around a half-buried log covered in snow that likely would be a problem for a real horse. "She's my master."

He felt Sally's sudden uncertainty about what that meant, and about what else Lily might be to him. He felt a quick surge of jealousy in Sally, tempered by her fear of being left alone again, and he turned his head so he could see her out of one eye.

"Lily is a good woman. I've been hers for a long time." He paused for a moment, wondering how much to say to her so soon. He couldn't make promises this early, not to a woman he'd seen only once before and who now was convinced he was the father of her child. "She's quite old. She's told me to watch for a new master, someone who would want to be with me for the rest of their life."

Sally's breath caught. "How's your search going?"

"I don't know yet," he said honestly, and she ducked her head, blushing and excited while at the same time afraid. Too soon, he thought. It was too soon to think of such things. It had been nineteen years since he'd seen this woman and he knew nothing about her other than what he could feel inside of her now and what he'd been told in the inn. He didn't want to leap in, unthinking, as so many of his fellows would, and end up in another bond that would give him everything he needed except for that deep soul tie. He loved Lily, would always love Lily, but she hadn't given that to him. He didn't blame her for this and she had his loyalty. He was her reward, she'd told him once, her reward for the hard life she'd had to live.

More, Mace didn't want to fall in love right away and then find out that Lily didn't approve of whom he'd found. He didn't want to have Lily tell him that Sally couldn't be with him after he'd already given his heart to her. For now, he tried not to think about it and instead focused on the issue of the boys and how they were going to get them back.

"Lily cares for orphans in the Valley," he explained. "Jayden is the youngest one left. She hasn't taken any new children for a long time. She's in her eighties now, and she's been doing this for thirty years." His voice turned sardonic. "There have been a lot of children, but most have moved out. There's just Jayden now, and a few older girls who are about to leave and get married."

"So Jayden was alone growing up?" Sally asked.

Mace half waded and half crunched across a spring that had a thin layer of ice covering six inches of water. Sally pulled her feet up to avoid being splashed, while Ruffles jumped to the other side. "It didn't seem that way. He was always following me around."

"He must have loved you."

Mace stopped, regarding her out of one eye in surprise. If Jayden loved him, it was buried under a morass of boy emotions that he'd never bothered to pay attention to before. "Why would he love me? Battle sylphs don't like men."

Sally smiled sadly and stroked his neck. "What does how someone else feels in return have to do with the heart?"

Mace snorted. "If he's supposed to love me, why did he run away?"

Sally's emotions turned very sad. "Maybe because he's like my Travish and wanted more?" she suggested. "How else was he supposed to get your attention?"

Mace just snorted again and continued on.

They traveled only a few more miles into the woods before Mace stopped, finding a clear piece of land, the ground soft with dried pine needles and clear of snow thanks to old overhanging trees. These left a wide area underneath that was tall enough to stand in and be protected from the wind. Reaching it, Mace knelt down, and Sally giggled as she dismounted. Happy, Ruffles ran around them both and then sat to scratch her ear.

Mace shifted into human form, Sally watching wonderingly as he did. There were still a few women in the Valley who were unnerved by the sylph ability to change shape; it was nice to see a woman immediately so unafraid.

It was cold out, so Mace gathered wood for a fire, setting it ablaze with a flick of power. Sally looked at that in delight, and she went to sit across from him, hands held out toward the flame.

"Do you think we'll find our son and your friend?" she asked, staring at the crackling blaze. Her confidence seemed less now, even though they were doing something. She wasn't a woman used to being allowed to do anything, Mace thought. Not since that night.

"Of course," he told her. The only other option was to see her sad, and he didn't want that.

Sally ate some of the food she'd brought, consuming it in small bites while she sat with her knees drawn up before the fire. Mace called Ruffles over and the dog lay beside him, her furry head on his knee, as he drew out some of her energy to feed himself. No one spoke, so there was no sound save that of the crackling fire and the clumps of snow periodically falling out of the trees.

It had mostly stopped snowing and the woods were peaceful. He'd find a squirrel for Ruffles in the morning, Mace decided. The dog wasn't hungry for now, but more interested in sleeping.

Sally finished her meal and wrapped her arms around herself. Now she was feeling nervous, thinking of her son and being worried for him, and concerned for herself as well. Probably she was wondering what would happen to them after this. His mention of needing a master hadn't sounded like a promise to either one of them, since it wasn't.

The evening passed. Sally sat across from Mace, watching the flames and smiling at him periodically, her emotions nervous and uncertain. Ruffles moved away and curled up on the edge of the clearing, her tail over her nose as she went to sleep.

Slowly, Sally's emotions started to change, shifting toward desire as she continued to sneak glances at Mace that she hoped he didn't see. Her breathing quickened, her breasts and lower regions beginning to tingle, as she thought about something Mace couldn't know for sure but at which he could certainly guess. She was remembering their night together, without regret and with longing. She wanted him to come around the fire to her, but for all her bravery had no idea how she was going to gain the courage to ask.

With a battle sylph, it was never necessary to ask.

Mace shifted onto his knees and went around the fire. Sally's nervousness surged, as did her desire, her entire body screaming for him. Touch her breasts, touch her thighs, touch the burning lips between them. Mace did, whispering his hand across her breast as he pressed his mouth against her neck, kissing the bare skin as she leaned her head back, her fingers frantically clawing her scarf off.

"Oh, I'd forgotten how good this feels," she gasped, reclining back. Mace followed her down, opening her clothes and his own as he did, savoring her pleasure and lifting his kisses up until he was moving his mouth against hers, their tongues gently touching.

Sally stroked his cheek, feeling the bones of his cheek and jaw. "The one thing I missed," she said, "was being able to kiss you. And talk to you."

"Now you can do both," he assured her. "And I can take on any shape you like."

She frowned, studying him. "I like this," she told him. "I like this form. Did you pick it yourself?"

"Yes," he said. He had, before he became Lily's. The only change she'd made was to tell him to remove all stubble.

"Then I like it," she said.

Mace smiled and bared her breasts, moving his hands in other ways he remembered her liking, filling her with the desire he felt inside himself, the way he'd let her know his want when he first saw her. It had been a long time since he'd done so and Sally had in fact been the last person he'd done so with. It was a natural part of lovemaking to a battler, a way of strengthening the bond between them and their partner, but Lily had never allowed it—she didn't like the surrender of control it meant for her. Mace shuddered as he let his lust go at last. He'd missed this more than he'd realized. From her gasps, he found that Sally had as well, and he bared her lower, moving down to show her just what he could do now that he had a mouth. This had her screaming, tensing against him for a long moment, before finally he moved upward again, kissing her as he gratefully slid himself inside.

They moved together, thrusting and gasping and holding

each other close, Mace buried deep in her emotions even if she couldn't feel his . . . not yet. She still reacted, though, part of her recognizing him, and he shook as he felt that connection, unexpected and sweet, carrying him deeply into her soul as though she *were* his master. There was a knot of tension and loneliness deep down inside her, he found, and he reached for it, loosening and finally releasing it in a glorious explosion. She shuddered against him, overwhelmed and wailing. Yet she was happy, so wonderfully happy, and Mace wrapped himself around her to keep her warm and let her feel safe, suddenly glad beyond imagining that he'd found her again.

Chapter Seven

The hills of Eferem, while nowhere near as steep as the high mountains of Para Dubh, were far hillier than anything in the Valley, and there were just so many damn trees. With the snows, they'd turned into a hazardous wasteland of frozen white that Mace was sure would have broken any normal horse's leg several times over. He, however, barely noticed the holes that threatened to twist or break an ankle, or the hidden gullies that an animal could fall into, other than for how a misstep might unseat Sally.

He did keep an eye on Ruffles, but the dog made her way easily, far more agile on the rough terrain than a horse. She also set the speed of their travel. Mace could walk until his energy ran out, but Ruffles was quicker to tire—as was Sally. The human woman sat his back easily enough, her knees gripping his barrel, but though he'd softened his spine for her comfort, he could feel how cold and tired she became as the day wore on, as well as how utterly determined she was to save her son.

His son as well. Mace felt her absolute conviction about that, her utter refusal to consider any other option. He wondered at her unconditional determination to hold on to the idea, knowing it just wasn't possible. Of all the battle sylphs in the world, and all of them with lovers, how could it be that he was the only one to father a child? And a *boy*. There were other battlers far more suited. There were even some who liked men. Heyou was friends with everyone, regardless of gender, and the battler Ril was mad enough to keep his bond to the same man who'd originally enslaved him. Even more insanely, his tie to both the man and his daughter were stronger than anything anyone else had in the Valley except Heyou. Each of those two would have been fine with a half-human son. Mace wasn't. It was wrong. It couldn't be anything other than wrong. But Sally said it was true, and if he wanted to feel that sweetness he had when he made love to her again, he could see already that he'd have to accept her son.

The day after they left Falloweld, they came out of the woods into a sloping valley, the trees continuing on either side and a not-very-impressive ridgeline ahead. According to Sally's imperfect knowledge, and to the maps he'd demanded from her brother before leaving, there was a river beyond. There seemed the best place to try and find the bandits, providing they were still in the area. He suspected so. If they were attacking convoys this late in the year, they must be prepared to stay the winter. Mace hoped so. He wasn't very interested in tracking them across the world. He wasn't even sure he could.

Without any covering trees, he had to shoulder his way through belly-deep snow, Sally on his back with her legs crossed and hanging on to his mane to keep from falling off. Ruffles followed, sniffing her way happily along the trail Mace cut. It was cloudy overhead, but there was no snow falling, and he looked up at the cliffs ahead, debating the best way to get over them. They weren't high, but they did surround the valley like a wall. He'd have to find a place he could climb, hopefully without having to make Sally walk.

Mace felt the bandits before he saw them, naturally. A sudden flick of human boredom came from the top of the ridgeline ahead, followed by alertness. Mace snorted, Sally straightening uncertainly as he reacted to the emotions of two men who were both surprised and suspicious.

"What is it?" Sally asked.

Mace stopped, his broad head lifted toward the ridge. The top was covered in trees, making it impossible to see anyone. "We've been spotted," he told her.

"Are we in danger?" she asked.

"No," he promised, and continued forward. These were just men. Mace was still of the opinion that Sally would have been in more danger left to the abuses of her family. It didn't matter that the bandits knew they were coming; they wouldn't be able to stop him.

After a moment's fear, Sally's determination to save her son returned, bringing with it all of Mace's uncertainties about the reality of his pedigree, as well as a growing delight in just feeling her courage.

It took twenty minutes to reach the foot of the ridge through the deep snow. The emotions of the sentries remained with him, not increasing from two. Why should they? They only saw a single woman with a dog riding alone on a draft horse. What possible kind of threat could she be? Mace snorted at that kind of stupidity and walked under the trees that marked the start of the ridge.

The ground rose abruptly before him, a jagged rise about seventy feet tall. There were spots that were sheer, but others were still graded enough that he could ascend without changing his form. Sally hung on to his mane with both hands, and her knees tightly gripped his sides as he went up the slope, pushing his way through the bushes. He stepped in a hole at one point, but the rock shattered before his leg did and he yanked his hoof free, moving forward without hesitation. Her tail wagging, Ruffles followed.

That was when he started to feel other men besides the sentries. Given the good view from the top of the hill, and the fact that it was steep enough to defend, it wasn't surprising that they were here. He felt a multitude of men and even a few women. Most of the men reeked of violence and greed, but none of these were aware of the newcomers.

He took note of each of the two sentries' reactions. One eyed Sally with a lust that Mace was fully prepared to tear out of him. The other was certain that there was more here than he was seeing. He expected a trap.

Mace kept climbing, making his way up the bluff slowly for his companions' sakes, and he took the time to study not just the feelings of the men on the ridge but those in the camp on the other side. He felt Jayden right away, recognizing the unique patterns of the fourteen-year-old against the surrounding morass. Those patterns had changed, though, and Mace snorted as he walked, ascending a ridgeline almost the same as a goat and ignoring the growing amazement of the sentries. Jayden had changed since he left home. The stubbornness and anger were gone. The boy who followed Mace everywhere had turned into a frightened creature, cowering and alone, but still with a core of courage deep down that wasn't much different from the one inside Sally, and was just as determined not to give up.

Mace stopped, his tail swishing uncertainly. He hadn't expected that. He'd expected to find the boy raging arrogantly, and to just toss him over his shoulder and cart him back to Sylph Valley. This person felt very much like a child again, desperately wanting someone to rescue him. More, as Mace zeroed in on those emotions, reading the nuances almost as effectively as reading a mind, he realized that Jayden was praying for *him* to be the one to come for him.

This reminded him again of what Sally had said, that the

boy loved him. He still didn't get why, since the love certainly wasn't returned, but still . . .

Mace had loved in his own way every single woman he'd ever slept with. It hadn't been the love of a master/sylph bond and it certainly hadn't been with the deep soul tie he longed for, but the love had always been there. It was the way he was made. Few had loved him back though. Most saw him as a sexual toy or a conquest; he'd felt it even as he pleasured them. Even Lily had only taken him at first to keep him from searching for a master among the girls she was raising. Only two had ever truly loved him back, one being Lily, after he'd become hers, and the other being the woman who rode him now. Now Jayden felt the same way. He wanted Mace to come to his rescue. At the same time, judging from the despair that swamped the courage he had, the youngster was certain it wasn't going to happen.

"What's wrong?" Sally asked quietly, laying a hand on his neck. Mace arched into it, even though he hadn't adopted the shape of one of those high-necked fancy equines. He liked to keep things simple. The hive mattered, women mattered. Human men didn't, but despite all his neglect, Jayden loved him—as a father or a brother or who knew what? How could Mace have been so self-absorbed that he'd never noticed? No wonder Jayden had run away.

"Have you found our son?" Sally asked, bringing up the other great confusion.

"No," he said, not contradicting her but not thinking about it either. "I feel Jayden. He's down there."

Her knees tightened around him. "Then our son has to be too! You have to find him!"

Mace tossed his head and tried, wanting to please her and to get this uncomfortable feeling of guilt out of his head. He looked for Travish's pattern, with nothing to go on other than his familiarity with the man's mother . . . and was surprised when he found it almost right away. The boy felt like Sally, with the same swirls and lines that formed her pattern but without that unique glow that marked her as a woman. He had his own luminescence, just as Jayden and all the other human men Mace ever encountered did, something that Mace had never paid much attention to before.

Travish had a beaten-down strength in him, the same as his mother, but he also had a terrible anger for whomever he saw as his enemies, along with a determination to succeed and prove himself, to be something other than the bastard son of a madwoman who claimed he was the son of a battler. Mace felt that anger, and also that the youth was with Jayden. Travish's emotions toward the boy were a mix of uncertainty and disbelief, overlaid with an absolute surety that Jayden was a liar. It seemed that Travish had been told in just whose home Jayden had grown up.

"I can feel him," he said. He immediately experienced Sally's exultation, as soothing to him as a balm after the emotions of the two boys.

Mace picked his way up the final stretch of slope and crested the hill, still unable to see beyond it due to the trees. There was very little snow on the ground, thanks to some tree cover, and no bushes either, the trees not allowing enough light for them. Mace moved forward across level terrain, sensing the sentries still watching out of sight. The camp was only a short way away, down in a smaller valley just beyond. "He's with Jayden."

"He must be taking care of him!" Sally exclaimed.

Mace stepped into a pit.

The bandits must have dug it to trap men, just in case someone topped the ridge. It was covered with sticks and pine needles to keep it hidden and was nearly six feet deep, the bottom filled with sharpened stakes that pointed up-wards. Mace's front legs went through the cover and he fell forward, his shoulders catching on the sides before he could land on the sharpened stakes. Sally shrieked and tumbled forward, barely stopped from rolling into the length of the trap by Mace throwing up his head and catching her in the stomach, tossing her clear and off to the side.

Ruffles crouched low to the ground, her ears flat and her tail stiff. She started to growl, glaring at the bushes where the sentries were hiding. Mace felt their intentions toward the dog and swung his head toward her.

"Evade," he grunted.

Ruffles stared at him, her ears coming forward at the command, and then she turned and ran, vanishing over the edge of the ridge and back the way they'd come. Her training included this command to save herself. She couldn't feed a sylph if she was dead, and any threat a battle sylph couldn't handle alone would be far too much for her. She'd find a place to hide and wait for him to find her.

That took care of Ruffles, but not Sally. He never should have brought her here, he realized. He just hadn't expected a group of bandits to actually be a problem, even with Lily's order not to kill. But as Sally sat up, a little stunned and cov-ered in pine needles, the two sentries came out of the woods toward her. They were both dressed in dirty, patched clothes; their faces were unshaven. They leered at her, one already rubbing his crotch and licking his lips. Sally gaped at them, white-faced.

There were things Mace could do, even without killing. He heaved himself out of the pit, pulling his forelegs free and rearing back, blasting both men with his hate aura as he did. The two reeled in shock. Halfway through rearing, Mace turned and threw himself forward, taking two steps and changing shape to human.

As the loathing hit them, overwhelming and unstoppable, one of the men ducked and ran, screaming. The one who'd been grabbing his crotch and planning to rape Sally simply gaped, his mouth hanging open. Mace slapped his hand over the man's face and pushed, sending the bandit flying backward into the trees. The other bandit vanished over the far edge of the ridge, though Mace could track his pattern. He could unfortunately hear him just as clearly when the man screamed for help.

It likely wouldn't have mattered whether he screamed or not. Mace had announced himself far too well already. Many battle sylphs could refine their hate aura to be felt only by a specific individual—someone standing right beside their target wouldn't feel any of it—and there were even battlers who could project an entirely different emotion to that second individual. Mace was more than old enough to have developed that kind of skill, but he'd never bothered. If he was irritated, he wanted everyone to know. Instead, he'd spent his years of enslavement perfecting the art of projecting his hate as far and to as many people as possible. Now was no different, and Mace's hate had been an even better alarm for the brigand camp than their sentry's screams.

He felt their familiar horror as the bandits were hit by his aura and their panic started to rise. He also felt hope and relief—Jayden, he realized. The boy thought he was being rescued after all.

For once the boy was right. Mace went to Sally and offered her a hand, helping her to her feet as he kept the aura strong; likely the bandits would run away out of terror and he wouldn't have to deal with them. He tried at the same

time not to project it to Sally, but he wasn't entirely successful, and the smile she gave him was wan.

"Come on," he told her. "This shouldn't take long."

Mace led her toward the camp, confident that the bandits
would retreat ahead of them. Sally followed, hand tight
against his own, both afraid and determined. Ruffles was a
distant flicker in the back of his mind, still running as she'd
been trained.

On the other side of the ridge, a path led down into the
narrow valley where the bandits had made camp, well worn
by foot traffic. This was more of a gorge than a valley, surrounded on three sides by rock walls. The river flowed over
the ridge from the east, making a narrow waterfall before
pouring down the length of the gorge and out. The camp
was well hidden, with the nearby walls scalable enough that
the bandits could flee in any direction if needed. There also
appeared to be caves into which they could retreat, some of
which likely exited on the other side of the ridge.

Right now, a lot of the bandits were splashing across the
shallow river to climb the ridges or vanish into the caves,
though not all did. Some hid where they were. Mace saw a
half dozen rough buildings on the wide bank of the river, all
weathered enough that he suspected the bandits had taken
this place over from someone else instead of building it
themselves. There were old racks for drying hides out in the
open, evidence that trappers might originally have owned
the camp.

Horses screamed where they were tied to a long line strung
between two of the buildings, ignoring the efforts of two
men who tried to calm them before they could break their
leads. Goats and even a few cows were panicking in a fenced-
off corral. The center of the camp was dirt that would turn
into mud whenever it rained. Right now it was frozen, the

mud ridged and rough. Everywhere there were crates of items, all clearly stolen.

Mace walked right into the center of it all, still projecting his hatred with Sally at his side. He could feel Jayden and Travish, and he focused on them, ignoring the rest of the bandits. The few women here he'd have liked to take with him, along with the boys, but the rest of the men could go hang. Perhaps the queen would let him bring some of the other battlers here after he returned, just to make sure that these villains didn't cause any problems in the future. She didn't like fighting, but for the right reasons she could be convinced.

"Fire!" a voice shouted, to his intense surprise.

Shapes armed with crossbows appeared around the sides of buildings and from behind the stacks of plunder. They were all male. Mace had already sensed and dismissed them, as he'd thought they were hiding. He hadn't thought they'd *shoot* at him, or more importantly, at Sally.

They were surrounded. As the bolts were launched at him and Sally, Mace changed shape, forming a solid wall of black flesh that completely surrounded her. Crossbow bolts struck him, causing great pain, but none went through. They hurt, though. Mace was surprised by how much. He'd never been harmed by a human in this way, and honestly he hadn't thought that he could be. But the sheer number of bolts now jutting out of him was as agonizing as the claws of another battle sylph, and he roared in pain, the hate he projected only increasing.

Men who should have run in terror didn't, obeying their leader instead. "Attack!" that voice shouted again.

Dropping their crossbows, which took too long to reload anyway, the bandits charged, howling as they came down at him with short swords. Eyeless, Mace sensed them, and he sensed as well how many there were. He was a fool. If he stayed wrapped around Sally, they'd cut him to pieces. If he changed form to fight back, one of them might hurt her. He felt her terror, along with her absolute certainty that he would protect her.

Mace lifted straight up into the air. Forget about pride, forget about expectations, forget about political missteps with Eferem—he had a woman to protect and a lot of personal stupidity to make up for. The queen had given her permission when it came to emergencies. He just wished she'd given the same exception when it came to killing. Changing to his natural shape, he retreated, rising dozens of feet into the air in seconds. Sally was safely inside him. The crossbow bolts that had struck him clattered to the ground.

He crested the ridge, then moved as fast and low to the ground as he could toward the valley on the far side, just in case his bad luck kept up and an Eferem battler saw him. From behind, he sensed the triumph of a group of bandits who shouldn't have been victorious, and the despair of a boy who'd once again been left behind.

Chapter Eight

Mace caught up with Ruffles only a mile from the ridge, out in the middle of the valley they'd so blithely traversed. He scooped the dog up into his mantle without slowing and fled to the hills on the far side, carrying both the animal and Sally to a covered grove not so dissimilar from the one in which they'd spent the previous night. It was far enough away that they wouldn't be in danger anytime soon.

He set both passengers down, the dog shaking and Sally stumbling at the sudden change, and became human, crashing to his knees in the thick bed of pine needles. His form appeared perfect, but he'd been hurt by those crossbow bolts, hurt far more than expected.

"Mace!" Sally gasped, dropping to her knees beside him and grabbing his arm. Ruffles frantically leaped up on the other side to lick his face.

"I'm fine," he told her, even as he let her ease him back onto the ground. Her quickly doffed cloak was wadded up and shoved under his head.

Mace looped an arm around Ruffles's neck, scratching her ears as he drew deeply from the dog's energy. He wasn't a healer, though; he could only fix his own wounds to a degree. They'd get better or they wouldn't, or he'd find a healer sylph. There weren't many options in between.

"You're hurt," Sally said, sitting by his side and cupping his cheek with one hand. She turned those beautiful eyes on him, and he mourned that he hadn't brought her son out. He shouldn't have taken her in. He couldn't have left her with her family, but he should have taken her to Lily and made sure she was safe before he tried this. He should have asked Lily to remove the no-kill order. There wasn't a mark on Sally, but it was his fault she was scared.

"I'm sorry about your son," he said. "I'll get him out."

"Shh," she soothed. She swallowed. "Thank you for trying."

"I haven't given up yet."

She smiled, filled with love for him, her hand still caressing his cheek. "I know." She paused. "I dreamed about you, you know. All those years I did, wondering what you were doing, what you were like, and if I'd ever see you again. I fell in love with you the first moment I saw you and I didn't know anything about you. Now I'm with you again and you turn out to be such a good man."

Mace blinked. "I'm not a good man." He wasn't a man at all.

Tears filled her eyes. "You are. You came back. I know it wasn't for me, but you came, and once you knew about me, you didn't leave me, any more than you're giving up on Travish or that poor boy you did come for."

Mace stared at the pine branches overhead. They were so tightly woven that even though it was daylight he couldn't see the sky through them. He could feel Sally's soul reaching for him, loving him so much it was almost frightening. He'd never felt such a thing before and felt like a hatchling, unsure of what to do. "Jayden was waiting for me," he told her. "I could feel how relieved he was."

"Of course he was. You're the closest thing he has to a father. He knew you'd come for him."

Mace was confused. "How? I was never there for him when he was growing up . . ."

"Never?" Her emotions were steady, her belief in him far more absolute than his own.

"Well, I was there, but I never did anything for him. I never did anything for the boys. Lily had so many, and I didn't really care."

"But you were there, showing him what a strong man should be." She smiled sadly. "Sometimes a boy doesn't need anything more."

She was quiet for a moment, just stroking his cheek and feeling her love and thinking. "It's sad," she said at last. "And strange. Our son fell in with those bandits because he didn't have you as a father. Your boy went because he did."

Mace watched her. The guilt he felt was somehow worse than the crossbow bolts, but the pain of both was easing under the strength of her emotions. Those feelings saturated him, drawing him to her, and he wondered if this was what Heyou had felt when he first met Solie. "I make a pretty piss-poor father."

"No one's perfect," she promised. "Even the Gift Giver from the Winter Festival. We just have to keep trying." That said, she leaned down to kiss him.

It was a soft kiss and comforting, not filled this time with years of passion and frustration. With her love singing to him it was a thousand times better, and he lifted his head toward hers, their mouths working together. She was happy that he was alive, he realized. She'd been just as convinced as he that he was invincible, and now she felt her remorse at his being hurt. She had loved him for years, and this kiss was partly her need to make up for causing him harm.

Mace didn't agree that she was to blame. She got enough of that from her family and he would have come out here anyway, for Jayden—for *Lily*—but now, thanks to Sally, he was finally doing it for the right reasons. He didn't mind a little bit of delightful payback, though, and so he reached up to stroke her as she lifted her dress over her head. She opened his breeches so that she could sit astride him and take him inside her, and she moved gently upon him, biting her lip as she looked up toward the sky.

He let her ride him to completion, too tired to do more and also too sobered by the depth of their connection. He could feel her, could become drunk on her, and he hadn't known until now how incomplete he'd always been. Neither of them expected anything of the other, but suddenly he knew that he wanted her for his master. He wanted her for the soul tie she could give him. She was his Winter Festival gift, and he was hers.

He didn't say any of that to her, though. They just shared her pleasure, and the climax when it came shook Mace to his core.

"I'll find Travish for you," he promised, cradling her afterward to his broad chest. "I'll find Jayden and I'll save him. I'll find my sons."

Chapter Nine

He went back that night, with the moon shining through a finally clear sky. He would have gone sooner, but he'd needed to sleep. This was a rare thing for a healthy sylph to do, and nerve-racking in a lot of ways. He'd only slept a handful of times in his life, and to lose all awareness of his surroundings the way he did was frightening, especially when he knew there was danger nearby. It was wrong. He was supposed to be the guard, not Sally. But she and Ruffles watched him sleep, sitting by the fire he'd helped kindle, and nothing happened.

Mace returned to the camp of brigands that night because he wanted the encounter done with. He wanted Travish and Jayden safe and all of them out of there. Moreover, he wasn't sure how much longer he could wait for healing. His injuries weren't fatal by any means, but he found it harder to hold energy and he was going though it much faster than he should. Ruffles was a good dog, but she didn't have the reserves needed to keep going like this; she was sleeping like the dead when he left her, nose buried under her tail. What he really needed was the Valley's healer, and he couldn't go to her until he had the boys. Saving them was as vitally important now as guarding his queen.

Leaving Sally in the safety of their camp with the fire to keep her warm, Mace shifted to cloud form and flew back toward the bandit camp, his attention focused ahead of him upon the men he could feel there. He hadn't been sure they'd stay. He'd seen a lot of people abandon their homes before for the merest threat of a battler. More than once, he had been that threat.

The bandits had already proven they weren't so cowardly. Once he might have thought them stupid, but they had managed to drive him away. Battlers had lost their reputation for disaster, he guessed. Solie herself had encouraged that, not wanting people to fear them. It had been decades since a battle sylph even flared their hate in Eferem, and these men didn't believe the stories of what they were supposed to be able to do. They understood the hate aura now, but they certainly didn't seem to trust in the other stories that a battle sylph could destroy a mountain. Really, they were even right in that conviction, since Mace wasn't allowed to.

He arched high over the camp, sensing them below. They'd lit bonfires around the perimeter as well as in the main square. They provided light while they watched the woods all around. No one slept that Mace could feel, and tensions were high. He tasted a lot of anger in the camp, and not nearly as much fear as he was used to. One man didn't feel fear at all, and Mace pinpointed him as the leader. He was the one who must have kept them fighting when Mace first arrived. Mace didn't like to think about how much control he had over these men to stop them from fleeing an enraged battle sylph's hate aura.

He swooped in before they saw him against the dark sky and hit the camp with his hatred again. Shifting shape, he landed heavily on one knee in the center of the open square, his face highlighted by the glow from the closest bonfire. Lifting his head, he stared across fifty feet of frozen mud to the man he'd sensed earlier, the one with no fear. He was a shaggy specimen, his face pockmarked by old scars and his hair greasy. He grimaced at Mace, mouth filled with missing or black teeth. His outrage was palpable.

Mace stood, his eyes never leaving the man. "I want two things. Give them to me and I'll leave. Don't, and I'll turn this camp into a crater filled with ash. You know what I am."

The bandits eyed each other nervously, some already retreating into the darkness, while their leader spat to one side. "What you want, freak?"

Mace ignored the insult. "I want two boys you have. Jayden and Travish. Hand them over. Now."

The bandit laughed. "Way I hear it, you monsters got no use for menfolk. And one of those two ain't a boy."

"He's still a boy. Hand them over," Mace repeated, increasing his hate.

The aura had more in common with a flash of plumage than an actual weapon, and some people were just immune. The bandit leader appeared to be one of them. His men didn't retreat, either. Mace knew this wasn't because they were unaffected, but because they were more afraid of what their leader would do to them than a battle sylph. The fact that Mace hadn't started off by simply killing everyone only helped reinforce that.

The bandit rubbed his nose and snorted a wad of phlegm into the snow. "Now, don't know if they'd be so interested in that. Why don't you ask them?" He gestured with his chin that Mace should turn around.

A strange itch burned between Mace's shoulder blades as he presented the bandit chief his back. Standing behind him were more of the bandits, watching silently, weapons pointed with varying degrees of confidence. Among them was someone Mace recognized immediately. He was dirtier than Lily ever would have allowed back home. His hair was a mess, and there were bruises on his cheek that Mace didn't like. He was terrified.

"Mace!" Jayden shouted, then winced. Someone had a grip on his arm, one tight enough to silence him.

Mace eyed the man who held Jayden. He was older than the boy but just as dirty. His eyes were hard with the hatred and bitterness Mace had already felt, and his pattern was so close to Sally's that there was no way he could be anything but her son.

"So you're Mace," Travish spat. "The one my mother keeps saying is my father." He laughed, the sound fraught with pain. He'd spent a lifetime paying for his mother's love. "What a joke that's been."

"Are you saying he *ain't* your da?" the bandit leader mocked.

Travish glared. "Do I look like I'm half freak?"

"Mace," Jayden whined. "I want to go home."

Travish shook the boy's arm. "Hey, you volunteered to join us."

Jayden looked desperate. "They said they'd kill everyone if someone didn't!"

Mace remembered what the townspeople had told him: Jayden's had been a noble sacrifice. But the bandits didn't respect it. The bruise on Jayden's cheek was days old, forcing one eye closed, and Mace didn't like the way the boy held himself. He could feel the youth's pain, and he knew Jayden would need the healer as well. Lily had been right to send him here.

He eyed the boy, really studying him for the first time, with his unnatural male energy and his terror that he'd be left here to rot. Under it all, Mace felt Jayden's endless admiration for him and his desperate need to be acknowledged, if only once. He regarded the child, his expression softening for a moment. Then he lifted his gaze to the angry young man who held him. The one he'd promised Sally he'd bring back.

"Let him go or I *will* kill you."

Terror flashed through Travish, but it didn't reach his eyes. He had his mother's courage, tainted with bitterness, and instead he pulled a knife, holding it to Jayden's throat. "You want to try?" he snapped. Jayden froze.

Mace frowned.

"This is how it's gonna be," the bandit leader said from behind him, making Mace turn. "You do what we say an' we'll let the kid live. Don't, an' we'll gut him like a fish."

Mace just stared at the brigand, well aware of Jayden's terror behind him. "What makes you think it matters to me?" he asked.

Jayden's terror increased, his surety that he was being abandoned after all sending him on a downward spiral faster than the battler could have imagined. Mace actually felt him give up, and something he hadn't known was there cringed in the depths of his own soul.

"Fine," he growled, acquiescing before the boy could feel worse. "But if you hurt him, nothing will stop me from killing every man in this camp."

Nothing except Lily's order.

The bandit leader nodded, smirking, but the hope infusing Jayden's pattern told Mace he'd made the right decision. He was of limited use to the bandits with Lily's order anyway. He couldn't kill for them, and without Ruffles he'd run out of energy and die. He just had to get both Jayden and Travish out of here before that happened.

Jayden would be hard enough. He didn't know how he was going to reach Travish at all.

Chapter Ten

They put him in a small building that had once been a stable, though now it was filled nearly to the rafters with stolen goods. The irony of being in a stable again didn't escape him, though the company wasn't nearly so good as the last time.

The bandit leader called himself Raven. His hygiene was appalling, but Mace had to admit that his mind was sharp and he was willing to take risks. Mace honestly didn't think the man realized the danger of what he was playing with—or perhaps he didn't care. He was an amoral killer after all. Mace had encountered such a monster before, and he could see this man's lack of a soul. Raven's enterprise fed nothing but greed and a lust for power, and the man saw the potential for that power increasing with the acquisition of a battle sylph. Mace could kill every single other person in the camp and Raven would still be willing to use him.

Seated on a crate marked as containing pottery from Para Dubh, Mace watched the bandit leader circle him, rubbing his hands. Mace kept his hate aura up, but Raven didn't care. He leaned over Mace's shoulder, his breath foul as he promised, "I'm going to use you to destroy every little shit town in this kingdom."

Mace didn't bother to respond or question why. It wasn't going to happen.

"It'll be beautiful," Raven continued.

Distantly Mace could feel Jayden, still in the camp but

somewhere out of sight. The bandits likely didn't realize that Mace could feel him. Most people didn't know much about sylphs, after all, and it was just as good that they didn't. Mace would know immediately if Jayden was hurt, and if the boy *was* taken out of his reach, he wouldn't be quite so willing to sit here. Right now, Jayden felt nervous but willing to wait, his courage returning again now that he wasn't completely alone.

"Soon," Raven purred.

Mace barely acknowledged him until the man clapped a dirty hand on his shoulder; then he turned his head to stare. The brigand just laughed and went out the door, leaving a lackey standing watch. His guard was sweating despite the cold, and Mace focused his hate on him, making him shudder even more. They stayed like that for some time.

Another man opened the door and came in. "I'll take over for a while," he said, and the first guard stammered thanks before fleeing.

Mace tilted his head to one side, pulling the hate aura back a bit as he studied his new guard. Travish hadn't inherited his mother's fair hair. His was dark and wavy, hanging down to his shoulders and badly kept, bangs in his eyes. He had a beard growing roughly in, and his clothes were filthy. No one here seemed to bother with hygiene. His teeth at least were good.

Travish was affected by the hate aura, but more than the fear in him there was a need to know, something akin to a ravenous hunger. "When the boy told me a battle sylph named Mace was going to come and rescue him, I wanted to beat him for being a liar. Now you're here." Sally's son crossed his arms, still standing by the doorway. "I never thought you actually existed."

"You thought your mother lied?"

Travish rolled his eyes, though guilt flickered deep inside

him. "Of course I thought she lied! Everyone thought she lied! I spent half my childhood banished to the kitchens because no one wanted to listen to her, and they sure as hell didn't want to see me."

"And now I'm here," Mace said.

"Yeah. Now you're here." Travish stared at him, and Mace let the hate drop a bit more, determinedly trying not to project it at him. None of the tension left either of them. "Are *you* saying you're my father?"

Mace couldn't quite make out the emotions running through the youngster. Part of Travish didn't want to believe. Another part, deep inside of him, desperately wanted Sally's words to be true, wanted her story to give him a place that he hadn't been able to make for himself. To be the son of a battle sylph would make him special, Mace realized, which had to matter to a man who'd been treated as a pariah his entire life.

The only problem was, Mace still didn't understand how such a thing could be possible. He wasn't human, and he couldn't *be* human, no matter how he refined his shape. He hadn't even been shaped as a human when he'd loved Sally. All he had was her word that he was the father.

"I believe your mother," he said. "If she says I'm your father, then I am."

Travish gaped at him, obviously not expecting such a calm, assured reply. His tension returned a moment later, though, and his mouth firmed. "That wasn't a yes."

"Do you want me to put you over my knee and spank you to prove it?"

Travish blinked at him and then laughed, the sound of it open and honest, amused. The reaction seemed to catch him by surprise. Mace blinked and continued to watch, his hands flat on his knees. He pulled back more of the hate and saw Travish relax.

"It's crazy. It can't be."

"How did your mother explain it?" Mace asked.

Travish shrugged. "She just said it was a gift."

"It's the Winter Festival. It's all about celebrating the magical gifts the Gift Giver gave and that you humans now give each other, isn't it?" It made sense to say this, even though he'd never thought of the festival that way before.

Travish glanced around at the stacks of goods. There weren't any Winter Festival ornaments in the stable; the entire camp was bare of them. "Yeah, well, *this* certainly isn't the place for any magic gifts."

He fell quiet, as did Mace. Travish was lost in his own thoughts, and Mace reeled the hate back even more, struggling to get the trick of not sending it to this man even as he projected it to everyone else. The trick seemed to be working, though he was certain Travish wasn't entirely spared. Mace didn't want to stop projecting to the rest of the brigands, though, and he frowned, wishing for once that he'd bothered to learn it in the first place.

"What is it?" Travish asked.

"I'm trying not to push my hate aura at you," Mace told him. "It's not simple to avoid a single person."

Travish flashed surprise. "Why would you bother?"

Mace lifted his hands, palms up. "You're not my enemy. Your mother asked me to bring you home."

Travish stared at him, surprised. Then his anger flared up again. "Home? If I've got a home anywhere, it's this place. I'm accepted here. If I'm the bastard son of a whore, then so are half the men here. No one gives a shit."

"No one would give a shit in Sylph Valley either," Mace told him.

Travish blinked. After a moment, he spoke again. "Sylph Valley is full of nothing but whores."

He sounded unsure.

Mace shrugged, though he loathed the use of the word *whore* and once would have been driven to violence by it. "Only to men who think a woman should have no choices in her life." He leveled his gaze at Sally's son. "Or do you think your mother was happy in that kitchen for your entire childhood?"

Travish had to look away again. He felt guilt for that, but there was a young man's bitterness and rage mixed in there as well, a desperate need for someone to blame.

Mace didn't know if he was going to reach the young man. He didn't know if Travish's bitterness was too deep for him to see any better path than the one he was on now, or if he could—or should—be forgiven for having taken it. Mace didn't know what his crimes were among these bandits. He'd held Jayden's arm until it bruised, and he was in a camp filled with stolen goods. How many of the original owners had Travish helped kill?

Yet Sally wanted him to get Travish out, and Lily wanted him to save Jayden. That was enough—for now.

"I want you to help me rescue Jayden," Mace told him.

"Why would I do that?" Travish sounded incredulous.

"Because he's now in the same position you were," Mace said. "And he doesn't deserve it any more than you did."

Travish laughed, his voice bitter and mocking, but Mace felt his pain as he backed toward the door. "I may be a lot of things, but I'm not a backstabber—and I'm definitely not stupid enough to cross Raven. Save Jayden yourself if you think you can. You're the damn battle sylph. Mother was always going on about it. How wonderful you were, how powerful." He spat on the floor. "Like it mattered. She could have just stopped saying it and kept her head down, and everything would have been easier. They could have forgot I was the bastard son of a whore and let me be part of the family. She's crazy. The whole family hates her because she's crazy." His lip trembled. "All she does is let things happen to her. She's a coward."

The young man went out and closed the door. Mace felt him on the other side, guarding, and he sighed. The boy's emotions were a mess and he obviously didn't want to talk anymore. Still, he'd left Mace alone, and that was a very welcome piece of stupidity—or perhaps intent.

Mace changed shape immediately, condensing his size and form and becoming a large black rat. He had to leave his clothes behind, but he didn't worry about that as he scurried to the back of the stable, making his way through the stacks of goods. The building was old, not well maintained, and he was easily able to squeeze out through a gap between two wall panels.

Outside, the sky was lightening toward dawn, but Mace doubted anyone would notice a rat even in full daylight; he could certainly sense enough other rodents making their way through the camp in search of food. Mace was in search of something else. He ran immediately to where Jayden was being kept, racing across the top of the snow along the outskirts of the camp and hoping that Travish didn't decide to head back in for a verbal rematch.

He might get blamed for this, Mace realized, but he put that thought aside. He would grab Jayden, get him out of the camp, and come back for Travish. If he had to follow his original, indifferent plan of throwing him over his shoulder and just leaving with him, he would. Travish would surely see the wisdom of not returning to a camp of bandits that the other battlers from the Valley were going to turn into a large crater.

Two brigands flanking him, Jayden sat in a lean-to by a fire, shivering and dozing in the early air. The men were drinking and laughing, waking the exhausted boy whenever they noticed him sleeping. Jayden looked to be too worn out to protest much, though Mace heard him swear at them when they jabbed his ribs, which only made them laugh. The guards were much taller than the boy, even sitting, and his slumped position lowered him even more.

Mace ran up behind the three, shifted into human form, grasped the heads of the two guards, and slammed them together. Jayden gave a gasp as they tumbled to either side, unconscious. Mace grabbed the boy, yanking him close before he could even turn. Changing shape, a moment later he was in his natural form, darting away from the camp through the trees, racing off in the hope of not being seen. He ached from his wounds, and this couldn't be a comfortable ride for Jayden, but he felt the boy's hysterical relief.

"Mace?" the youth gasped.

Mace couldn't answer, not in this form. Jayden would have had to be his master for a telepathic link to be possible. He thought for a moment instead, and formed a tentacle inside the inner pocket in which he carried the boy, reaching out to squeeze Jayden's shoulder.

The boy started to cry. He was sobbing, his breath hitching as he gasped out apologies and promises to never run away again. Mace really didn't know how to deal with that, and finally just stroked the boy's hair with the tentacle, just as he would have tried to comfort one of Lily's female orphans. It worked much the same here, doing nothing to stop the crying but helping to ease the hysteria. Mace sighed and kept flying, well aware of his own guilt. It had been easier when he still didn't care, but that was in the past. He stroked Jayden's hair and carried him to safety, letting the boy weep.

He'd left Sally and Ruffles in the woods at the other end of the valley. Mace flew toward their hiding spot, hugging the tree line on the south side so that no one on the ridge would see him. He'd leave Jayden with Sally and Ruffles and head back for Travish. He still hurt, but if all went well they'd be returning to the Valley within the hour. He was more than big enough to carry all of them, and the humans could, he hoped, keep Ruffles from doing anything disgusting while she was inside him.

Mace darted into the covered clearing where he'd left the females. It was deserted.

Lurching about with all of his senses, Mace physically froze. There was no sign of Sally, not visually and not patternwise. The ground was torn up, and Mace made a mournful sound, setting Jayden down and shifting to human shape, spinning around with a growing sense of horror.

"What's wrong?" Jayden asked, wiping his eyes. "Can't we just go home?"

Mace closed his eyes and focused, reaching out with his senses for both Sally and Ruffles. The dog was apparent to him immediately; they must not have frightened her during the capture. But they wouldn't have to. Sally was brave, but she was also smart enough not to try and fight against a group of armed men. Mace had dropped her here, in a copse only a few miles from the bandit camp. Then he'd gone back, focused on the camp itself, not on his surroundings. How hard could it have been for a few men to skirt the valley and take both Sally and Ruffles? How could he have been so unmitigatedly stupid? He'd never underestimate a human man again, he promised himself. Not if he survived long enough to outlive the world.

He stared back toward the bandit camp, standing nude

among the pine needles and snow, since he'd abandoned his clothes, his mantle throbbing from the pain of his wounds. He couldn't feel Sally over this distance without a master bond, but he could touch Ruffles. She was there, and Sally had to be with her.

"Mace?" Jayden whimpered as the battler closed his eyes. "I'm sorry I ran away. I am. I shouldn't have gone with them, but they said they'd kill everyone."

Mace opened his eyes and looked down at the boy, really seeing him this time. There were all the usual male traits that he'd always ignored, feeling they made men inferior to women. Below that, though, he found a desperate need to be acknowledged, to be loved. To be worthy of attention from the person Jayden believed to be the greatest warrior in the world. He wanted to be just like Mace, and he couldn't because he hadn't been hatched a battle sylph. Surprisingly, finally realizing that made Mace feel rather small.

He reached out and clapped a hand on the boy's shoulder, felt him instantly tense. "Going with them to save the others was the right thing to do," he said. "It's what a battle sylph would have done." Well, a battle sylph would have killed the bandits, but the courage was the same, the instinct of hive over self. For Jayden, the courage to do that actually had to be greater than anything a battler would need. "You . . . you honor me."

Jayden stared at him for a moment and then started to cry again, obviously trying to stop and furiously wiping his eyes. Mace couldn't leave him here. Not with how Sally had been plucked from the same place. And he couldn't take him back to the bandit camp; he wasn't so stupid that he'd make the same mistake multiple times. He had to get Jayden to safety.

Oddly, he *wanted* the boy to be safe.

Chapter Eleven

The ritual of visiting and gift giving in Falloweld had turned into a full-out party, likely at the thought that there was a battle sylph out hunting down the bandits who'd been terrorizing them for so long. The inn was filled with townspeople and families all raising their glasses in a cheer, as though there had never been any danger at all to a woman, two boys, and a dog.

A lot of those glasses dropped when Mace crashed in, slamming the door into the wall as he did, and dropped his natural shape for his human one while he set Jayden down. They gaped at him, at his nudity, and at the filthy boy standing in the circle of his arm.

"What?" Falon managed.

Mace pushed Jayden a few steps forward. "Feed him," he ordered. "He saved your lives. I'll be back in a few hours. Treat him as anything less than a hero and I'll destroy this entire stinking inn."

Before they could say anything, before they could protest, Mace was out the door again and back in his natural shape, flying toward the bandit camp. He didn't worry about Eferem misreading or attacking him now; there simply wasn't enough time to consider any alternative. He was running through his energy faster than normal, thanks to his wounds, and he needed to feed. He also needed to save Sally. This was the kind of emergency his queen would fully understand and he was terrified of not getting back in time.

He raced straight back, skimming the treetops until he reached the ridgeline and roared up the steepest side. If he was lucky, both Sally and Ruffles would be held where he could easily get to them.

He wasn't lucky. They were in the center of the camp, Sally sitting on a crate, with Ruffles lying at her feet. All of the bandits were there, standing around the two females and looking in every direction. Sally seemed unhurt, but her fear was palpable. So was the bravery that spoke to his soul.

It didn't take them long to spot Mace's lightning. Someone shouted, and they were all gawking up at him, closing ranks around their captives. Most of the men were terrified, but at Raven's order they acted. The bandit captain stood beside Sally, one hand playing with her hair.

"Get down here!" he shouted. He exuded fury, outrage at having been defied, and as Mace hovered there, the bandit chief's hand gripped Sally's hair and yanked her head back, ignoring her cry of pain. "If you don't want her dead, you'll get down here!"

Mace wanted to kill him. Never had he wanted to destroy someone as he did right now, and he raged at Lily's command. Not even against Jasar's control had he fought with so much desperation, and the men below him stared up in terror as the blackness of his form turned nearly white with the crashing lightning inside him. His mouth gaped wide, teeth formed of pure energy, and he roared his fury, rearing up. He would disobey. He would disobey this thoughtless command, this order restraining justice. He would kill the man, free Sally, take her in his arms, and make her his master. His love. His soul tie. He screamed, gathering his power . . . and nothing happened.

Below, Raven grinned, his teeth a sickening nightmare. He laughed, recognizing he was for some reason untouchable.

Not able to do anything else by his very nature, Mace carefully formed vocal cords for his cloud shape. It wasn't easy, and his voice came out strange, but he didn't want to land. Not until he figured out what to do. He couldn't fight. Instead, he came closer to begging than he'd ever imagined he would. "If you do, you'll never get me to do what you want."

Raven sneered. "How about I just torture her instead? You want her little finger? One of her eyes?" He yanked Sally's head farther back, leering down at her. "How about I just take her right here?"

"No!" Sally cried, her courage rising as she tried to push him away. Raven backhanded her, and Mace roared in renewed fury. His hate aura flared out. Raven only grinned and grabbed Sally's breast, squeezing it until she started to sob.

"Stop it!" a new voice said.

Raven turned. From only a few feet away, Travish glared at him, the boy's fists clenched at his sides so tightly that they were trembling. He had a black eye to match Jayden's now, and a swollen lip, both apparently rewards for letting Mace escape. He stared at the man who held his mother and lifted his chin. "You don't have to hurt her."

"Really?" Raven almost looked delighted.

"Travish," Sally wailed, reaching toward him even though Raven had a painful grip on her hair. "Don't, he'll hurt you!"

"You know her?" Raven demanded, his amusement immediately turning to anger. The other men were eyeing Travish as though he'd suddenly become an enemy.

The young man swallowed, shooting a glance at Mace before looking directly at Sally. "She's my mother."

"Your mother?" Raven laughed, howling at the thought of it. "Your mother!" His face twisted abruptly with hate again and he yanked Sally onto her feet, his hand still holding her hair. Travish jerked as though it were he being pulled, and Sally shrieked, trying to claw Raven's hand free behind her head. Ruffles leaped to her feet, barking and whining.

"You're sworn to *me*, you worthless pile of shit!" Raven shouted. "These are the people who mocked you your entire life! Who made you weak! They treated you like a damned servant when you should have been their master! They made you nothing and you defend them?"

Travish looked torn, staring at Sally, who stared back at him, her eyes wide. "My mother never did," he whispered.

"Your mother's a whore!"

Mace acted. It was a desperate move, but the brigands were all focused on Travish, at least for the moment. He lunged forward, all his energy focused into a single, scything blade of power that lashed away from him, thin as a leaf. It sliced through Sally's hair in the inch between her skull and Raven's hand. She fell forward, free.

The bandit dove for her, grabbing her shirt instead of her hair. In the next instant, seeing the threat and filled with her own bravery, Ruffles leaped at him, clamping her jaws on his forearm. Raven howled, yanking his belt knife out of its sheath.

"No!" Sally screamed, rolling over and grabbing his legs, pulling him off balance. He dropped the knife. Several of his men moved into action.

Mace barreled through those men between him and Sally, half of whom had been going to aid their leader, the other half of whom had been staring. He hit them and rolled, his large semisolid body flattening them to the ground but not killing them. Rolling back upright, he threw himself at Raven, his lightning-filled jaws gaping wide.

The bandit leader saw him coming and took advantage

of the few seconds where Mace had been fighting through his men. His face a soulless study of hate, he punched Ruffles in the eye so hard that the dog yelped, letting go, and he grabbed Sally, ignoring his injured arm and her struggles as he pulled her up and against him, his arm around her throat and a second dagger at her chest. The point pressed lightly to her coat, right above her heart.

Mace skidded to a halt, roaring with all of his hate and fear. Raven just snarled, unmoved by Mace's form or his hate. "Move and I kill her," he promised. Sally's eyes were huge with terror. The dagger's point was pushing through the fabric of her coat, and Mace saw her gasp in pain. Slowly, hating Raven more than even his original master, Mace sank to the ground.

"Good," Raven snarled. "Now—"

He stopped speaking, his expression suddenly bemused. He stayed that way for a moment before his arms dropped and he started sliding sideways. Sally stumbled forward with a yelp, her hands raised protectively before herself, and she turned and looked behind her, the same way Mace was staring. Both of them saw Travish standing behind Raven. His hands were empty, his soul throbbing with a hate that wasn't any different from that of a battle sylph with a hive to protect. His dagger jutted out of the lifeless Raven's back.

Chapter Twelve

Without Raven, the rest of the bandits were easy to force into retreat. Mace lashed out at them with his hate aura and quickly formed tentacles with which he beat at them. Leaderless, they fled out of the gorge and up the ridge, screaming their way in all directions. He let them go, too tired to give chase, and he drew as much energy from Ruffles as she could spare.

Sally stood in her son's arms, crying against his chest while he stared over her head at Mace both shocked and horrified, numb now that his rage was spent. Mace shifted to human form and looked at the pair.

Travish gaped down at Raven's body. "I couldn't let him do that," he whispered. "Not to my own mother."

Mace nodded. He was tired, sore, and actually feeling the cold. He could sense how Travish's regret for what Raven had done to Sally went to the young man's very core, though not all of his regrets were so deep. "Why were you letting him do it to anyone else?" he asked bluntly, and felt the young man's spearing pain. It speared through Mace as well, as he thought of how he'd treated men himself over the years. He'd ignored them or frightened them, and he'd enjoyed their fear. He'd thought Heyou and Ril both mad for loving men. Now he wished he'd listened to them a long time ago and seen what they did. Men mattered as much as women, and both this boy and the one waiting back in Falloweld mattered to him more than any.

"Let's go," he said, not wanting to discuss it any more.

They arrived at Falloweld with a heralding roar from Mace as he set himself down in the main street. The inn was packed, half the town still there to hear the news. No one was going around giving any gifts now, not recognizing the strength of the gift in their presence. The sound of dozens of conversations faltered as Mace shifted to human form, disgorging his passengers. Sally and Travish stood together at his side, while Ruffles pressed nervously against his pant leg—he'd put his clothes back on before leaving the bandit camp.

Faces pressed against the windows all around, staring out at them.

"Oh, no," Travish gasped, stepping back with fright. "I can't stay here."

Sally reached out and put a hand on his arm. "It's all right." There was a calmness to her now, a balance she hadn't had before, though Mace sensed her nervousness at her family's imminent reaction.

"We're only here to get Jayden," he said.

Both of them looked at him. Mace leaned down to take Sally's hands, well aware of all the people watching through the window and the now-open door. They were coming outside, spreading out in the street to see them, and he said nothing to them, wanting them all outside where they could see. "If you want," he told her, "you can come to the Valley with me. I have a home there for you, and I want you there. *Both* of you."

While his mother's eyes filled with tears, Travish's held on to his doubt. It would be a long time going away. "No one's going to trust me after what I've been."

Mace just stared at him. "I'll have to introduce you to our chancellor. If you think your past sins are bad, you'll have nightmares at his."

There was a commotion at the door to the inn. "Let me through!" Mace heard Jayden yell, just before the boy pushed his way out of the whispering crowd and stopped on the front porch, staring at Mace uncertainly. Mace felt all the boy's old doubts: that he'd be ignored, that he'd be left behind, that he'd be seen as a duty and nothing else. That Mace had only come for him because he'd been ordered.

Mace opened his arms. "Come here."

Jayden's eyes widened, and then the fourteen-year-old ran to him.

Mace held the child and looked at Sally. "Do you want to come with us?" he asked her.

"Yes," she whispered, tears on her cheeks.

"And you?" he asked Travish.

For an instant in that bandit camp, he'd felt the fire of a battle sylph in the boy. For that and for Sally, Mace was willing to accept that Travish was his son, just as he was willing to take Jayden as his son as well. Most of the other battlers in the Valley would think he'd gone mad, but Ril and Heyou would understand. If the boy came.

Travish eyed the townspeople watching them, all of them muttering but standing back for fear of the battler. Mace could feel their anger at seeing the young man whom they'd always considered a bastard and then decreed a traitor. There was no future here for him except the jail or the noose. Deep down he had the soul of a battle sylph, though. In the Valley he'd have a home.

"I guess I have no choice," he muttered. But at least he

was willing. Mace nodded. What he did in the Valley was up to him, but at least he would have more choices.

As for Sally, she had the most choices of any of them. He'd have to sit down and explain exactly what a battle-sylph master was and what it meant. He'd introduce her to Lily, and for once in his life he'd make it clear. He loved Lily and he belonged to her, but in Sally he had the chance for more. He could feel the hope of a soul tie in her, the one thing all battlers wanted and so few found, even with female masters. If Lily truly loved him, she'd agree. He knew his Lily. She might laugh at him, but she'd let him go in the end.

Falon appeared at the doorway of the inn, pushing his way through the crowd and staring down at his sister and nephew. Everyone was outside now, holding their mugs and staring at them. Falon had made very good trade on his sister's misfortune. "You're back."

"Yes," Sally said, regarding him.

He sighed, looking disgruntled, annoyed, and relieved all at once. "You better get in here, then." He eyed Travish. "I'll decide what to do about him later."

"No," Mace announced, his voice loud enough to carry over the crowd. "They're not staying."

Falon gaped. "But it's the Winter Festival. They're supposed to be with family."

"That's why they're coming with me," Mace told him. "I know more about family than you do."

"You're a battle sylph!" the man protested. "This is their home!"

Mace raised a hand, palm facing outward. Falon gaped at him, going pale. "Move," Mace told him, and the human bolted.

All of them moved, running out into the street and snow. Mace was very controlled about his blast, and the explosion that consumed the inn went straight up, taking the roof and everything inside the structure along with it. Sally gasped, her delighted emotions showing what she really thought about what he'd done, while Jayden stared in amazement and Travish started laughing.

Falon gaped at the destruction of his inn, his face white.

Mace lowered his hand. Neither the queen nor Lily had forbidden this, though he suspected he'd hear about it soon enough. It was worth it.

"This was never a home," he told the man. "Perhaps the next one you build will be."

Chapter Thirteen

Lily was missing Mace more than she'd thought she would. She'd taken him as her own almost on a whim, and certainly to prevent him from going after the girls in her charge, but she'd grown very fond of him. His needs never faltered, though, and sometimes it had been hard to love him. She'd tried to give him what he needed, just as she took care of the orphans in her charge, but she knew she wasn't as loving as he deserved. He'd never complained, which was one of the things she loved about him the most.

This was the longest time he'd ever been away from her, though, and she sat alone in her kitchen by the fire, waiting. The orphans she'd raised were all with their own families now, for the biggest celebration night of the festival, and the two adult girls who still lived here were at the main hall, helping with the town feast. Lily had insisted they go, not wanting anyone with her so long as Mace and Jayden were gone. They'd promised to return later, and she had no doubt the girls would. Both had a strong dedication to duty, instilled in them, she hoped, by both herself and Mace.

She sensed Mace before he arrived, tired and in pain, and heard his voice speak into her mind. *I have Jayden*, he said. *He's all right.*

Lily sagged with relief for a moment before she pulled herself upright in her chair again.

There's more, Mace continued a second later, his mental

voice suddenly seeming almost nervous. *You said to find a new master if I could . . . I have, if you'll accept her. She's a woman I knew before I met you. I've brought her and our son. Even if you don't accept her, I want them to live here in the Valley. I . . . Lily, I love her.*

Lily blinked, absorbing that. She'd had no doubt that Mace would find someone new, simple creature that he was, but she hadn't quite expected this. For him to say this? That he *loved* this woman? He'd never told Lily that he loved her, and she'd never thought anything of it. Their bond had always been good enough for her.

She pushed that thought away for more practical matters and the other thing he'd said. *Our son?* she thought toward him, not used to mental speech even after all these years.

We were lovers for one night, he told her. *She gave birth. She says she's been with no one else and that he's my son. I believe her.*

I see, Lily replied. She'd judge that for herself.

They arrived a few minutes later, Mace letting the group in through the front door. Lily rose to her feet but stayed by her warm fire, letting them get organized rather than going out and risking a cold draft. She truly felt them more than ever. Given her breathlessness from just standing, she suspected that Mace might have found a new master just in time, though she had serious misgivings about the woman's claim.

Then the group was in the kitchen, and Lily frowned down at a contrite Jayden before turning her attention on the newcomers. The young man looked as though he hadn't had a bath in years—a condition she'd see remedied before she'd let him sit in any of her chairs—and the woman . . . She was beautiful, though battlers didn't care about beauty, and she was old enough for Mace's story to be true, though that would mean she'd been very young indeed when she was with him. He'd been a suit of armour at that point, Lily reminded herself with a hint of amusement. A bit catty of her, she supposed, but this woman was proposing to replace her in Mace's bed, even if it was a place she didn't want to be anymore.

She nodded to the woman. "Welcome to my home," she said.

"Thank y-you," Sally stammered, looking nervous.

Lily turned to her battle sylph then, putting her hand to his cheek and gazing up at him. He was in pain, but there was patience in his need. He could wait, as he always did—and there were other things going on here that Lily felt couldn't.

"Dear one," she said, "please take these two boys to the barn and scrub them clean."

"It's very cold," he pointed out.

"Then you should hurry."

He ushered them out. Travish looked uncertain, and Jayden was already whining. The dog Mace had taken as an anchor followed, pressing up against Jayden and wagging her tail happily. The boy had his hand shoved deep in her ruff, and she looked as devoted as any dog had ever been to a boy who would play with her.

Lily watched them go and turned to Sally.

"I think I need a bath too," the woman admitted.

"In a bit, dear. When the boys are done." Lily eyed her sternly. "I wanted to ask why you lied to Mace. I will not hand my battler over to a woman willing to lie to him, let me be clear about that."

She stiffened. "I never lied to him!"

Lily sniffed and turned to the stove to get two mugs of tea. "Battle sylphs can't get human women with child, dear." She gathered the mugs and turned, seeing Sally at the table with tears in her eyes.

"I never went to another man," she said.

Lily set the mug down in front of her, realizing what wasn't being said. "What does that have to do with it, when the man forces the issue?"

Sally looked away, weeping. "I . . . The night after Mace . . . I went to the barn to remember. I'd never gone out at night before, but I missed him. There was a man there, a drover from a passing merchant train and . . . he . . ." The tears fell, a secret Lily knew she'd been carrying a long time now coming out so that she could stay with the being she loved. "He was drunk. He held me down and . . ." She couldn't finish.

After a moment, she said, "After he passed out . . . I took one of the lanterns . . . The straw was so dry, it burned so fast. They all thought it was an accident, and I never . . . I never said . . ."

Lily leaned down and hugged the younger woman. "It's all right, dear. You don't have to say any more." This was a dangerous woman indeed, she thought. How perfect for Mace.

"Mace *is* Travish's father," Sally said fiercely, hugging her back.

"The best families are always found, dear," Lily allowed.

Mace appeared in the doorway, having sensed their strong emotions. "What's wrong?" he asked.

Lily straightened. "Nothing, dear. I was just telling Sally that I think she would make a wonderful master for you."

Mace glanced between them, not sure he entirely believed that, based on what he'd just felt, but both women were staring at him, Lily impassively and Sally wiping her face. Was it really worth knowing? he wondered, and decided it wasn't. He had the two women he loved, and their spirits were brightening even as he watched them. His doubts about this meeting left him. Lily approved, even if there was a little secret smile on her lips. Lily had always had her secrets.

"The boys are nearly done," he said at last. They might

not pass Lily's inspection, but at least they didn't reek anymore.

Lily nodded. "Good. Find them some clean clothes from the press, dear." She looked down at Sally. "I have a dress that will fit you once you've bathed. I haven't enough food for all of you, so I thought that we could go and enjoy the town feast. It should already have started." She looked at Mace. "And the healer sylph will be there for *you*."

Mace watched Sally wipe away the last of her tears, all the tension going out of her. She was going to be accepted here, and she realized it. "But I didn't bring any presents to give," she suddenly worried. "That's always a big thing in Falloweld."

"You brought a gift," Mace assured her. "Yourself and our son."

Sally smiled at him.

When Lily regarded him with bemusement, he told her, "And you gave me a gift as well—sending me after Jayden."

"Indeed," she said. "And what gift do you bring?"

"Mace is a gift," Sally told her.

"Of course," Lily agreed. "For as long as I've known him, he always has been."

The Crystal Crib

Helen Scott Taylor

*To Mum and Dad for all the wonderful
Christmases you gave me.
~Helen Scott Taylor*

Chapter One

Sonja's neck prickled as she approached the grand entrance to the hotel at Santa's Magical Wonderland in Iceland and halted beneath a banner that read: LIVE YOUR DREAMS THIS CHRISTMAS. Against a backdrop of snow-cloaked wooden lodges, shuttle carts shaped like white cats zipped along carrying smiling moms and dads with giggling kids. A cacophony of Christmas tunes blasted from the rides in the nearby theme park, lending the whole scene a manic out-of-this-world feel, as if a cartoon had come to life.

Her instincts were usually accurate, but Sonja couldn't spot anyone watching her—apart from two scruffy, black birds perched on a wire above the road. She squinted at them, a sense of unease wriggling up her spine. Perhaps she just felt guilty for coming here without telling her aunt.

Rubbing her neck, she walked under the impressive ice-palace facade of the Magical Wonderland hotel and into the foyer. A familiar sense of isolation closed around her as she threaded her way between the happy family groups. Twin girls dashed past, holding a younger boy firmly by the hand, and she paused to watch them catch up with their mother and have a group cuddle. When she was younger she'd longed for a brother or sister, although she'd have been satisfied with just a mother or father.

With a sigh, she ignored the people and concentrated on assessing the place with a travel professional's eye. Despite the crowds, the hotel had a welcoming ambience. A huge Christmas tree hung with shiny decorations reached to the top of the glass-domed atrium, while the ice-palace theme gave the place a sense of fantasy.

The resort staff wore green velvet outfits trimmed with white fur. A receptionist wearing the name badge FRIDA looked up and smiled as Sonja approached the desk.

"May I help you, madam?"

"I have an appointment with Vidar." Using the managing director's first name made Sonja cringe, but she'd been told this was how people addressed each other in Iceland because they didn't have normal surnames.

Frida's gaze sharpened with interest before she checked her computer screen. "You are Sonja?"

At her nod, the woman extended a hand, indicating she should come around the end of the reception desk to a door marked PRIVATE. On impulse, Sonja grabbed a red and white button with the slogan LIVE YOUR DREAMS THIS CHRISTMAS as she passed a display of resort freebies and dropped it in her pocket. She'd collected buttons when she was a little girl and still kept up the habit. Perhaps it would bring her luck when she met Vidar. Frida punched in a security number and held open the door.

They entered a plushly carpeted hall. The door closing behind them shut off all noise, leaving a sudden silence. Another woman dressed in uniform admitted Sonja when she reached the other end of the corridor. She gestured her toward some leather chairs arranged around a low glass table.

"Would you like a cup of coffee, Sonja?"

"Oh, no thanks." Her stomach did nervous somersaults. She closed her eyes and opened her mind to the loving presence of the spiritual being she thought of as her guardian angel, who always soothed her mind when she was upset or nervous. His quiet strength filled her, steadying her nerves. When she was a little girl, she'd assumed everyone had a spirit to comfort them until her aunt threatened to put her button collection in the trash if she ever told anyone.

Silently she rehearsed her pitch to secure a room allocation at deep discount for her aunt's travel company, Destination Heaven. If she secured this plum deal, her aunt would have to admit she was ready to handle the foreign destinations. She wished she'd had time to work up marketing plans to show Vidar, but his letter inviting her aunt Una to a meeting had only arrived yesterday.

A buzzer sounded. The second woman ushered Sonja toward a set of double doors. "Vidar will see you now."

Sonja's heart jigged. Her fingers touched the button in her pocket. "May my dreams come true," she whispered. She swallowed a few times and cleared her throat.

She breezed through the door, trying to imitate Una's confidence. One look at the man who rose from his chair to greet her and her step faltered. Vidar stood tall, his powerful physique showcased by a dark suit. His shaggy black hair gleamed under the office lights while stubble shadowed his lean, bronzed face. He obviously wasn't a native Icelander. Her research indicated that he'd founded the resort in the late fifties, but that couldn't be correct as he only looked to be in his midthirties.

He stepped out from behind his desk and extended a hand, his lustrous golden gaze devouring her as if he'd never seen a woman before. Sonja's heart thumped as the firm warmth of his palm swallowed her hand.

"Sonja."

He spoke her name in a thick velvet whisper, as if it were

sacred. The seductive foreign lilt of his voice zinged along her nerves. She had the weird feeling that she knew his voice, knew *him*. Even though she'd never seen his face before.

"Hello, Vidar, thank you for meeting with me."

For long moments he scrutinized her. She couldn't drag her gaze away from his compelling golden brown eyes.

"Where's Una?"

His question broke the spell, and she dropped her gaze to the white cat-shaped pin in his tie. Did he know her aunt, or had he used her aunt's Christian name because of Icelandic convention? Sonja tried to pull back her hand, but his grip tightened.

"She's taking a martial arts course in South America. I thought your letter sounded too good an opportunity to delay the meeting until she returned." Sonja winced at her overly eager response. She might as well get down on her knees and beg for his business.

"Hmm." Even his murmur had a husky foreign tone that echoed through her, raising goose bumps on her arms.

"I have my aunt's permission to negotiate a deal on her behalf." It was a little white lie but the only way she'd ever get a chance to prove herself.

Finally, he released her hand. He waited for her to be seated in the leather guest chair before he dropped back into his seat on the other side of the desk. With a brooding look, he ran the side of his hand over his lips.

"What has Una told you about our customs?"

"My aunt's told me a little about Iceland." A lie, but he wasn't to know. Her aunt flatly refused to tell her anything about the country of her birth or her parents.

Vidar stared at her some more and shook his head to himself. "You're the spitting image of your father." He gestured toward her. "Exactly the same blonde hair and blue eyes."

Sonja touched the long hair spread over her shoulders, willing Vidar to elaborate. "You know my father?"

"Uh-huh." He tapped his fingers on the desk, frowning in thought. "Would you like to meet him?"

"No . . . Yes." Sonja's pulse raced. She pressed a hand to her heart. Did she want to meet him? As a child she had fantasized about her father coming to rescue her from her strict aunt. But in twenty-six years, he hadn't even sent her a birthday card. Nowadays, she imagined telling him exactly what she thought of irresponsible men who abandoned their kids.

"He'll be at the Yule Fest I'm attending tonight. Come with me," Vidar said in a low, compelling voice. "You must be curious about him."

She imagined coming face-to-face with her father in the middle of a party. How stunned he'd be to see her. How nervous she'd be to see him.

"That's settled then. I'll take you with me."

"No!"

His elegant dark eyebrows rose. "Do you have a problem with me?"

"You? Of course not." Darn, now she had offended him. But arriving at a party full of strangers with a man she didn't know to face the father she'd never met . . . She wasn't that brave. "If you give me his contact details, I'll call him." Or maybe she wouldn't.

Vidar laughed—a low amused chuckle, as if she'd cracked a joke. "Your father is not the sort of man you just call."

She set her jaw and clasped the briefcase on her lap. She hadn't come here to find her father. They were getting off track. Just because Vidar owned one of the most successful theme parks in the world, she mustn't let him browbeat her. "Let's discuss business."

He laughed again, this time a weary, self-mocking sound

that disturbed her. "You'll get your deal after the Yule Fest, Sonja. Don't worry." He pressed an intercom button on his desk. "My guest is leaving, Hildur."

Vidar rose. Sonja had no option but to follow suit.

"I'll see you tonight then," he said.

"I haven't agreed to come with you." She wanted the deal badly but not if it came with strings attached.

"There's no need to be nervous about meeting your father. I'll be with you. Go to your cabin and get some rest. You'll be out late tonight."

She bristled at his high-handed attitude. It was on the tip of her tongue to tell him to shove his deal somewhere unmentionable when the reassuring presence of her guardian angel flooded through her. Her fears slipped away, and she realized that she must take this opportunity to meet her father. If she returned to England without seeing him, she would never forgive herself.

"Where is the Yule Fest?"

"Valhalla—that's Odin's ice palace. There'll be a lot of people there."

The resort's theme was a combination of Norse mythology and Santa Claus folklore. She couldn't come to much harm surrounded by other guests. "All right, I'll come with you, Vidar. Thank you."

"I'll collect you from your cabin at around six." For the first time he smiled, a slow stretch of his lips and a sparkle in his eyes. A shiver of awareness fluttered through her.

Only when she was outside his door did she wonder how he knew that she had never met her father.

Vidar stared at his office door, the memory of Sonja's slender form and the silky fall of blonde hair replaying in his mind. His body was tense with arousal just from sitting opposite her.

He slammed shut the file on his desk and cursed. *"Skitur!"* The last time he'd seen her she'd been a tiny baby. He'd been curious to discover how she'd turned out, to put an adult face to the child he'd protected over the years. Never in his wildest dreams had he imagined she'd look like *that*. Her long blonde hair and deep blue eyes so closely resembled those of Troy the Deathless that her appearance should put him on guard. Instead, he'd fought to concentrate on business rather than dwell on her full lips and the soft swells of her breasts beneath her blue jacket.

How could he want to kiss her when she reminded him of Troy? He swiped the back of his hand over his mouth. She was an innocent he'd pledged to protect. He would do well to remember that fact.

Sharp tapping sounded on the window behind his desk. Even before he pivoted, he knew he'd find his father Odin's damn raven spies at the glass. His breath rushed out in irritation. He wrenched open the slider and the two birds swooped into the room.

The air around them shimmered as the birds took human form, their straggly black hair trailing over shoulders hunched beneath long dark coats. "Why did Una not accompany Troy's daughter?" Huginn demanded, while his brother Muninn cowered behind him, afraid to meet Vidar's gaze.

He wanted to throw the creeps out. He'd had enough of them hanging around watching his every move. But that would condemn them to suffer at his father's hands and earn him a night of torment. He clenched his hand, feeling the bite of the slave ring on his little finger. "My guess is Una never saw my letter. Sonja came without her knowledge."

"We'll report to our lord Odin."

"Tell him his plan can still proceed. I'll bring her to the Yule Fest myself."

The ravens sidled toward the window then changed into their feathered forms and flapped away. Vidar slammed the slider closed, leaned his forearm against the wall, and hung his head. He'd been depending on Una to protect Sonja while he kept his father and hers apart.

Odin had insisted they hold Sonja's safety over Troy's head to make him behave. The flaw in his father's plan was that Vidar would never obey an order to harm her. He'd argued that bringing Sonja here would only inflame Troy's anger, since he'd been adamant his daughter should never learn her true identity. There was no way to spare her from the shock of discovering her heritage. But if he were careful of what he said, he could hide the reason he'd invited her to the Yule Fest. And he would make damn sure she never heard mention of the Crystal Crib. He didn't want her to discover her tragic history.

Chapter Two

At six p.m. sharp, a knock sounded on Sonja's log cabin door. She scowled at it, still not sure if she wanted to attend the Yule Fest or meet her father. Vidar's invitation implied she would only get the business deal if she went with him. But he couldn't be blackmailing her into attending a Yule Fest! The idea was ridiculous. She must have misunderstood.

A second knock roused her from her indecision, and she opened the door. Vidar stood outside, swathed in a long fur coat, the hood framing his face. With his unusual golden brown eyes and tawny skin, he looked exotic and out of place in this snowy world.

"Good evening, Sonja. Are you ready?"

"Yes." If she were ever going to make her mark and impress her aunt, she must take risks to get what she wanted. And this might be her only chance to meet her father.

Over her pantsuit, she pulled on her champagne wool coat, then added her pink gloves and matching beret. When she stepped outside, Vidar scanned her from head to toe.

"You'll freeze dressed like that."

"Isn't the party inside?"

He gave her a veiled look. "You'll still need warmer clothes."

She spread her arms and looked down at herself. "I only brought an overnight bag. This is all I have."

With a resigned breath, he ushered her into one of the

resort's shuttle carts. He squashed into the driver's seat beside her. She hugged her coat close, acutely aware of him pressed against her in the confined space.

The cart headed out of a small gate manned by a security guard and took a narrow snow-covered track into woodland. Sonja peered back over her shoulder at the receding lights of the resort. Apprehension fluttered in her chest. "I assumed the Yule Fest was in the theme park."

"Uh-huh," he said, as if his mind was elsewhere.

"Vidar!" He glanced her way at her sharp tone. "Where're you taking me?"

A wave of reassurance swept through her like a gentling hand smoothing out her worries, even as her mind told her something was wrong. "The Yule Fest is a little out of the way," he said. One corner of his mouth quirked, nearly making it into a smile. "You'll enjoy the next part of the journey."

He stopped the shuttle and cut the engine. Sonja had been so focused on the resort disappearing behind them that she hadn't noticed the view up ahead. Her breath caught at the sight of a glittering sleigh harnessed with a white horse. Decorated with golden lanterns and colored bows trimmed with silver bells, the magical carriage rested on a patch of pristine snow.

"It's beautiful."

Vidar shrugged. "Seen one, seen them all."

He grabbed something from the sleigh and tossed it on her lap. She stared at the fur coat with distaste.

"I don't wear fur."

"It's not a fashion statement, Sonja. It's a necessity."

"I prefer to stick with my own coat."

She was a little chilly, but it was nothing she couldn't handle for a short while until they got inside. She handed back the fur. He dropped it in the sleigh; then he pushed a fleecy blue coat into her hands. The material felt just like fur. She squinted at it. He raised his eyebrows.

"Okay, I'll wear this one," she decided. She'd never seen a blue animal.

Vidar checked the harness on the horse while she changed coats. She slipped in the snow when she climbed out of the shuttle, but before she could blink he had a steadying arm around her waist. Her heart skittered as he hugged her to his side and guided her to the sleigh. She could get used to this type of gentlemanly behavior.

Once she and Vidar were seated, the sleigh glided forward, bells jingling. A thrill zinged through her. "This makes me think of Santa Claus. All we need is a sack of gifts and some reindeer." She turned to grin at him but found him staring at her, eyebrows drawn together.

"You missed out on Christmas when you were a child, didn't you?"

What was he, a mind reader?

She shrugged. "I survived." She pushed down the sharp pang of pity for her younger self and stared at the passing tree trunks as the sleigh slid along the forest track.

Vidar's hand covered hers and the guardian angel's familiar loving presence swept through her like a warm wind chasing away the clouds. She glanced at Vidar, confused that they had both chosen that moment to comfort her. Vidar smiled, the shadows in his eyes disappearing.

"You're in the right place to enjoy Christmas," he said. "Perhaps you should try out some of the rides in the park. Maybe I'll join you."

For the first time in years, a magical anticipation filled the air, as if Christmas morning had arrived and anything was possible. Her fingers strayed to her jacket pocket where she'd stashed the resort button. Maybe dreams did come true.

After a lifetime of hoping, Sonja was about to meet her father. She didn't kid herself he'd be pleased to see her, but at least he might explain what had happened to her mother and why he'd deserted her.

Tiny flakes of snow swirled around them. The forest thinned and the track became less defined. In the far distance, jagged icy peaks pierced the leaden sky. Sonja's face stung with the cold, so she pulled the hood of the blue coat up over her hat.

"Where are you taking me?" she shouted, the wind whipping away her words. Vidar just snapped the reins, making the horse move faster. Out of the whiteness, a deep shadowy ravine loomed in front of them.

"Vidar, stop!"

Sonja's heart slammed painfully, and she snatched panicked gulps of arctic air. She grabbed for the reins but Vidar caught her wrist to restrain her.

"You're safe," he shouted. A whisper of calm stroked across her churning thoughts. "Sit still and hold on."

She clutched his arm and pressed her face into his furclad shoulder.

"I'm not going to kill us," he breathed against her ear.

Her rational mind knew his words made sense; her survival instinct wasn't taking any chances. She dragged her face up and glanced at the rapidly passing ground, wondering if she dared jump.

"Trust me, Sonja." His words flowed into her, soothing and reassuring.

Then the horse leaped over the precipice. Her breath jammed in her lungs. Sonja squeezed her eyes closed. But the sickening stomach-flipping fall she expected didn't happen. The sleigh shuddered and bumped; then the ride smoothed.

After a few frantic beats of her heart, she cracked open her eyes. Instead of falling, they climbed into the swirling cloud of snowflakes.

With her gloved fingers still fastened in a death grip around Vidar's arm, Sonja peered down at the snowy valley hundreds of feet below them. She scrabbled to make sense of what was happening. They were at least two miles from the resort, so the sleigh couldn't be a theme-park ride.

Shocked and angry, she punched him in the arm. "How are you doing this?"

A flash of remorse crossed his face. "I live in a different world from you, Sonja."

"You're telling me flying horses are normal in Iceland?"

"Not horses."

Her gaze jerked back to the creature pulling the sleigh and her eyes bugged. A huge white cat the size of a tiger strained against the harness. A little squeal broke from her throat. In Norse mythology, the goddess Freya had a flying carriage pulled by giant cats. Like any sane person, she'd assumed that was fantasy.

"I'll stay by your side at the Yule Fest. You've nothing to fear," Vidar promised.

"The Yule Fest!" They were hanging in the air in a sleigh pulled by a giant cat and he thought she was worried about a party? "I don't care about the stupid Yule Fest," she shouted. "Take me back. Now."

"Don't you want to meet your father? We're nearly there."

Her breath rushed in and out, in counterpoint to the thudding of her pulse in her ears. She closed her eyes for a few seconds and tried to calm herself. "Where exactly is this Yule Fest?"

"My father's place."

His father lived in the freaking sky? "Who is your father?"

"Odin."

"Odin—as in the Norse god?" Sonja wrinkled her cute little nose at Vidar, obviously wondering if he were mad.

Vidar nodded, wishing he could protect her from the horrors of his world—namely his father.

While she was here, he had decided to stay out of her mind unless he needed to calm her or soothe her fear, but he couldn't resist slipping into her thoughts to test her reaction as the glittering icy turrets of the gods' kingdom of Asgard came into view. Her wonder mingled with apprehension, but she didn't panic. He was proud of how well she coped. But he shouldn't have expected anything less. After all, she was the daughter of a man notorious for his emotional control.

Vidar steered his snow cat Gleda to the icy ledge and halted the sleigh among the parked vehicles. Gleda stretched, raking her claws across the ice. He jumped out and patted his cat's flank. "Hey, girl, play nice. No fighting while I'm inside."

"Surely that's a dangerous animal." Sonja pressed herself in the corner of the sleigh, starring wide-eyed at the cat.

"They can be, but I've had Gleda since she was a cub." He held out a hand to Sonja, crushing down his pleasure when she trusted him enough to leave the safety of the sleigh. He mustn't fall for his own ploy and start believing this was a date.

"This is your father's palace?"

"Valhalla."

She ran her hand over a wall of ice. "It must be damn cold living here."

A startled laugh burst from him. "Too right. I hate it."

She halted, hanging on to his arm so he had to stop

with her. "If my father's here . . ." She turned uncertain blue eyes on him and something inside him tightened to the point of pain. If she were hurt tonight, he would never forgive himself for dragging her into the conflict between Odin and Troy.

"Your father is of our world, Sonja."

Her fingers tightened on his arm. "So, what does that make me?"

He didn't want her to get upset and bolt. Odin must see her at the Yule Fest or there was no telling what the crazy old man would do. "Come and meet Troy. See for yourself."

"My father's name is Troy?" she asked, her voice breathy.

Vidar squeezed her hand as guilt pulsed through him. She trusted him, and he was setting her up.

He pushed down her blue hood and smoothed out the long golden strands of her hair with his fingers. Her soft pink beret was somehow innocently cute and damn sexy at the same time. And he shouldn't think about her like this. He needed to get tonight over and send her home safely.

They approached the high arched entrance to the palace. The tiny gold fire imps and multicolored flower fairies decorating the tall Christmas trees on either side of the doorway swooped out of the branches and buzzed around their heads in a glittering cloud. Sonja pressed against his side with a squeal. "My god. I thought they were decorations."

"They are. Hungry ones." Vidar dug a jelly bean out of his pocket and handed it to her. "Hold it out on your flat palm. The dominant in the troop will take it." She gave him an uncertain glance but did as instructed. A tiny pink woman landed on her hand, wings buzzing too fast to see. She curtsied, then grabbed the treat and flew back toward the Christmas trees with a cloud of colorful fairies in her wake.

Sonja laughed and held out her hand for another jelly bean.

"Let the flower fairy queen eat hers first or you'll upset her."

Sonja watched the tiny fairies, her blue eyes glowing with wonder as Vidar led her past the Christmas trees and into the entrance hall. The six female Valkyrie warriors on guard tensed visibly while their gazes tracked Sonja across the room.

A pine Yule log burned in the center of the palace's cavernous main chamber, creating a puddle of meltwater on the ice floor. It produced a pleasant smell, and a golden glow that gave the illusion of warmth. The low murmur of conversation stopped as Vidar entered with Sonja on his arm; then the chatter of speculation rose. Everyone in the room knew why he'd brought her. Everyone except Sonja. Guilt burned through him again, and he pushed it away. He couldn't allow Troy and Odin to fight as they had twenty-six years ago when Troy last visited Asgard. If there were a slim chance that Sonja's presence might help keep the peace, he must use her.

"My god, Vidar."

Sonja's eyes rounded as she stared up at the eerie floating light globes illuminating the room. He followed her gaze, trying to see the scene as she did.

Her perusal of the room stopped on a group of tall silver-haired light elves. "Flipping heck. Who are they?"

"Light elves," he growled.

Some of the male elves returned her appraisal, interest clear in their slanted turquoise eyes. Irritation flashed through Vidar as a couple of them broke away from the group and headed toward her. After a fleeting glance at Sonja to make sure she wasn't watching, Vidar pushed aside the flap of his coat and rested a hand on the hilt of his sword. The elves glared but returned to their friends.

"Watch out for them. They use fairy glamour to disguise themselves as human and then seduce the tourists."

Sonja chuckled. "I'll add that to the marketing blurb for your resort under unique attractions."

Vidar stifled an angry breath. He'd come armed to prevent a confrontation between Troy and Odin, not to protect Sonja from sex-mad light elves.

She turned her attention to his father, who slouched on his dirty ice throne at the far end of the room, scowling down at the revelers with his one good eye. Vidar's brother Thor sat on the ground at Odin's side, his scruffy red head rested against the ice throne, already drunk by the look of him.

"There's no need for me to introduce you to Odin and my brother Thor."

"They look grumpy."

Vidar gave a wry laugh. "You might say that."

Sonja's fingers suddenly dug into his arm. "That man's my father, isn't he?"

Vidar followed her gaze across the room. The Irish fairy queen had arrived late, but now Ciar stood in the center of a group of admirers. Fire flickered in her red hair while blue flames licked around her hands and dripped from her fingertips, leaving sooty pockmarks on the ice floor. Troy the Deathless stood behind her, pale and motionless as a marble statue. He still played at being her bodyguard when it suited him, even though he'd grown more powerful than she, centuries ago.

Troy's blue gaze fixed on them, an arctic whip of accusation. Vidar placed his hand over Sonja's grip on his arm, making sure her father understood the reason for her presence. Troy bent to whisper in Ciar's ear; then he slipped through the crowd toward them.

Despite his flamboyant clothes, he moved with the controlled grace of a fighter. Vidar prayed that Troy behaved himself, because when he finally decided to take revenge on Odin for the past, nobody would be powerful enough to stop him.

Chapter Three

Sonja couldn't tear her eyes from the man striding toward her through the crowd. Everyone in his path stepped aside as though repelled by an invisible force field.

This man—her father—didn't even appear human. His skin glowed, and an aura of elemental danger surrounded him. Panic ticked in her throat. A primitive survival instinct screamed at her to hide. She stepped back into the security of Vidar's arm.

So intently did she watch her father's face, she only registered his ostentatious ermine-trimmed scarlet brocade coat and the froth of lace at his throat when he reached her.

"Vidar the Valiant." Troy's softly spoken words held little inflection but drove through her with the cold thrust of a blade. He stared at Vidar with lacerating intensity. Then his gaze dropped to Sonja and he smiled. His change of expression was as unexpected and shocking as the sun flaring bright at midnight.

"Sonja, daughter, this is an unexpected pleasure."

She'd thought her father might ignore her or be rude to her. She hadn't expected him to be pleased to meet her. Her brain stalled, and she couldn't get a single word out of her mouth.

His eyes softened as his gaze flicked over her. His hand rose, his fingertips softly brushing her check. The tension in her body fell away. A moment of perfect peace sang through her before the reality of the situation filtered back and the blissful sensation faded.

Her resemblance to her father was amazing. After Vidar's comment she'd expected him to have blue eyes and long blond hair, but even the shape of Troy's features was similar to hers, if with a strong masculine cast.

"Why . . . why haven't we met before?" *Why did you abandon me?*

Her father angled his head to stare at Odin, who resembled a tramp, hunched as he was on his grubby throne, with his straggly gray hair and crumpled clothes. "Ask our host," he said in a lethally soft voice.

Vidar's body stiffened behind her. Sonja glanced over her shoulder to see his jaw clench. "What does he mean, Vidar?"

Her question hung unanswered. The crowd had fallen silent and stood watching.

"Not the time or the place for this, Troy," Vidar said. His arm tightened around Sonja.

Troy's gaze flicked down to where Vidar held her before returning to his face. "Never is, my old friend." He pivoted away and started walking back toward the woman with the fiery hair.

"Wait!" Sonja cried, stepping forward, her hand raised as if she could summon him back. She had so many questions she wanted to ask. "Can I see you again?"

With fluid grace, Troy swung back toward her. Regret flashed across his face, replaced immediately by merciless determination. "No."

The word reverberated around the room. He turned his back on her again. After a few seconds of mortified shock, her gaze skated over the onlookers, who stared back at her as if she were a freak.

Suddenly, she couldn't get enough oxygen. She ran toward

the door, jostling people out of her way. She barely spared a glance for the female soldiers in the entrance hall. When she burst outside, she gasped aching lungfuls of frigid air. The tiny fairies from the Christmas trees swarmed around her head, chattering and laughing. She batted them away.

She hadn't expected her father to be interested in her. So why did his rejection hurt so much?

"Skitur." Vidar cursed as Sonja dashed away through the crowd. Her distress strummed along his nerves. He clenched his hands and resisted the instinct to follow and comfort her; he could not leave the Yule Fest until he was sure Troy wouldn't cause trouble.

He paced after Sonja's father and caught up with him before he rejoined the Irish fairy queen. "We need to talk," he said.

Troy wheeled around, his hand reaching over his shoulder for the sword strapped to his back. He gripped the sword hilt but didn't draw. "You are a man without honor, Vidar. When I persuaded Odin to release Sonja from the Crystal Crib twenty-six years ago, we agreed that she would be told nothing of our world and never be involved in our conflict."

Frustrated anger twisted Vidar's guts. *He* would have adhered to the agreement. "Odin had other ideas."

"Odin always does." Troy slashed a glance at the grizzled old man hunched upon his ice throne. Odin's good eye was fixed on them, the other hidden behind an eye patch.

Troy released his sword hilt and raised his hand, throwing a light dome around himself and Vidar for privacy. For a split second his face fractured with emotion, but then his barriers snapped back. Regret rode heavy on Vidar, a memory of a time long ago when they had loved each other like brothers. Before Troy's father Loki had killed Vidar's brother and spurred Odin into an orgy of violent retribution that still echoed horror through the halls of Asgard.

"I am not the aggressor, Vidar. I never was."

"Nor I, Troy." They stared at each other, the bad blood between their families too bitter and venomous for any hint of friendship to have survived. "I did my best for you when my father wrought revenge. If not for me, Sonja would have died in her crib."

"Yet now she's grown you put her in harm's way?"

"She's under my protection."

"That rather negates your threat to harm her if I don't behave."

"You know I would never have followed through."

"I should raze this icy hell to the ground for what Odin did to my family." Troy's jaw tightened, and Vidar's hand went to the sword hidden beneath his coat—not that it would do him any good if Troy decided to unleash his power. "But I enjoy watching your father squirm while he awaits my vengeance. One day I'll punish him, but not tonight. Go after my daughter and return her safely to the human world."

Vidar let his hand drop away from his sword. Once they had been equals, young men sparring together, learning the pleasures and dangers of the world they inhabited. Now he doubted he could even stand against Troy in hand-to-hand combat. But he dared not show weakness. "Give me your word that you won't cause trouble."

"I give my word I will wreak havoc if you don't look after my daughter."

"Understood." That was the best he could hope for.

"And . . . Vidar." Troy waited for him to meet his gaze before he continued. "You will never tell Sonja that her power's trapped in the Crystal Crib."

Vidar gave a sharp nod. That was something on which they agreed.

The light dome dissolved with a pop, and Vidar strode away through the crowd, ignoring the frantic gestures of his father who would want details of his conversation with Troy. He surged out through the door into the darkness.

Odin's shape-shifter spies waited perched on the edge of a carriage in raven form, no doubt ready to follow him. Vidar balled a handful of ice crystals and hurled the missile at the bigger bird. Huginn shot into the air in a flurry of black feathers.

"Get lost!" Vidar shouted as Muninn followed his brother.

Sonja stood alone near their sleigh, her arms wrapped around her body, her teeth chattering. He strode up behind her and gathered her into his embrace. "I'm taking you back to Santa's world."

"How are you involved with me and my father?"

When she tried to turn around and look at him, he held her tightly against his chest. He should have prepared for this question. "You're cold and tired. Let's talk when we're back in the warmth." After he'd had time to come up with an answer.

She didn't object as he hustled her past the sleeping snow cat and into the sleigh. At a word from him, Gleda stood and stretched, flicking her tail. He pulled back on the reins. They reversed off the ice platform and headed toward the woodland where he'd left the theme park's shuttle.

Sonja huddled deep in the fur coat he'd disguised as a thermal fleece, staring at something in her hands.

"Are you all right?"

When she didn't reply, Vidar clasped both reins in one hand and used his fingers to tip up her chin. He'd thought she might be crying, but she stared at him dry-eyed, the same guarded expression on her face that Troy wore so well. She'd arrived at his office earlier that day excited and enthusiastic. In a few short hours, he'd killed her excitement and drained her enthusiasm. *Bloody good job, Vidar.*

He lowered the mental guard he'd raised to block their bond and let his consciousness flow around her. A cold impenetrable wall of resistance met his attempt to enter her mind. For the first time in her life, she'd shut him out. He stared at her in shock. It made no sense unless she'd guessed he was the presence in her mind.

"Sonja, talk to me."

She dragged in a breath. "Dreams don't come true." She tossed away the small thing she'd been holding and he realized it was a resort logo button.

"Are you all right?"

"What do you want me to say, Vidar?"

"Tell me what you thought of your father."

"You were right. I look like him." Her voice stayed level, almost unemotional, but the protective shield around her mind wavered and a flash of misery escaped. She felt unwanted, unloved. A pain stabbed the vicinity of his heart.

"Your father only stayed away from you for your own good."

She cast him a disbelieving glance.

"It's complicated, Sonja."

"And I'm too stupid to understand, I suppose."

"That's not what I meant."

He couldn't take her back to her room and leave her miserable. With a twitch of his wrist, he changed Gleda's direction.

Sonja's head tilted. "Where're we going now?"

"I want to show you my favorite view."

He slowed the sleigh as they approached the flat icy rock. The sleigh's metal runners scraped onto solid ground.

Despite Sonja's melancholy, her curiosity picked up when Vidar stopped the sleigh. An occasional snowflake spiraled out of the dark sky toward the endless expanse of glittering frost-glazed landscape below.

Vidar slid close and curved a supportive arm around her shoulders. She resisted the temptation to lean back against the reassurance of his body. She had a sick sense that she was the butt of a joke. Everyone at the Yule Fest obviously knew who she was, and had enjoyed the spectacle of her father rejecting her.

Green light flashed across the dark sky. "There." Vidar pointed as the colored lights pulsed around them. "Humans call it the aurora borealis. It's really the light elves showing off."

She sensed Vidar looking at her and couldn't resist a quick glance his way. He grinned and her stomach did a strange flip. She'd never experienced such a strong connection with a man before. It was as though on some level she'd known him all her life. She had started to trust him by the time they reached the Yule Fest, despite the fact he'd sprung his strange world on her with no warning. But after what happened at the party . . .

"Explain what went on at the Yule Fest tonight, Vidar."

He pulled her tightly to his side and the heat from his body seeped through the fur, warming her. Streaks of green, blue, and pink shimmered across the sky.

After long minutes when she thought he wasn't going to answer, he leaned close to her ear. "Tonight you got caught up in a family feud. Just forget about it, *elskan mín.*"

She wished she could rewind tonight and delete what had happened. But she'd met her father. "Forgetting's not an option."

Vidar's breath hissed out and he tightened his arm around her. "I know you feel that Troy abandoned you, but he did it to protect you."

"Protect me from what?" She swiveled around to see Vidar's expression. The golden glow of his eyes took her breath away each time she looked into them. His face was so close to hers she felt his breath on her skin. Her world narrowed to the man in front of her. Her fingers flexed against his chest. "Didn't Troy want me in his world?"

"It's not that simple," Vidar whispered. His hand slid up her back to pull off her hood. His warm palm cupped the back of her head. "Sonja . . ."

He was going to kiss her. She should stop him. She had so many questions he hadn't answered. Yet her gaze dropped to his lips. He closed the gap between them, his mouth finding hers, hot and smooth, dangerously seductive. Her aunt always said not to mix business with pleasure. But this was way past business into uncharted territory.

The hot tip of his tongue touched her lips, and her mind blanked as he deepened the kiss. Her hand tingled, longed to burrow beneath his coat in search of skin. But it was too cold to start removing clothes.

She barely noticed the squawking and flapping sound until Vidar pulled away from her and looked up. Her heart raced, wanting more of him as if she'd been waiting for him all her life, even though she knew little about him and his world scared her. The two black birds that had been circling above them peeled away and disappeared into the darkness.

Vidar cursed and rubbed a hand across his face. "They're

bad news. I need to get you back to your room. Have you scheduled a flight home?"

The speed at which he moved from intimacy to getting rid of her left her breathless. "You want me to leave?"

Cold bit into her at the uncompromising gleam in his eyes. "It's best."

"I left the return date open," she said, her voice barely more than a whisper.

"Check flight times when you get back to your room. Take the first available flight to London."

"Are black birds a bad omen or something?"

"Forget about them. I just want you off this frozen rock as soon as possible."

No room for confusion there. Both Vidar and her father had mood swings that threatened to give her whiplash. It was on the tip of her tongue to ask about her deal with the resort, but she would find another way to impress her aunt. Her head was spinning with everything she'd experienced since she arrived. One day in Iceland was long enough to last a lifetime.

Chapter Four

Sonja sat on the bed in her room with her laptop balanced on her crossed legs and booked her homeward flight. She'd finally met her father and found a man who she connected with deeply, yet Vidar and Troy both wanted her gone. Why did nobody want her? She felt more alone than she'd ever been in her life. She'd always known she was different from other people because of her guardian angel, but she wouldn't allow herself to seek his reassuring presence. After her disturbing visit to the ice palace in the sky and her glimpse of the weird people at Odin's Yule Fest she no longer trusted anything out of the ordinary.

The first available flight to London was in the morning, so that meant she was stuck in Iceland for a night. She booked an early cab, packed her bag and fell into a restless sleep. Fractured images of her father and the weird people at the Yule Fest alternated with heated memories of Vidar's kiss and the feel of his body pressed against hers.

She woke in the still of the night and blinked into the darkness. A streak of illumination from the light outside pen-etrated between the curtains. Tinny Christmas music still played in the distance, although the time was well past mid-night.

Something dropped onto the pillow beside her head. Sonja raised herself on an elbow and picked up a black feather. In the sliver of light, it gleamed blue-green like oil on water. Where had that come from?

Movement in the shadows snagged her attention. She sat up, squinting at the corners of the room. The darkness stirred. A scream burst from her lips. Fingers clamped over her mouth from behind, wrenching her neck sideways against a bony chest.

"Shhhh. Shhhh," a male voice hissed in her ear.

A second figure loomed out of the darkness in front of her. He stripped away the bedcovers from her body. She clawed at the hand over her mouth while her legs were pulled over the edge of the bed and her ankles tied together.

When the hand left her mouth, she dragged in a frantic breath and screamed as her wrists were jerked behind her back. Then a gag tightened between her lips. She struggled, kicked, grunted, and banged her head back against the bony chest until sparks swam in her vision. She must escape now. Once they took her from her room, no one would find her. Anyone who checked would think she'd left for her early flight. She opened her mind, longing for her guardian angel, but he wasn't there. More than ever, she needed his calm support to help her cope.

Dark, suffocating fabric covered her face. Her breath came in short panicked gasps while they manhandled her. The material enclosed her, and she fell awkwardly. They had put her in a bag. The tight binding on her ankles and wrists bit into her skin as she was carried.

Her head banged against something. Pain speared down her neck, bringing tears to her eyes. Cold hit her and the festive music blared louder. Then she landed with a bruising thud on a hard surface. Muffled voices argued for a moment, then she felt movement as if she were in a carriage or sleigh like the one Vidar had used.

Why had she come to Iceland? She hated the damn place. She opened her mind to her guardian angel again, begging him to come to her. She implored him for help, as she had many times over the years when she'd felt lost and alone and she'd had nobody else to turn to. The image of Vidar merged with the angel's presence in her mind. *Vidar, Vidar . . .* She repeated his name—a silent mantra to keep her sane.

Suddenly, his presence flooded through her, shoring up her shredded control with a tender supportive embrace as if he held her in his arms. Vidar was her guardian angel. Vidar was the loving presence in her mind. How was that possible?

Vidar jolted awake to find himself slouched on the sofa before the log fire in his retreat. A flash of terror streaked along his mental link with Sonja, and her anguished call burst through his mind. After years bonded to her he responded automatically: calming, soothing, in the same way he had since she was a baby. He blinked and swiped a hand over his face as his thought processes caught up with his instinct. He'd left her in her cabin at the resort hours ago. She should be asleep. What in the Furies had happened to her?

Staggering to his feet, he knocked the shot glass and empty vodka bottle to the floor. His temples thudded, making him wish he had held off drowning his sorrows over having to send Sonja away to protect her until she was safely out of the country. He pulled on his boots, grateful now that he hadn't got around to undressing, and headed toward the door. At the sound of whistling wind battering the protective heat shield over his front door he wheeled around to snag his fur coat off the back of the sofa. He wouldn't be much use to her if he froze to death.

Outside his cabin, frigid air laced with snow slashed his face. If only he could leave this miserable frozen place and return to his mother's people in Italy. If only he wasn't Odin's son. If only he could be with Sonja. His life was filled with *if onlys* . . .

He pushed two fingers between his lips and whistled, squinting through the blizzard at the snowy slope above his cabin. His snow cat Gleda bounded toward him, freezing droplets flying in all directions as she skidded to a halt at his feet.

He slapped her shoulder affectionately, wiped the worst of the snow off her fur, and threw a leg over her back. His heart thundered in response to Sonja's panic, but he would rescue her or die in the attempt. Vidar leaned forward to speak directly into Gleda's ear so she heard him over the roar of the wind. Then he tangled his fingers in her silky mane. His stomach lurched sickly as she flung herself off the icy ledge over the ravine, yet the feeling had little to do with the drop.

Sonja landed with bone-jarring force on the ground and lay still inside the dark, airless bag, gathering her wits for what she would face next. Her teeth chattered uncontrollably. On the journey, the chill had penetrated the bag and her fleecy pajamas to pierce the very marrow of her bones. Now she was lying on a surface so cold it could only be ice.

The bag loosened and the fabric peeled back from her face. She blinked at a gleaming expanse of white. The large space was empty, but a long sooty stain on the floor in the center of the room looked like the remnants of the Yule Log that had burned at Odin's Yule Fest.

Still tied, she wriggled around to peer behind her. Odin sat bundled on his ice throne. His long gray hair and beard hung in matted clumps over his stained coat. A huge wolf crouched on either side of his throne, golden eyes glued to her as if waiting for the command to attack.

"Huginn, turn her round," Odin ordered. His voice sounded like a glacier grinding rocks to dust.

A skinny man with long dark hair and pointed features pulled the edge of the sack, sliding her around in a graceful arc to lie at Odin's feet. The gaze from the god's single visible eye raked over her accusingly. His scowl deepened, creasing his ancient face like old paper.

"She has the look of the Deathless One," Odin said.

Sonja lay still so she wouldn't antagonize him, but she listened intently.

Another man who looked like Huginn's twin stepped into view. They had to be her two kidnappers. "Is she dangerous?"

"Of course not." Odin flapped a dismissive hand. "Her power's bound to the Crystal Crib."

"Shall I remove her gag so you can question her?" Huginn asked.

"I'll cast the runes first." Odin pointed his staff at a table across the room. "Muninn, my bag."

The more timid of the two kidnappers retrieved a brown leather bag with a drawstring top. Odin shook the bag then dug inside and scattered on the ground a handful of rectangular wooden pieces marked with symbols. He stared down at them, absently scratching his beard.

"Hmm." His gaze moved back to her and he puffed out a blast of stinking breath.

"Can you use her against Troy?" Huginn asked.

"The runes say she's the catalyst for great change."

Muninn shuffled closer and stared down at the wooden pieces with a frown. "Is that good?"

Odin cuffed him around the head. "Change is never good,

you imbecile." Odin's face scrunched into deeper creases so his good eye nearly disappeared beneath his bushy gray eyebrow. "She might discover her power and become a threat like her father."

Was it possible she had inherited power from Troy? The idea of flying or being super strong like Superman appealed to her. She imagined the shock on Odin's face if she broke free of her bonds and zoomed off into the night.

Just another stupid dream. The vision faded, and she sank back into her chilled misery. She didn't have any power. The only way she would escape was if Vidar or her father rescued her.

Vidar's warm, reassuring presence hummed more strongly in her mind, easing her fear. The sound of raised voices behind her made her crane her head around. Her heart jumped as Vidar paced in and bore down on them, his face a mask of anger.

"What in the Furies are you doing?" He swept past her, kicked the scattered wooden runes aside, and crouched between her and Odin. "Are you all right, Sonja?"

"Leave her be, Vidar," Odin boomed in a voice that made the floor vibrate.

"She's no threat to you," Vidar snapped without turning. He loosened the gag and pulled it away from her mouth. She dragged in her first decent breath in hours, filling her lungs with cold air flavored with the hot spicy tang of Vidar's scent.

The tension inside her eased as Vidar untied her and helped her to her feet. His presence in her mind felt so familiar and natural she yearned to stay with him even while her common sense demanded that she get out of Iceland and never return.

Vidar pulled off his fur coat and helped her into it, fastening the front to keep her warm.

"You'll get cold without your coat, son," Odin said sulkily.

"*I'll* get cold!" Vidar shook his head in disbelief. His father was losing his mind. "Are you trying to incite Troy to violence? He'll bring Valhalla down around your ears if he discovers you've kidnapped his daughter and left her to die of exposure."

"I want to keep her as insurance—freeze her again."

"She's too big for her Crystal Crib now," Huginn piped up.

Sonja stiffened beneath his arm. "What's that?" she asked, through chattering teeth.

"Nothing important." Vidar hoped the others didn't elaborate. "Let me take her back to her cabin at the resort. If she goes home tomorrow Troy will stay away and you can relax for another few decades."

Odin peered up from beneath the brim of his hat, his mouth a flat sulky line. "No." The word echoed around the room with finality. "She's my insurance."

Vidar sucked in a breath, released it slowly. He could reason with his father on many subjects but not on Troy; the old enmity had poisoned his father's mind. He glanced at Sonja, wishing he was able to send thoughts into her mind to explain that he didn't mean what he was about to say: "I'll keep the woman tucked away so she's at hand if Troy returns to cause trouble."

Odin grunted. "Only if she wears my ring."

Vidar stilled, acutely aware of the slave ring on his little finger—a more effective jail than any cell.

Odin pulled the enchanted gold ring Draupnir from his finger and laid it on his palm. The metal jumped and flexed. A second gold band grew out of the original before separating with a pop. Odin tossed the new ring to Vidar, who snatched the cursed thing from the air and clenched it in his fist.

"You don't want to press a human into your service, my lord." He would not allow Odin to ruin Sonja's life as his own had been ruined.

Odin bent to pet one of his wolves. "She's only half human. No one could accuse Troy of having humanity."

Despite Troy's fearsome reputation, he had more humanity than Odin. Vidar's grip tightened on the ring.

"Give Draupnir's progeny to Troy's daughter," Odin commanded.

Vidar's breath grated in and out of his lungs. Once Sonja slid his father's ring on her finger, she would never escape the old man's control. "Consult the runes first." He crouched to gather up the wooden pieces he'd kicked aside. He dropped them back into the bag on his father's lap.

"Let me put it on. I can take it off again later," Sonja whispered.

Vidar cast her a look of dissent that he hoped would keep her quiet.

Odin stirred the runes in his bag, grabbed a handful, and scattered them on the ground. He bent forward to examine them; his face screwed into a frown.

With Huginn and Muninn also engrossed in the runes, Vidar backed up, taking Sonja with him. All he had to do was get her out of Iceland and she'd be safe from Odin.

"Have you got the sleigh here?" she whispered as the distance between them and the throne widened.

Vidar put his finger to his lips.

Odin's attention lifted from the runes. Familiar agonizing pain shot up Vidar's arm from the slave ring, slicing through bone, spearing along muscle. He slammed down the shutters on his link with Sonja as his legs buckled and he collapsed to his knees with a cry of pain.

When the torture ceased, his bones throbbed and his muscles ached. Sonja was on her knees before him clutching his shoulders. "Vidar, what's the matter?"

Troy had been right to cut her off from this world. If only Vidar had stood up to his father and refused to invite her to Iceland, she would not be in danger. "Go," he grated between clenched teeth. "Ride Gleda back to the resort."

She framed his face in her hands. "I won't leave you like this."

"Get away from me. I don't need a human's help." He infused his voice with savage contempt to make her leave.

Her hands dropped away from his face, her expression uncertain. But she'd missed her chance. Huginn scampered up and pinned her wrists behind her back.

"Flipping heck, not you again." She struggled but was no match for the wiry strength of the raven-men. Vidar longed to reach out to help her, but his abused muscles wouldn't obey.

Muninn snatched up the ring intended for Sonja that Vidar had dropped and pushed it onto her finger. Vidar closed his eyes, and his head fell forward. Now Sonja would be trapped in Iceland forever.

Chapter Five

Once the gold ring was on her finger, Odin beckoned his two creepy henchmen back to him and left through a door in the wall behind his throne. The two massive wolves trotted out at his heels, leaving Sonja and Vidar alone in the huge echoing ice chamber.

Vidar remained on his knees, head bowed, breath ragged. His naturally tanned skin had lost its usual golden hue. He looked pale, defeated.

Tugging the fur coat tighter around her body, Sonja crouched before him, trying to control her chattering teeth long enough to speak. "Can you get up?"

His gaze rose to her face. "Why didn't you escape?"

All her life Vidar's loving presence in her mind had given her the strength to cope when times were tough. How could he believe she would run away and leave him now that he was in trouble?

She reached for his limp hand and pressed it against her cheek. "We can both go now."

With her support, Vidar scrambled to his feet and they headed to the door. The two female warriors standing guard eyed them as they passed through the entrance hall, but made no move to stop them leaving.

Sonja clutched Vidar's arm, her feet frozen in nothing but the pink fluffy socks she'd worn to bed. "Will you take me back to the resort? I can still make my flight if I hurry." She didn't want to be parted from Vidar if he really was her guardian angel. She had always loved her angel so that meant she loved Vidar, but this whole situation was too weird. She needed time to get her head around it.

Vidar stopped at the door. His breath heaved in and out on a sigh. "Now you wear Odin's ring. You're trapped here."

She stared at the ring on the third finger of her left hand and frowned. The band had been loose when Odin's lackeys put it on her. She tugged but it wouldn't budge. "Don't tell me this is supposed to be a wedding ring." The sting of bile burned the back of her throat.

Vidar laughed, bitterly. "More like a manacle. It ties you to Iceland."

"How? It's a ring." But even as the words left her mouth, she conceded it was no ordinary ring. She'd watched in disbelief while Odin's ring spawned the band that now hugged her finger like a leech.

"We'll talk when we get back to the resort."

They exited into the swirling snowstorm. "Gleda," Vidar called. His huge snow cat approached out of the whiteness.

Vidar swept Sonja into his arms, deposited her on the cat's back, and then climbed up behind her. "Hang on tight." He reached an arm on either side of her to grasp handfuls of the cat's mane; then he shouted a command against the wind.

The cat trotted to the edge of the ice platform and jumped into the abyss. Sonja hung on to the beast's fur for dear life as her stomach somersaulted. She clamped her thighs against the creature's sides until her muscles ached. The bite of the wind stole her breath, so she closed her eyes and buried her face in the cat's fur, praying they reached the ground in one piece.

Wind whistled past her ears, whipping at her hair. Just as she wondered if they would ever stop falling, the cat jolted beneath her. Powerful muscles flexed as the creature bounded along a trail between the pine trees surrounding the resort. Lights sparkled in the distance, and she heard the reassuring sound of corny Christmas tunes.

The creature halted just inside the tree line, its sides heaving. Vidar jumped off and pulled her into his arms. Sonja rested her head against his shoulder, suddenly exhausted, her body ready to shut down after the traumatic night. The security guard opened the small gate for Vidar with a friendly greeting as if it were normal for him to arrive out of the forest in the early hours of the morning carrying a woman in her pajamas.

Once they were inside her cabin, Sonja went to the bathroom to clean up, then changed into dry clothes and wrapped herself in the bed quilt. Now that the ordeal was over, she had started to wonder if she'd been confused about Vidar and her guardian angel being one and the same. If he'd had a mental link with her all her life, surely he'd have mentioned it by now. The whole idea sounded crazy when she tried to put it into words.

Vidar put on his coat and turned up the heat to its maximum. "I hate the damn cold," he said, rubbing his hands together.

"Then why run a theme park in Iceland?"

Leaning back in his chair, he gave her a weary smile. "My father's such a sweet old guy; I can't bear to leave him."

She snorted and pressed the quilt over her mouth. He held up a hand and flashed the ring on his little finger.

A chill swept through her that had nothing to do with temperature. "You said something about it being a manacle, but a ring can't stop *you* leaving."

Even as her comment fell into the silence, she realized how foolish her incredulity sounded when she'd just been rescued from an ice palace in the sky and ridden a flying cat. She fingered the ring on her own hand and nervously said, "Okay, explain."

"My father's ring's called Draupnir, a magical artifact forged by dwarves thousands of years ago. You saw how the ring multiplies. Through the parent ring he controls anyone who wears one of the others."

"Why did he make you wear one? Surely he trusts his own son."

"He trusted me just fine until I defied him and did something to help Troy."

"But to make you stay here against your will is primitive!"

"Primitive's his middle name, Sonja. Words like freedom and democracy aren't in his vocabulary."

"Have you tried to leave?"

He cast her a what-do-you-think glance.

"Don't you have any power to fight back?"

"Only what I inherited from my mother. She was queen of the Folletti—they're a type of Italian fairy." Vidar spread his hand, and a small golden flame flared from his palm.

Sonja's heart rate shot from calm to manic in a second. "How . . . ? Is that real fire?"

"I'm a fire elemental, but my power's pathetic. Did you see Ciar, the Irish fairy queen who was with your father?" He whistled through his teeth. "She's a walking furnace. Even Odin gives her a wide berth. She's the reason your father escaped . . ." His words trailed away and he stared down at his hands.

"The reason my father escaped what?"

"That was a long time ago, Sonja. No need to rake up the past."

She wanted to know more about the feud between their families, but not as much as she wanted to get out of Iceland

and leave all the madness behind. She checked her watch before rising to her feet. Her cab was due any minute. She packed the last few things in her overnight bag, slipped on her coat, and zipped up her boots.

Vidar frowned. "What're you doing?"

"Leaving."

"Didn't you understand what I said about the ring?"

Sonja glanced at the gold band gleaming on her finger. She'd soaped her hand and tried to pull the ring off when they arrived, but all she'd done was aggravate her chapped skin.

Tears gathered in her eyes, and she blinked them away. She felt raw and vulnerable at the thought of leaving Vidar and losing any chance of seeing her father again. But her father had already made it clear he didn't want to see her, and Vidar had wanted her to leave before this last incident. How could she stay here? "What am I supposed to do, spend the rest of my life in a cabin at a theme park?" Living with her aunt wasn't much fun, but everything she knew was in London.

Vidar stood and rested a hand on her shoulder. "Odin won't let you leave, Sonja."

"He doesn't want you to leave because you're his son. That doesn't mean he'll stop me from leaving." She tried to blank out what Odin had said about keeping her as insurance.

"He'll hurt you if you try to leave."

She clutched her hairbrush to her chest. The scary things that had happened over the last few hours felt surreal now. A stupid ring couldn't possibly stop her from leaving Iceland.

A knock on the door banished her doubts. She jammed her hairbrush in her bag before zipping it up.

"Sonja . . ." Vidar pulled her into his arms and pressed his lips to her temple. He leaned back and stroked the long strands of hair away from her face. "If I hadn't written to

Una, you'd still be safe in London. But then I would never have met you."

A terrible thought hit her. "What does my aunt have to do with this?"

His hands dropped from her face, and he turned away. "Don't go there, Sonja."

Fine. Una's obsession with fitness and martial arts started to make sense if she was muddled up with Vidar's world. She'd get answers from Una when she arrived home. A shuttle cart collected them from the cabin and took them to meet the cab waiting at the main building. Vidar opened the door for her, then circled the car and joined her in the back.

"You don't have to come—"

"Yes. I do."

On the drive to Keflavik Airport, she stared out the side window, unsuccessfully trying to ignore the gold ring pinching her finger. "Vidar . . . what does it feel like . . . when the ring constrains you?"

He stared at her, his jaw clenched, his golden eyes gleaming as if lit from within. She wondered if that was his fiery nature showing. "It feels as if your joints are ripping apart and your muscles stretching to tearing point. It's said the old dwarves captured the screams of prisoners tortured on the rack and added that to the gold."

Nausea burned her throat and she pressed a hand over her mouth. She refused to believe a ring could do such a horrible thing, especially to her. She would leave.

"I'll stay with you until you board the plane. If you feel even a hint of pain, come straight back."

"You don't think I'll get away, do you?"

He gripped her hand so tightly it hurt. "Don't go. Come back to my place, *elskan mín*."

Her guardian angel's presence caressed her mind, loving

and persuasive. She closed her eyes, sinking into the feeling. She had loved the angel in her head for as long as she could remember. Now the sensation had subtly changed to include a zing of sexual awareness, and she was finally certain the feeling came from Vidar. But why hadn't he spoken to her about the connection? Didn't he want her to know? She had so many questions. She didn't want to leave him, but she wouldn't confine herself to Iceland like an animal pacing an imaginary fence too frightened to step outside. "I know you've got the resort to think about and that's obviously a huge consideration, but if I get out, will you try to follow? I've only just found you. I don't want to lose you."

Vidar flopped back against the seat and shook his head. "Believe me, I'd leave the resort in a heartbeat if I thought I could be free of my father. I'd have no trouble selling the place. But I told you, I've tried to leave and I can't. There's no hope for me."

The international airport was busy with tourists arriving for Christmas, many of them with red and white stickers on their bags proclaiming LIVE YOUR DREAMS THIS CHRISTMAS. Sonja saw one of the resort buttons on the ground with the same slogan. She kicked it out of her way, but Vidar bent to retrieve it and dropped it in his pocket. Vidar accompanied her in silence as she checked in and headed to security. She expected him to say good-bye at the security point, but he breezed through with nothing more than a few words to one of the officers.

"How did you do that?" she whispered when she caught up with him by a cafe.

"Glamour. I made them think that I'm dressed in a security uniform."

"You're wearing your fur."

"You see through my glamour. We have an . . . an affinity."

Why had he waited until she was about to leave to mention their link? Sonja wound her bag strap around her fingers. "I know we have an affinity. I sense you in my mind." She glanced up to gauge his reaction.

He gave her an arrested glance. "I've always tried to be subtle, so you don't notice."

"Oh, I noticed. I feel as if I've been linked with you on some level my whole life."

"Sonja, *ástin mín*." Vidar halted, ignoring the people walking past them, and pulled her close. He curved a hand around her cheek. "I pledged to protect you when you were a baby, and I'll always be there for you when you need me, even if we never meet again."

Tears filled her eyes. His sadness whispered through her and suddenly she wasn't sure she wanted to leave. Her job and the few possessions she had in London didn't matter. What mattered was people. The only person she had in London was an aunt who'd never cared much for her—and she'd even started to wonder if Una really was her aunt.

She gripped the front of his coat. "Vidar . . ." She closed her eyes and pressed her face against his neck. Vidar had always been the most important person in her life, even when she had only known him as the guardian angel in her mind. But what would Odin do to her if she stayed?

Vidar kissed her hair, pressed his lips to her ear. "Although I want you to stay, if you are able to leave, you must go. Be free of my father."

The announcer called her flight. Desperation tore through Sonja. She didn't want to leave Vidar but she didn't want to stay either. This was so unfair.

"Sonja." Vidar eased her away from him. "Time to go." He kissed her hard, and she kissed him back, angry with fate for letting her find her angel while making it impossible for her to stay with him. She infused the kiss with all the love and churning emotions in her heart to show him what she couldn't put into words. He pulled away. "Remember: any pain and you come back to me."

Her heart thudded as she lined up to present her boarding pass. She did a mental audit of the health of her body. Apart from the hollow ache in her chest, she felt no discomfort. She glanced back at Vidar when she passed through the gate.

He shouted, "I'll be right here."

Sonja's breath faltered as she followed the line through the boarding tunnel. She felt light-headed and part of her longed for pain, for any reason to stop her boarding. When she reached the plane door, an air steward smiled at her and checked her boarding pass, directing her to her seat. Then she stepped over the threshold.

A burning shaft of agony ran up her arm, arrowed along her limbs, burrowed into her chest and belly. The bag dropped from her fingers and she stumbled, collapsed. Someone shouted. Hands gripped beneath her arms. The heels of her boots bumped over the metal threshold as she was pulled back into the tunnel.

The reassuring sense of Vidar's presence flooded her mind, blocked the pain. Strong arms surrounded her; then everything went blissfully dark.

Chapter Six

Sonja woke on a bed snuggled beneath a heavy quilt. Her head pounded and her body ached as if she'd been used as a punching bag. A rustle of sound caught her attention. She turned over warily and opened an eye. A log fire crackled, casting dancing patterns of light over a forest green sofa and honey-colored wood.

Where was she? She tracked back in her mind and remembered boarding the plane. Her breath hissed in as an echo of pain flashed through her. The ring *had* trapped her in Iceland. A gamut of emotions followed the realization: anger at Odin for daring to confine her, fear over what would happen to her now, but also relief that she had an excuse to stay with Vidar.

The sound of footsteps heralded Vidar's approach from a small kitchen in the far corner of the log cabin. "You're back in the land of the living." He smiled down at her and placed a steaming mug on the nightstand before hunkering down beside the bed. "Hot chocolate with a nip of something to revive you."

He bent his head, his dark bangs flopping over his face, and pressed a kiss on the back of her hand. Her breath rushed in, carrying the hot, spicy smell of Vidar mixed with the sweetness of chocolate.

"How long have I been unconscious?"

"Long enough for me to lug you back to my retreat and put you to bed."

Her eyes opened a little wider when she realized she must be in his bed.

While Vidar fetched his own mug from the kitchen, Sonja sat and pulled her knees up to her chest. She tried to smooth the creases from her black tailored pants but gave up and drowned her sorrows in a blissful chocolate mouthful with a kick of alcohol. She held off reality for half a cup of hot chocolate, then the strangeness of her situation swamped her, and she returned her mug to the nightstand unfinished.

She spread her fingers, gazing at Odin's ring. "How can I get it off?"

Vidar sat beside her and gently wrapped his hand around hers. "Forget the ring. There's nothing you can do about it. My brother Baldur cut off his own finger to rid himself of the ring but it just appeared on one of his other fingers."

Sonja shivered.

Vidar drew her hand toward him and kissed her knuckles. "Stay here with me, *elskan mín*."

She stared around the tiny wooden lodge. The place was toasty and snug but little more than one room. Inside her head she'd sensed Vidar all her life, but moving in with him when they'd only known each other for a couple of days was crazy. Yet where else could she go? "I'll be in your way."

With a wry laugh, he cozied up to her. "No . . . you won't." His hand settled at her waist, and he eased her around to face him. "We've been together in mind and spirit for a long time. Our connection is strong."

He leaned his forehead against hers. Her eyelids fell as the familiar comforting sense of him swept through her, calming her fears and smoothing her worries. His lips brushed her forehead.

"There're things I need to explain, Sonja. Things you have a right to know."

Vidar rose, and she immediately missed his touch. He fetched a small cream silk bag from a shelf before returning to the bed. After unfastening the drawstring, he upended the bag over his palm. Three linked blue crystal rings dropped out—similar in shape to a Celtic knot.

"This is your Magic Knot."

He rubbed a finger wistfully across the rings then placed them in her hand. A shimmer of awareness spread across Sonja's skin before stirring through her. The air around her subtly shifted, and she felt she could reach out and touch the layers of light and warmth. She held up the strange jewelry. Flickers of firelight danced within the crystalline structure as if the rings themselves contained fire.

"The three rings of your Magic Knot hold the essence of your mind, body, and spirit," Vidar said. "Keep them safe."

Sonja turned confused blue eyes on him, and Vidar's heart went out to her. Why hadn't he refused when his father demanded he involve her in the feud with her father? She didn't deserve to be tangled up in the conflict. But even as the thought passed through his mind, a selfish part of him admitted that he wanted her here.

He shifted closer to her and brushed his fingertips around her palm, circling the three crystal rings. The urge to touch her rode him like the need to breathe.

"Is the Magic Knot really magic?" she asked.

"I suppose it sounds like it to you, but it's simply a part of life. Humans have them as well, but they've internalized them."

Tiny lines appeared between her eyebrows, and his fingers itched to stroke them away.

"You're saying I'm not human?"

Vidar almost laughed. "Sonya, *ástin mín*, you've met your father."

She wrinkled her nose. "Point taken."

"I'm not human either." He gave into temptation and smoothed the pad of his thumb over her cheek.

"So if these stones really are part of me, why did *you* have them?"

"It's complicated." Vidar rubbed a hand back and forth over her quilt-covered legs, soothing. Explaining what had happened to her when she was a baby without freaking her out was going to be difficult, if not impossible. She had coped with so many revelations in the last few days; he didn't want to shatter her perception of herself any further. Yet he owed her the truth.

He was damned if he told her, damned if he didn't.

He rose and went to stare out of the small diamond-shaped panes of glass in his door. On the icy terrace outside, Gleda lay curled in a tight furry ball against the blast of snow-laden wind sweeping up the ravine. This lonely life he'd tolerated for so long would be transformed if Sonja stayed.

She came to stand beside him and squinted out through the window. "Where are we?"

"In the uninhabited interior of the country, where nobody can find us. I have an apartment at the resort, but this is where I retreat for privacy."

For long minutes she stared outside, gnawing her lip. He gave in to the need to touch her again and smoothed his palm in comforting circles on her slender back. The touch seemed to rouse her, and she turned to him. "Tell me the full story about this feud between our families, Vidar. I need to understand."

Should he tell her the whole truth and watch her world

crumble around her? Or should he lie and protect her feelings—and his own? He sucked in a breath. "Go and sit by the fire."

He followed her to the sofa and sat beside her. He sent calming thoughts along their mental link, wrapped her in his strength so she could cope with his revelations.

"Our families had a falling out."

With a frustrated breath Sonja said, "Don't talk to me as though I'm a child."

Vidar fought against his instinct to protect her. "Okay, here's the short version—Troy's father killed my brother."

Sonja pressed a hand to her mouth. "My god. I'm sorry. When?"

"A long time ago." He couldn't bring himself to reveal just how long, or he'd have to explain about the Crystal Crib.

Sonja stared at him in silent horror for a few moments, then blinked as if waking up. "That doesn't excuse the way Odin's treated me."

"Odin believes the sins of the fathers shall be visited on the children and grandchildren. He took revenge on Troy's father, Loki. He also killed one of Troy's brothers and condemned the other to spend the rest of his life in wolf form."

Sonja's eyes widened. "Wolf form?"

"Fenrir is a wolf shape-shifter. Odin trapped him in his animal form, so it wasn't as strange as it sounds."

Sonja flashed him an incredulous look that said his explanation was every bit as strange as it sounded. "What about my father?"

"Troy escaped with his life, but Odin took you and your mother away from him." A memory he'd buried long ago crept into his mind: Troy as a young man before he came into his power, kneeling at Odin's feet, begging him to return his wife and baby daughter. Vidar clamped down on the swell of anger the memory roused. Because he'd helped Troy and his family, Odin had punished his disloyalty with the curse of the slave ring.

"What happened to my mother?" Sonja asked, her voice barely a whisper.

Vidar shook his head. "She's gone, Sonja." He had never discovered what happened to Troy's wife, but she was human and surely long dead.

Sonja looked down and rubbed distractedly at the creases in her trousers. Despite her calm appearance, Vidar sensed her churning emotions. Instinctively, he encircled her with his arms and eased her against his chest, offering physical comfort as naturally as he'd always soothed her mind.

"I survived," she whispered.

He smoothed his hand down her silky blonde hair again and again, as if he could wipe away her pain and confusion. "Yes, you did, *ástin mín*."

"So why didn't I live with my father?"

His heart contracted at the tremor in her voice. "Your father loves you, Sonja. He would fall on his own sword if he thought it would protect you." No lie. He'd watched Troy sacrifice his life for his child—only to discover that he couldn't die.

"Really?" She raised uncertain eyes to him and he realized, with a crushing sense of sorrow, that she'd grown up without anyone to love her.

Except him.

The child he'd comforted and protected out of a sense of duty had grown into a woman. Along the way, his concern for her well-being had grown into love, a miracle for him in the dark cold land where he'd been bound against his will for centuries. But the pleasure only lasted a moment. It was his fault that Sonja was now condemned to live that same life.

He held her tightly, realizing he must tell her the complete truth of her past. Just not yet.

"So, how did you end up with my Magic Knot thingy?"

The trouble with telling half-truths was that the gaps had to be cemented with lies. "I wanted a way to check that you were safe, so I took your Magic Knot and formed a bond with you. That meant I could be with you in mind and spirit wherever you were."

As her questioning blue gaze met his, he realized exactly what he'd revealed.

"We're bonded in some way?"

"Yes, *ástin mín*." And the bond of mind and spirit no longer satisfied him. His body yearned to make their link physical. He decided he would complete it by giving her his own Magic Knot.

But first, he would make love to her.

Chapter Seven

Vidar's golden eyes flared with desire, his face a taut mask of control. Sonja's heart tripped and raced. She splayed her hand on his chest, felt the flex of his muscles and the thud of his heart, while his hunger for her caressed her mind. She'd lived with this man in her head and her heart for as long as she could remember. Being with him now felt like the most natural thing in the world.

He lowered his mouth to hers and slowly brushed her lips with his own. Yet, even as he kissed her, she sensed doubt reining back his need.

Gripping his shoulders, she said, "This *is* what I want, Vidar." From the moment he'd touched her Magic Knot and become her *guardian angel*, there could be no other man for her.

He curved a hand around her cheek. "Part of me feels this is wrong." He frowned and squeezed his eyes closed. "I pledged to myself I would protect you. Not take advantage of you."

She touched a fingertip to his full bottom lip and trailed her finger from one corner of his mouth to the other. "Then let me take advantage of you."

Nibbling at his lips, she relaxed under the enervating wash of pleasure as he responded. She knew exactly how to make Vidar forget his reservations. Her hand skimmed down his chest, and she dragged her fingernails lightly across his belly just above his belt. He gave a needy little grunt and gripped the back of her head to deepen the kiss.

While they kissed, her fingers worked loose the buttons on his shirt. The smooth, warm skin that met her palms sent streamers of heat through her. She traced the sculpted ridges and hollows of muscle and bone, memorizing his body, eager to see him as well as touch him. With a little gasp, she broke the kiss and shoved his shirt off his shoulders. Feathering her lips across his chest, she breathed the intoxicating scent of him.

Her hands fell to his belt, but he stilled her fingers with the flat of his palm. "Sonja . . ." Amusement edged Vidar's velvet drawl. "Slowly, love. Slowly." Glancing down at his bare chest, he smiled. "You have me half naked and you haven't even taken off a sock."

Vidar stood, bringing her to her feet with him before freeing her of her jacket. As soon as her arms were out of the sleeves, her hands returned to him, cruising up and down the sinewy strength of his forearms. She wanted him naked on the bed, yet he was maddeningly slow, taking his time as he unfastened the top button of her cream silk shirt. He trailed his fingers across the sensitive skin he revealed, sending an electrifying shiver through her.

"You're teasing me," she accused.

He laughed, his eyes sparkling. For the first time since she'd met him, he looked truly happy. "It's called foreplay. I thought women liked to take things slowly."

She pouted in mock offense, enjoying the game.

"What do you want me to do? Rip off your clothes and throw you down on the rug in front of the fire?"

"That might work."

"Don't tempt me." Curling an arm around her waist, he jerked her flush against his body. A sigh of satisfaction escaped her before she wrapped her arms about his neck. Their lips met in a hard, hungry kiss. She speared her fingers through his hair, moved against him, drowned in the sensation of his mouth. She didn't notice his wandering hands had unfastened everything until he eased back to pull her shirt over her head and she lost her bra as well.

Excitement thrummed between them as his hot gaze traveled over her. "Sacred elf-fire, Sonja, I knew you'd be beautiful, but . . ." He swallowed hard. "Change of plan, we'll take things slowly next time."

He swept her into his arms. Raining feverish kisses over her face and neck, he carried her to his bed, deposited her gently on the mattress, kicked off his shoes, and came down beside her with a grunt of satisfaction. The heat of his mouth caressed a sensitive spot at the base of her throat. Unbearable need rolled through Sonja. He strung a row of kisses around her breasts. She grabbed handfuls of his glossy black hair and urged him on. His mouth explored her skin, driving her mad with wanting as he circled first one nipple then the other with the tip of his tongue. Then the wet heat of his mouth closed around her breast and she stopped thinking altogether.

Somewhere in the very back of Vidar's mind, the voice of his conscience told him he should set everything straight with Sonja before he made love to her. But he was long past the point of talking, almost past the point of thinking.

Tasting the silky softness of her skin, he ran his tongue over her nipples, kissed his way down the gentle rounding of her belly. He eased her trousers down her legs, rewarding each newly exposed inch of skin with a kiss. Then he paused to marvel at the beauty of the woman on his bed—his fantasy come true. The golden halo of her hair spread out on the pillow, while her eyes burned for him like blue flames. With her long slender limbs and full breasts, she was both beautiful seductress and innocent maiden, firing his desire and making him want to take things slowly at the same time.

He didn't deserve her. Yet he couldn't stop. He moved up the bed, sprawling half across her body to claim her mouth in a searing kiss. Her seeking hands went to his belt. She pressed her palm over his erection, stroked him through the fabric.

His breath hissed out. Fire blazed in every cell of his body. If he didn't find release soon, he would combust. He reared back, bracing his upper body on his arms. "Yes. Go on."

She held his gaze for a second before her eager fingers worked his belt loose and unfastened his trousers. Her hand enclosed him. The tentative touch sent an explosion of desire racing through his body. He jumped back off the bed and stepped out of his trousers.

She watched him from beneath her lashes, the tip of her tongue playing at the corner of her mouth. Did she do that on purpose to drive him wild? He leaned down and pressed his lips to her belly, breathing in her female fragrance. A moan of desire escaped her, and she flexed beneath him, parting her legs.

"Sacred elf-fire, Sonja."

Vidar gripped her feet, pushed her knees back against her belly, and positioned himself between her thighs. With one hard thrust, he entered her. Her eyes widened at the suddenness of his move, and her surprise flashed along their mental link.

What was he doing? Trying to shock her, make her push him away?

"Sorry." He withdrew, sat back on his heels, and screwed closed his eyes, trying to understand why he was sabotaging his chance for happiness.

The bed shifted as she moved. "Vidar . . ." Fingers trailed along his jaw, over his lips. He opened his eyes. The deep, almost luminous blue of her gaze trapped him, her breath a sweet whisper across his face. She gave him a naughty grin. "If you stop now, I'll have to tie you to the bed and take you by force."

She lay back, arranged herself sensually on the bed, and beckoned him. His doubts burned away in a rush of electrifying eroticism. He followed her down, catching his weight on his elbows. He curled a lock of golden hair around his finger and stroked it across her lips.

Sonja smiled, and a place inside him that had been hollow was suddenly filled with warmth. He might not deserve to love her, but he did.

She looped her arms around his neck and pulled his head down. The feverish intensity of her kisses wiped all thought from his mind. Her legs wrapped around him. This time he entered her slowly. Instinct took over. He opened himself to her completely, flowed into her mind, tasted the essence of her spirit. A frisson of unbearable pleasure expanded between them, joining them in the ecstasy of mind, body, and spirit.

"Sonja, *ástin mín*." She was his, so perfectly his.

Her breath came in fractured little gasps. She dug her fingernails into his back, clutched him tight, and he never wanted her to let him go. Her pleasure rose, swirling around him, and he sensed her air elemental nature more clearly than ever before. His fire responded: flared in a scorching burst of sensation that seared along his nerves with almost painful intensity. When it was over, he sagged against her, his face pressed into the sweet curve of her neck.

In the wake of the pleasure, painful realization hit him so hard it brought tears to his eyes. He'd confined Sonja to the

Crystal Crib without any idea what he'd given up to appease his father's anger. He'd lost years of loving her to satisfy one cantankerous old man's need for revenge. Never again would he ignore his conscience.

Sonja's fingertips traced circles on his back while his awareness of the room returned. He eased his weight up onto his elbows so he didn't crush her and touched her cheek. "I want to give you my Magic Knot. Bond completely," he said.

"Yes." She smiled, so sweet and full of love.

But would she still look at him like that when she knew about the Crystal Crib?

Sonja curled against Vidar and dozed for a little while, but she was so conscious of the hard muscular length of his body pressed against her that she couldn't settle. She wanted more of him.

Opening her eyes, she watched him sleep. His sooty lashes lay in dark crescents against his lean bronzed cheeks. Her throat tightened with love to see him looking so peaceful, even while her body quivered at the prospect of making love with him again. She slid down the bed and rained tiny kisses across his chest, gradually working her way over the taut muscles of his abdomen and lower.

He woke with a gasp and pushed up on an elbow. "Sonja, love . . ." He blinked at her as she dropped a kiss on his hip. "We need to talk."

"Not more talk." She wrinkled her nose. She was well aware they had issues to discuss, like where she would live and how she'd earn a living, but that could wait until later. She ran a teasing finger over his belly and thighs. Already things were starting to perk up down there. She grinned at him, excitement tingling through her. For the first time in her life she could do what she wanted without her aunt watching her every move. How ironic that Odin's ring had confined her, yet set her free to be with Vidar.

She straddled his thighs and smoothed her palms up his body until she lay on top of him. Then she wiggled her hips and his breath shuddered out. His hands settled at her waist and she rubbed her lips across his, teasing him with the tip of her tongue. Although he kissed her back, she sensed reluctance. A tiny chill took the edge off the heat in her belly.

Breaking the kiss, she rested her head on his shoulder, suddenly uncertain. The first time they'd made love had been wonderful for her, but perhaps she'd overestimated his enthusiasm. She kissed his neck and stroked tiny circles on his chest. Perhaps he was just tired.

"Sonja." Vidar rolled over, depositing her on the bed beside him. He propped his head on a hand. "We need to discuss the past and how it affects us."

Goose bumps rushed across her skin, so she pulled the quilt over herself. He must mean about the disagreement between their families. "I'm sorry my grandfather killed your brother, but that doesn't have to be a problem for us, does it?"

Vidar rubbed a hand over his face and wouldn't meet her gaze. The tiny chill inside her hardened to a ball of ice.

"Vidar, you're scaring me."

"I'm sorry. I don't want you to worry . . . but you have to know something. You weren't born twenty-six years ago, Sonja. You were born a lot earlier than that."

"What?" She squinted at him in the firelight. "You're not making any sense."

"Two thousand years earlier, to be precise."

"Yeah, right." The tension in her gut released. She laughed, expecting him to smile. He didn't.

Silence stretched between them until her ears hummed. He was freaking serious.

"That's crazy! There were cars and planes and stuff when I was little."

Yet, why was she trying to counter such a ridiculous claim?

Vidar sighed as if what he was about to say ripped at his soul. He climbed off the bed and pulled on his pants before joining her again. Resting his back against the headboard, he leaned his forearms on his raised knees and said, "There's no easy way to explain this, so I'm just going to say it. Everything I told you about the past was true, but I left out a couple of things. Troy's father killed my brother two thousand years ago. That was before Troy developed his power. Odin wanted to kill you and your mother along with Troy as part of his revenge. I managed to persuade him not to kill you. Instead, I had you frozen in a Crystal Crib by a frost fairy."

Sonja's gaze riveted to Vidar's face. How could the man she'd made love with be so old? She'd thought he was maybe thirty-five. That would have made him nine when she was born and explain how he'd been old enough to take her Magic Knot to keep tabs on her. But . . . two thousand? She couldn't even comprehend living that long.

"Did you hear me, Sonja?"

"I don't believe you're two thousand years old."

He closed his eyes and pinched the bridge of his nose. "We're talking about what happened to you." He reached for her hand and squeezed it while he repeated what he'd said. This time the words hit home.

"I was frozen. Like cryogenics?"

"I suppose the crib must have worked in a similar way."

She heard his words. But that's all his explanation was:

just words. "I don't remember anything before I went to kindergarten . . ." She curled her fingers into the quilt. "What happened to my mother?"

"She ran away and we never found her. But she was human, Sonja." Vidar's grip tightened on her fingers. "She must be long dead."

Sonja's gaze lost focus. She tried to imagine her mother living out her life without her husband and daughter. "Didn't my father try to find her?"

"I'm certain he did. Troy had little power then, but he's always been determined."

"And you had me frozen?" She glanced up at him, and he held her gaze, his golden eyes anguished.

"I'm sorry, Sonja."

She pulled the quilt off the bed, wrapped it around her shoulders, then stood staring at nothing.

"Are you all right, *elskan mín?*"

"Stop calling me that," she snapped. "What does it even mean?"

"Sweetheart," he whispered, gruffly.

Her anger vanished as quickly as it had flared. She wanted to make sense of everything, but her brain refused to work. She wandered around the end of the bed and plopped down on the sofa in front of the fire. She was two thousand years old, and Vidar had frozen her in a Crystal Crib.

He crouched beside her. "I grabbed your Magic Knot when Odin would have crushed it and killed you by breaking the link between your body, mind, and spirit. That's why I touched it."

So, he hadn't even intended to bond himself to her.

"If you hadn't frozen me, I'd have lived and died centuries ago like my mother . . ."

"Perhaps," he allowed.

Her gaze left the flames and sought his face. "What's that supposed to mean?"

"Your father's known as Troy the Deathless. If you've taken after him, there's a strong possibility you can't die."

Chapter Eight

Vidar persuaded Sonja to return to bed with him and try to sleep, claiming she would feel better in the morning. He fell asleep quickly. But even snuggled in his arms she couldn't settle. She wriggled out from under his arm, then pressed a kiss to his shoulder before climbing out of bed.

Her restless mind turned over what Vidar had told her. She rationalized that as she'd been in stasis during the years she'd spent in the crib, she was really only twenty-six. But she couldn't get her head around the fact that Vidar had lived in Iceland, trapped by Odin's ring, for two thousand years. And then there was Vidar's comment about her never dying.

Sonja pulled on her clothes and went to the small kitchen to fix herself some hot milk. She was pouring it into a mug when a subtle shift in the atmosphere sent prickles racing up her spine. Now that she had her Magic Knot, she sensed the air around her like water, and it had just been disturbed. She gripped the handle of the milk pan tightly to use as a weapon, sucked in a breath, and turned.

She'd expected to see one of Odin's sneaky henchmen. Air rushed out of her lungs in relief to find her father standing at the entrance to the galley kitchen. His skin glowed pearly white in the semidarkness. His black jacket accentuated the pristine white lace at his throat and his golden hair. The only spot of color in his black and white ensemble was a huge rainbow-hued gem on the gold spike holding up his hair.

"Sonja, my child." His words whispered around her, quieting her surge of fear.

"I didn't think you wanted to see me again," she said.

"I harbored the futile hope that my disinterest would keep you safe." He stepped forward and his strong fingers brushed the slave ring on her hand. "I was wrong. If we're to fight back, you have much to learn."

Vidar stirred in the bed on the far side of the room. Troy's head turned at the noise. "I need time with you alone," he said, walking across the room. He threw a bubble of light over the bed, obscuring Vidar.

"Don't hurt him!" Sonja hurried across to Vidar, a knot of anxiety tightening in her chest.

"My light shield simply gives us privacy. No harm will come to him."

Troy gestured her closer. She hesitated before moving toward him. Her father took her hand and stepped behind her, holding her close to his body.

"What're you doing?"

"Relax," he said, his silky tone draining her tension. "Time for your first lesson in survival."

The room disappeared, and a startled gasp burst from Sonja's lips. For an instant she was in limbo; then her feet touched the floor and the room reappeared—except they were now by the door facing the sofa.

"Flipping heck. What just happened?"

He smiled sadly, stroking wisps of hair behind her ear with gentle fingers. "I should have been there to teach you this when you were young. I persuaded Odin to release you from the Crystal Crib twenty-six years ago, but I thought you'd be safer from the dangers of my world if I stayed out of your life and you were raised as human. I was wrong."

Sudden overwhelming sadness flooded Sonja at the thought of what her lonely younger self had missed. Her father pulled her into his embrace. She closed her eyes and pressed her face against his chest. With his heart beating beneath her ear, and his firm, comforting hands on her back, she could almost ignore the lace tickling her forehead and imagine he was a normal father.

"How did we transport across the room," she asked softly.

"We call it walking unseen. Only air elementals like us have the power. I'll help you master the skill."

She looked up into the intense blue of his eyes. "Do I take after you in other ways?"

He kissed her forehead. "One step at a time. First we must solve your immediate problem." He raised her left hand so Odin's ring caught the light. "Have you suffered any ill effects from this abomination?"

Briefly she explained her unsuccessful attempt to fly out of Iceland, watched her father's face tighten into a mask of fury. "Odin has pushed me too far this time. Dress warmly. We're going to persuade Odin to take back his ring." The repressed violence in his tone made her tremble.

Returning to Valhalla was right at the bottom of her to-do list, but if her father could persuade Odin to remove her ring, perhaps he could help Vidar as well. Sonja pulled out of her father's arms and turned to wake him.

"No." Her father's hand landed on her shoulder.

"Can't you help him get rid of *his* ring?"

"If Vidar stands with us, Odin will probably kill him."

A crash and a blast of frigid air dragged Vidar from sleep. He opened his eyes to see Gleda standing in the doorway of his cabin, nose in the air. His snow cat only ever burst inside when she sensed trouble.

Warily pulling back the bedcovers, Vidar glanced over his shoulder to check on Sonja. She was gone.

"Sonja!"

He leaped out of bed and scanned the room. Her bag gaped open. The pantsuit and boots she'd been wearing were nowhere to be seen, and his fur coat had disappeared.

He strode into the kitchen and wrapped a hand around the mug of milk he found there. Still warm; she hadn't been gone long. Vidar grabbed his spare fur out of the chest at the foot of his bed, shrugged it on, and followed Gleda to the icy ledge outside his retreat.

Wind whipped up the ravine, nearly blinding him. The pearly gray sky indicated that it was morning. Squinting, he scanned the steep white hill that angled up above the building. Only Gleda's paw marks disturbed the pristine snow. Someone must have taken Sonja away, because she couldn't have left on her own.

Gleda raised her nose to the air in the direction of Valhalla and roared, the sound echoing along the valley. The chill seeped into Vidar's bones. Only Troy or Odin would take Sonja from his cabin. Either way, she was likely in danger.

Entering his cabin, Vidar dressed, strapped on his sword, jammed his feet into boots, and donned his fur. Then he returned to Gleda, who'd kept vigil outside, her golden gaze fixed on some distant point.

Vidar climbed on her back and leaned forward to speak into her ear. "Good girl, Gleda. Find Sonja."

The snow cat tensed her muscles and leaped off the ledge. Gripping her mane, Vidar silently prayed that Sonja was anywhere but Valhalla. When the glittering icy peaks of the palace appeared out of the murky sky, his heart plunged.

He had saved Sonja's life once before, but at a terrible cost to her. This time he would not compromise. He would not allow any harm to come to her. The day had come for him to stand against his father. Unfortunately, he doubted he would survive.

Sonja and Troy materialized in the entrance hall outside Odin's throne room after walking unseen from Vidar's retreat. Troy wriggled his fingers out of the death grip Sonja had on his hand. "Breathe, my child."

She gasped in a breath, her lungs aching. It would take her a long time to get used to the strange nothingness as her body faded into the air. During their journey, she'd smelled the cold clean scent of ice but didn't know how her father had navigated to Valhalla.

Two of Odin's female Valkyrie guards stepped forward to intercept them. "We're here at Odin's invitation," Troy said in his silky musical voice. "Step aside."

The two guards resumed their positions, allowing them to pass. Troy pulled Sonja's hand through the crook of his elbow and led her into the throne room.

She leaned in to him and whispered, "How come they believed you without question?"

"I have an honest face." When she laughed in disbelief, her father smiled. "The skill is called silver tongue."

Sonja squeezed Troy's arm, the first traces of affection blossoming. "I want to know everything about you."

He cast her a startled glance. "Everything? What a horrifying prospect."

Their voices echoed around the empty chamber. The dirty throne sat at the far end of the room like a malignant growth on the shiny white ice. She had expected to be scared, but her father's presence gave her strength. She was even looking forward to seeing Vidar's father get his comeuppance.

"How will we find Odin?" she asked.

"He knows we're here," Troy said, setting a leisurely pace down the room while his gaze flicked between the various entries and exits. "By the time we reach the throne, he will have arrived."

When they had twenty feet left to walk, the door on the back wall opened. Huginn and Muninn emerged before standing aside to flank the door. Odin stepped out. He glared at Troy and Sonja, then scurried toward his throne, his uneven gait revealing a limp as his staff clacked on the ice.

He dropped onto the throne and heaved himself back with a grunt. His single golden eye gleamed malevolently beneath a bushy gray eyebrow. He rapped his staff on the ground. Huginn and Muninn dashed forward to take up positions on either side of the dais.

Both henchmen wore gold rings. Did Odin control everyone who served him with magic?

Vidar's brother Thor lumbered through the door, clutching a gleaming blue crystal pod beneath his meaty arm. He deposited it on the ground at Odin's feet and stepped back. Sonja squinted at it, trying to make out what the blue crystal thing was. Realization hit and she froze. A baby's crib.

Her fingers dug into the silky fabric of her father's sleeve. "Is that what I think it is?"

Troy covered her tense hand with his own. "Don't let him play on your fears." Halting ten feet in front of the throne, he gently disengaged Sonja's hand from his arm. She expected her father to explain why they'd come and make demands. Instead, he became inhumanly still, an aura of menace filling the silence.

Odin pulled a leather bag from inside his coat. He dug in a hand and scattered wooden pieces across the ice beside the crib. Leaning forward, he scanned the runes. "Threaten me all you will, Troy. I have you trumped," he announced.

A searing spike of pain shot up Sonja's arm from the ring. She yelped. Her father curled his fingers around her hand, enclosing the ring. The pain ceased abruptly, and heat flowed up her arm, washing away the ache and easing her fear.

"Hurt my daughter again, and I will destroy Valhalla and all within."

"Even you can't remove the ring from her hand," Odin crowed. With a defiant glance, he rested one dirt-encrusted bare foot on the Crystal Crib. He was taunting them, trying to goad her father into losing his cool.

"I puzzled over your motive for drawing me here in anger," Troy said. "Now I understand. You forced a slave ring on my daughter's finger simply to lord it over me. You've become foolish old man. Isolated at the top of the world, you've lost touch with where the real power lies."

"Power does not lie with you," Odin spat.

"You feared my father's power, so you killed your own son and set Loki up to take the blame."

"Enough!" Odin scrambled to his feet and banged the bottom of his staff on the ice. A crack of thunder split the air. Sonja's ears rang.

"'Full of sound and fury, signifying nothing,'" Troy murmured.

He released Sonja's hand before drawing a short black sword from the scabbard across his back and raising it. Lightning burst from the blade's tip, arcing across the room to hit the side of Odin's throne. The dirty ice exploded, showering those nearby with slush. Huginn and Muninn jumped aside, brushing the muck off their clothes. After a few moments Huginn slunk back to his master's side, but Muninn had obviously had enough. He sidled toward the door.

Odin glanced at him, and the raven-man fell to the ground, writhing in pain.

"Rats leaving a sinking ship," Troy said under his breath. Then louder: "Remove Draupnir's child from Sonja's hand and I shall leave you in peace."

Odin kicked the Crystal Crib, causing it to slide a few feet toward them. "Don't think you can dictate to me, Troy the Deathless."

"Will you leave me no choice but to kill you?" Sonja's father asked wearily.

Raised voices sounded behind her. Vidar raced into the room and sprinted toward them, his long fur coat flying. "Sonja, are you all right?" He skidded to a halt at her side, grabbing her arm, as if to prove to himself that she was solid and alive.

"Come and stand at *my* side, Vidar," Odin roared.

Sonja's burst of pleasure at seeing him died beneath an onslaught of fear. "Go to your father," she encouraged. She couldn't bear the ring to hurt him again.

He gazed at her as if she'd lost her mind. "My place is at your side. I chose you two thousand years ago when I defied my father to save your life."

"What're you talking about?" Odin bellowed. "Come here, Vidar."

Vidar met Troy's gaze in unspoken accord. He drew a sword from beneath his coat then faced his father. "No more," he said, his voice soft but firm.

Odin's head dropped forward, his leather bag of runes clutched against his chest. For a moment Sonja thought he might back down, now that he'd lost Vidar's support. But then he said, "You never were to be trusted."

Vidar fell to his knees, teeth gritted, the sinews on his neck taut with pain. His ring was clearly punishing him.

"Father, do something!" Sonja dropped to the ice at Vidar's side, tears in her eyes.

"Stop this, old man," her father demanded, his voice a slash of warning.

"Thor! Wake up, son!" Odin shouted. "Do as I told you!"

The red-bearded giant stomped forward from the back of the room. He swung his hammer up in an arc and down to smash the Crystal Crib. The crystal structure shattered into a hundred blue shards.

"No!" Vidar's tormented shout rang off the walls. He reached for her, his hand closing around her wrist. "I never meant this to happen. I love you!" he shouted.

The noise faded as if she had cotton wool stuffed in her ears. The room wavered. Energy leaked out of her body as if someone had ripped a hole in her soul. Her father's arm wrapped around her back, and she sagged against him. Clear crystal blue color ringed her vision . . . then closed around her.

Chapter Nine

The racking pain from the ring faded, leaving a residual ache, but Vidar ignored his discomfort and turned to where Troy held Sonja's limp body in his arms. "She's alive? Tell me she's alive!"

The air elemental's normally inscrutable expression fell away, and his face tightened to a mask of fury. The air around him prickled with barely contained power as he gently laid her on the ground. "She's dead," he said.

Odin rattled his staff against the ice in triumph. "Not invincible after all, are you, Troy?"

Vidar vaulted to his feet, heedless of his bruised muscles, wanting only to close his hands around Odin's throat and squeeze until the monster shut up. Troy caught his shoulder and jerked him back. "No. We use this opportunity," he said.

"Opportunity!" How could Troy call his daughter's death an opportunity?

Distraught, Vidar lashed out, but Troy deflected his weak blow. Vidar fell to his knees at Sonja's side and took her face between his hands. Her skin was warm, but when he reached to touch her mind, he found only a whisper of her presence.

Troy crouched beside him. "She's still close. The remnants of the Crystal Crib and your bond hold her here. She's inherited my gift, Vidar. Call her back."

New hope surged. He had told Sonja she might have inherited her father's ability to return from the dead, but Vidar had hardly dared hope it was true. He closed his eyes and recalled the sensation of touching Sonja's mind and spirit. Behind him sounded the deadly hiss of metal sliding over metal, as Troy drew his sword to stand guard over them.

In his mind Vidar called Sonja to return: pleaded, cajoled, and commanded by turns. He clasped her hand, and the cursed ring fell from her finger into his palm. Vidar's eyes snapped open. Odin always joked that Draupnir only released its victims in death. If Sonja returned from the dead, she would be free of the ring, free to leave this miserable place and have a life.

Without him.

Deep crystalline blue cradled Sonja in its familiar protective embrace. Her fear and uncertainty faded as the power stolen from her and locked in the Crystal Crib for two thousand years flooded her being. Far away, a man called her name.

His voice tugged at her chest, trying to drag her to him. A memory of love and tenderness whispered through her. Sonja wanted to go to him, but that meant leaving her safe blue haven. He called again, closer this time. An image formed in her mind of his lean body and dark hair, lustrous golden eyes that flared like flames when he looked at her. *Vidar.*

A gossamer web enclosed her heart, tiny filaments of connection that she sensed bonded her with him. Her blue haven dissolved, and she found herself again in Valhalla. Fragments of blue crystal covered the floor in a starburst of destruction. The memory of Thor smashing the Crystal Crib tumbled back through her mind on a wave of grief. When the crib shattered, she'd felt as if one of her vital organs was ripped out. She picked up a large crystal shard and clutched it lovingly to her chest. Her lost power streamed into her from the shattered blue crystal until she pulsed with energy.

Vidar called her name again and she turned, searching for him. She saw Troy standing like an avenging angel over her prone lifeless body, sword raised, protecting her physical form until she returned. He radiated light like a minisun, giving her focus. But she didn't think he could see her.

Her heart fluttered as the translucent filaments joining her to Vidar quivered with his grief. Squinting against Troy's brilliance, she followed the glittering strands to a shadowy form hunched over her body. It didn't look like Vidar. She paused warily, raising the crystal sliver to protect herself, but the translucent strands pulled her closer to the dark figure. She studied the shadow and realized that it was Vidar. He was concealed beneath a dense, dark mesh.

Sonja dug her fingers underneath the mesh and tugged, trying to free him, but it clung, unbreakable wire. She looked around for help. Odin stood out like an oily black stain in the air. Trails of dark threads ran from the ring on his hand to other shadowy figures that must be Huginn, Muninn, and Thor.

Anger flashed through her, quickly chased by determination. A burst of tingling energy ran along her arm to sizzle across the blue crystal shard. She would not let Odin imprison Vidar through the ring's evil any longer!

Taking care not to cut the translucent strands that linked her with Vidar, she used the sharp-edged crystal to slice away the dark mesh covering him. When the final black threads fell clear, Vidar flared with a bright orange glow. *Fire.* His welcoming heat streaked along their bond, drawing her back into her body. She opened her eyes and gasped in a breath.

"Sacred elf-fire, Sonja." Vidar pulled her into his arms and hugged her so hard she couldn't breathe. When he released her, she clung to the front of his fur coat, reveling in the solid strength of him.

"Are you all right?" she gasped.

"Am *I* all right?" He hugged her again. "Crazy woman. You're the one who died." He cradled her head and kissed her cheeks, nose, and lips. He pulled back, frowning and touching the crystal fragment in her hand. "When did you pick up this?"

Odin cursed, grabbing their attention. He glared at his ring. "Huginn, Muninn, bring me my errant son." Neither raven moved, their gazes locked on Troy, sword still upraised.

Sonja grabbed Vidar's hand and pulled the slave ring off his finger in case Draupnir could re-create the imprisoning mesh. Vidar stared at the loose gold band; confusion followed by hope flashed across his face.

"How . . . ? The ring fell off your finger when you died, but mine shouldn't have come off."

"I'll explain later."

"Well parried," Troy said. "Now we riposte." He dipped and snagged the two rings. "On your feet, Sonja. I need your help."

She couldn't imagine how her fledgling power might help Troy overcome Odin, but she scrambled upright, hanging on to Vidar's arm.

Troy held up the rings. "Did you foresee this consequence of your actions in the runes, Odin?" he asked contemptuously. Flickers of crackling energy danced around his hand, sparking off the rings. He turned to Sonja. "Raise the point of your crystal dagger."

"Dagger?" Sonja blinked at the crystal shard. She had a weapon in her hand and her father expected her to use it. The total weirdness of the situation suddenly hit her like a truck, nearly knocking the legs from under her. "I won't hurt anyone. I can't."

"No time for self-doubt." Troy gave her a meaningful glance.

Vidar placed a steadying hand on her back. His energy filled her, strong and fortifying. Sonja dragged in a breath before raising the point of the glinting crystal blade.

Troy dropped both gold rings over the tip, then wrapped a hand around hers. A wild hurricane of energy raced through her; then she sensed her father's fine control focus the tempest down to a point of fearsome power. Lightning flashed out of the end of the crystal dagger, shooting toward the ceiling. With a wrenching groan, the ice there fractured. Huge chunks rained down, thudding to the floor all around them. Sonja covered her head, while Vidar wrapped his arms protectively around her. Troy threw a light shield over them, and the ice bounced off with an electric sizzle like high voltage cable.

Odin staggered. Losing his grip on his staff, he collapsed to his knees. "Help me!" He grabbed for the hem of Thor's coat as his son lumbered toward the door, hammer over his shoulder, fleeing the destruction. He missed, and howled as he sagged to the ice, his limbs twitching, his wrinkled face screwed up.

"Incredible," Vidar whispered in Sonja's ear. "Troy's focusing your combined power into the two child rings to attack Odin through Draupnir." The storm of ice fragments settled. The roof of the chamber was now open to the sky.

"Hold your focus," Troy commanded, and he released Sonja's hand.

Her heart pounded as energy from the air poured through her into the crystal. She felt as unprepared as a kid given the steering wheel of her father's car, but she wasn't about to show weakness in front of Odin.

Troy paced forward, crunching shattered ice and crystal underfoot, his expression merciless. Vidar wrapped an arm around Sonja, boosting her strength. He gripped her hand on the crystal shard. Heat shot through her, and flames leaped from the tip of the crystal.

"*Skitur!*" Vidar snatched away his hand. "My fire . . . How?"

"Who knows, just help me!"

Vidar's hand closed over hers again, and heat flooded her. Flames burst from the end of the dagger, engulfing the rings. Huginn and Muninn transformed into ravens and flapped up to the ceiling, circling, cawing loudly.

"Have mercy on an old man," Odin gasped, reaching for Troy's polished black boot. Sonja's father took a half step back out of reach.

"You punished Vidar with a slave ring for the sin of saving my baby daughter's life. Why should I show you mercy?"

"Stop, please."

Troy's breath hissed out, and his sword hovered in the air above Odin, ready to strike. "Relinquish Draupnir and your suffering ends."

"No!" Odin banged his fist against the ice, an angry whine rising from his throat.

"He'll never give up the ring," Vidar whispered.

Sonja trembled, terrified that Troy might slaughter Odin right there in front of her.

Her father angled the point of his sword at Odin's throat. "There's another way to break your hold over Draupnir," he said.

"I curse you, son of Loki. I curse you," Odin ground out between clenched teeth.

Troy smiled grimly, pressing the tip of his sword against Odin's throat until blood trickled onto the ice.

"Stop!" Odin's bony hands fluttered together, and he tugged Draupnir from his finger. "You win . . . this time." He held up the ring. The tense agonized lines of his body eased

as he recovered from the way Troy had reversed the energy
flow and attacked him through the ring.

Sonja lowered her crystal knife and sagged against Vidar,
exhausted but relieved.

The tip of Troy's blade touched Odin's throat again.
"Renounce the ring," he commanded.

"Isn't it enough that I've taken it—?"

"Renounce it. Now."

"I release thee." Defiance flashed in Odin's single gold eye,
only to be replaced by fear at another jab from Troy's sword.
"I release thee, Draupnir, gift of Brokkr and Eitri, to seek ye
a new master." He glanced longingly at the ring, then tossed
it away.

A rent opened in the air, sucking in the ring. Searing elemental power burst through the chamber, whipping up a
whirlwind of shattered ice that knocked Sonja and Vidar to
the ground. Sonja lay still until the turmoil faded, Vidar
covering her with his body. Once the air cleared, he grabbed
her hand and helped her to her feet. Heart skipping with
apprehension, she peered through the steaming, shattered
ice for Troy. By some miracle, her father was still standing
over Odin, untouched by the chaos.

"Don't let him kill me, son," Odin shouted to Vidar.

Two tall, dark-haired men appeared out of the murky air.
Sonja needed a few seconds to recognize them. Huginn and
Muninn now stood tall and straight, a bright intelligent
glint in their eyes. Huginn's gaze flitted from Troy to them
and back. "Kill him, or we will."

"Why put him out of his misery?" Troy moved aside so
they had a clear view of the pitiful sight of Odin curled on
the floor, looking like a vagrant in his dirty clothes. "Let us
not deny him years of wretchedness in a shattered palace
with no servants to do his bidding and no sons to bully."

Huginn narrowed his black eyes and nodded. "Very well." His outline shimmered; then the black raven rose into the air, larger and sleeker than before, to be joined a moment later by his brother. They flew toward the door and out.

Troy pivoted away from Odin and strode toward Sonja, sheathing his sword as he came. Sonja's heart thudded, praying this was an end to the conflict between her family and Vidar's.

"You did well, daughter." Troy brushed his knuckles across her cheek with a smile. "Take good care of your crystal dagger. It will focus your power whenever you need it."

His gaze settled on Vidar. He touched his fingers to his brow in some kind of a salute. "There's nothing holding you here now," he said.

Vidar returned the gesture. The two men stared at each other candidly, their eyes intense with unspoken acknowledgment of past friendship, shared pain, new beginnings. Then Vidar gave Sonja a cautious smile. "We'll go somewhere warm. Perhaps I'll visit my *mother's* family."

"The Folletti," Troy said, his gaze drifting thoughtfully into the distance. "Italy will be a fine place to continue Sonja's education."

Did that mean he was coming with them? She exchanged a glance with Vidar. Much as she wanted to get to know her father and discover how to use her power, she wanted time alone with Vidar. In some ways she knew him so well, but in other ways they had a lot of catching up to do.

"Go on ahead," Troy said with a glance over his shoulder. Odin had stood and was shuffling toward the door in the back wall. "I'll find you after I've tidied up here."

Chapter Ten

Two weeks later, Sonja flew from London to Italy to meet Vidar. She waited impatiently for her bags before hurrying out to find him. Even in the middle of the bustling crowd he stood out, looking very Italian in his dark glasses with the collar turned up on his leather jacket.

She abandoned her luggage cart to throw herself into his open arms. While they'd been apart, she'd only had to think of him for his presence to fill her mind, but she'd missed seeing him, touching him, making love with him.

She wormed her fingers inside his jacket while he kissed her. "Did you miss me?" she asked breathlessly when they came up for air.

He grinned. "Always, *elskan mín*."

"Shouldn't you call me something Italian now, like *bella*?"

"Angling for compliments?"

She grinned back at him. "Always, my love."

Vidar loaded her bags in a black BMW before driving her along the Amalfi coast. The serpentine road followed a fairy-tale route around sparkling blue bays and through quaint villages of tiny whitewashed houses stacked up the steep coastal cliffs. Sonja finally relaxed, releasing the last few stressful weeks in London, moving her few belongings out of her aunt's house into storage and sorting out her affairs. Her aunt hadn't been her aunt at all, but a Valkyrie tasked with guarding her. Saying good-bye to someone she'd known all her life but never really known at all had been as surreal as everything else that had happened to her recently. Vidar had spent the time initiating the sale of Santa's Magical Wonderland to a Norwegian company, and she sensed he would miss the place. He'd told her that throwing himself into developing a business in the human realm had been the only thing that had kept him sane over the last few years. As for the rest of his life, he'd mentioned some years spent with her father when they were young men, and a devastating war between the light elves and the dark elves that had lasted for centuries. Now she and Vidar would have time to talk, she hoped to discover everything he'd done over the last two thousand years.

The car slowed as they approached Positano. "That's the ancestral home of the Folletti," Vidar said, pointing. "They're still a small fairy troop, although there are too many for the house now and some of them have dwellings in the surrounding hills."

Sonja stared out the car window at the white villa on the cliffs, entranced by the labyrinth of tiny balconies and narrow stone staircases. Green shutters, bright ceramic pots overflowing with huge red poinsettia blooms, and terracotta tiles provided a patchwork of color.

Vidar maneuvered the car into a garage that was little more than a cave beneath the house, and she followed him up a stone staircase hewn into the rock to an entrance hall full of darkly polished wood and colorful ceramic tiles. "The place has changed a lot since I left." He sounded upbeat, but she caught a hint of wistfulness in his tone. His mother had died centuries ago, so returning must be a bittersweet experience.

Leaving her luggage in a corner, Vidar led her through a comfortable sitting room to a glass door. White pillars circled with vines marked the corners of a covered terrace furnished with an ornate metal table and chairs.

He offered her a plate of biscotti and poured from a pot of tea left on the table by a maid. "I thought you might be hungry."

Sonja stood at the balcony rail, munching the crunchy almond cookie while watching a fleet of brightly colored fishing boats bobbing far below on the blue sea. Vidar wrapped an arm around her waist. She leaned her head against his shoulder.

"The speed at which my life's changed is bizarre," she murmured. "Speaking of the bizarre, is my father here yet?"

Vidar cleared his throat. "There's something I need to tell y—"

"Ah, you're here." A delicately beautiful woman with long black hair and blue eyes glided out to greet them. An ivory silk wrap encased her slender body, but she was obviously naked underneath the fine fabric. She embraced Vidar before casting an assessing gaze over Sonja. "*Buon giorno*, Sonja. You have your father's beauty."

"Sonja, meet Arminia, she's the reigning queen of the Folletti and a very distant niece of mine."

"*Buon giorno*," Sonja replied.

A moment later Troy came out, and Sonja blinked in amazement. Each time she'd seen him he was impeccably dressed. Even after the conflict with Odin, he'd hardly had a hair out of place. Now his feet were bare, the top button on his trousers was undone, and he was shirtless.

"Sonja, child." He touched her cheek. "Have you practiced walking unseen?"

She tried not to stare at the amazing pearly skin of her father's naked chest. "I've been too busy."

"I'll practice with you later and help you to master your other skills."

"We'll leave you to show Sonja around," Arminia said to Vidar. "We'll meet you for dinner." Then, with a seductive sideways glance at Troy, she turned and flitted back inside.

Troy watched her go before returning his attention to Sonja. "We'll talk when you're rested." He followed Arminia.

"My having a rest is *not* what's on his mind," Sonja exclaimed as soon as he was out of sight.

"Sorry I didn't get a chance to warn you your father's here," Vidar said. "I get the impression Arminia has been seeing him for a while, but she'll never get him to commit to her. He has a bit of a reputation for fighting hard and playing hard."

"Oh my god, he *doesn't*." She turned to Vidar with an embarrassed laugh.

He gave her a wry grin. "Look on the bright side. It means that you likely have a few siblings. If we find out who they are, we can visit them."

"Gosh." She leaned against Vidar, suddenly feeling as if the earth were shifting beneath her feet again. Meeting her father had been a revelation, but to think she had brothers and sisters somewhere . . . She'd gone from having no one except her reluctant pseudo aunt to having a lover, a family, the whole world at her fingertips. This Christmas all her childhood dreams were coming true. It made up for all the years when she'd missed out on Christmas gifts. When she'd set out for Santa's Magical Wonderland, had she known deep inside that she'd find her *guardian angel* there?

Vidar hugged her to him. "I have a surprise for you."

She turned in his arms and speared her fingers through his hair to pull his head down. "I hope it's a huge king-size bed with silk sheets." Pressing her lips to his, she melted into his embrace.

He eased back and stroked wisps of hair away from her face. "You'll love our bedroom. But first I want to take you somewhere else."

"Not another Yule Fest, please. I can only cope with one of those a year." He gave her a mysterious smile, then led her along a warren of staircases and tiny corridors, through ancient warped doors and under low stone arches where he had to duck. They emerged in a garden of tiny linked terraces literally hanging on the edge of the cliff. Hidden among the greenery was a stone bench in an alcove set with shells. Sonja inhaled the scent of mild salty air as the sea lapped against the rocks below them.

Vidar stepped forward to gaze down at the water. "Years and years ago, I used to come here to think." His leather jacket outlined the masculine width of his shoulders, tapering to his narrow waist. Itching to touch him, Sonja followed him and laced her fingers with his.

"It's good to be home," he said, his voice thick with emotion. "The only thing I'll miss about Iceland is Gleda.

"When my father summoned me all those centuries ago, I dashed off proud to be the son of a god, eager for adventure and excitement. I had no idea I would never see my mother again. But if I hadn't gone to Asgard, I wouldn't have been there to save your life, and I wouldn't have bonded myself with you. Chances are we'd never have met." He turned and buried his face against her neck. She stroked his hair, trying to imagine what her childhood would have been like without his loving presence in her mind.

They clung together for long silent minutes, Sonja lost in thoughts of what had happened, and what might have been. "Can't change anything," she said softly.

"Wouldn't want to," Vidar replied, his breath warm against her ear. "I saved your life, but you saved mine as well. I don't think I'd have survived two thousand years trapped in my father's service if not for the bond I had with you. Even when you were just a babe in the Crystal Crib I always sensed the warmth of your spirit on the edge of my consciousness like the distant promise of spring in the middle of a cold, harsh winter." He pulled three linked red crystal rings from his pocket and said, "I want to give you my Magic Knot to complete our bond."

Entranced by the fire dancing inside the stones, Sonja reached to touch. Vidar closed his fingers around the rings, his expression serious.

"Before you accept, you need to understand that in our culture exchanging Magic Knots is equivalent to becoming engaged. Only, it's irrevocable." He met her gaze. "It means forever, Sonja. For people like us, forever's a long time."

Sonja's heart raced, and she sucked in a steadying breath. She still couldn't comprehend the concept that she would never die. "I want to spend my life with you," she said softly.

She unfastened the chain holding her own Magic Knot around her neck. Vidar swapped her stones for his and helped her put the gold chain back on. The three red rings gleamed supernaturally bright against her powder blue sweater.

She reached to touch them, but he caught her hand.

"Wait a moment." He pressed his lips to her three crystal rings before tucking them into a small silk bag he pulled from his pocket; then he guided her to the stone bench and they sat down. "Now put my stones against your skin."

She dropped the ruby rings inside her sweater where they nestled on the end of the chain between her breasts. Heat blossomed inside her. The familiar feeling of Vidar intensified, gained clarity, expanded within her so that she lost track of where she was, her senses overwhelmed. She clung to him, and he wrapped his arms around her.

"*All right,* ástin mín?"

She was about to answer when she realised he hadn't spoken aloud.

His thoughts brushed her mind: naked skin, heat, pleasure. Her eyelids fell. Desire pulsed through her. "Vidar . . ."

"Yes," he said in a dark velvet whisper.

Her hand flattened on his thigh. "Take me to our bedroom quickly, you tease. I want to give you your Christmas gift."

He pulled her onto his lap with a chuckle and reached in his pocket. "Close your eyes." She obeyed and felt him pin something to her sweater.

"Is this my Christmas gift?"

"Not exactly, but you've definitely earned it."

She opened her eyes and looked down to find a shiny red and white button from the resort. "Live your dreams this Christmas," Vidar whispered.

They did.

INTERACT WITH DORCHESTER ONLINE!

Want to learn more about your favorite books and authors?
Want to talk with other readers that like to read the same books as you?
Want to see up-to-the-minute Dorchester news?

VISIT DORCHESTER AT:
DorchesterPub.com
Twitter.com/DorchesterPub
Facebook.com (Search Pages)

DISCUSS DORCHESTER'S NOVELS AT:
Dorchester Forums at DorchesterPub.com
GoodReads.com
LibraryThing.com
Myspace.com/books
Shelfari.com
WeRead.com

✂ ☐ **YES!**

Sign me up for the Love Spell Book Club and send my FREE BOOKS! If I choose to stay in the club, I will pay only $14.00 each month, a savings of $8.97!

NAME: _____

ADDRESS: _____

TELEPHONE: _____

EMAIL: _____

☐ I want to pay by credit card.

☐ **VISA**   ☐ MasterCard.   ☐ DISCOVER

ACCOUNT #: _____

EXPIRATION DATE: _____

SIGNATURE: _____

Mail this page along with $2.00 shipping and handling to:
Love Spell Book Club
PO Box 6640
Wayne, PA 19087
Or fax (must include credit card information) to:
610-995-9274
You can also sign up online at **www.dorchesterpub.com**.

Price includes shipping. Offer open to residents of the U.S. and Canada only.
Canadian residents please call 1-800-481-9191 for pricing information.
If under 18, a parent or guardian must sign. Terms, prices and conditions subject to change. Subscription subject to acceptance. Dorchester Publishing reserves the right to reject any order or cancel any subscription.

CPSIA information can be obtained at www.ICGtesting.com
Printed in the USA
BVOW040418230911

271950BV00001B/9/P

9 781428 511620